PRAISE FOR MELISSA FOSTER

"You can always rely on Melissa Foster to deliver a story that's fresh, emotional and entertaining. Make sure you have all night, because once you start you won't want to stop reading. Every book's a winner!"

—*New York Times* bestselling author Brenda Novak

"What sets Melissa Foster apart are her compelling characters who you care about . . . desperately. I dare you to read the first chapter and not be hooked."

—*New York Times* bestselling author M. J. Rose

"With her wonderful characters and resonating emotions, Melissa Foster is a must-read author!"

— *New York Times* bestselling author Julie Kenner

"Melissa Foster is synonymous with sexy, swoony, heartfelt romance!"

— *New York Times* bestselling author Lauren Blakely

"I'm highly addicted to her stories, and still want to kick my own behind for taking so long to finally read her."

—*The Power of Three Readers*

"The author's writing was amazing, and to be completely honest here, to get me to read a subgenre I would not normally touch with a barge pole shows that her writing can make even the pickiest reader fall in love with her books—you just have to give them a chance."

—*Cara's Book Boudoir*

"Melissa creates quite a palate of feelings for the reader to experience all through the novel."

—*Cruising Susan*

ONLY
for
YOU

MORE BOOKS BY MELISSA

Have you read Melissa's Love in Bloom big-family romance collection? Each book may be enjoyed as a stand-alone novel or read as part of the larger series. Characters from each family appear in other Love in Bloom family series. For more details on the Love in Bloom series, visit www.MelissaFoster.com.

SNOW SISTERS

Sisters in Love
Sisters in Bloom
Sisters in White

THE BRADENS

Lovers at Heart
Destined for Love
Friendship on Fire
Sea of Love
Bursting with Love
Hearts at Play
Taken by Love
Fated for Love
Romancing My Love
Flirting with Love
Dreaming of Love
Crashing into Love
Healed by Love
Surrender My Love
River of Love

Crushing on Love
Whisper of Love
Thrill of Love

BRADEN NOVELLAS

Promise My Love
Our New Love
Daring Her Love
Story of Love

THE REMINGTONS

Game of Love
Stroke of Love
Flames of Love
Slope of Love
Read, Write, Love
Touched by Love

SEASIDE SUMMERS

Seaside Dreams
Seaside Hearts

Seaside Sunsets
Seaside Secrets
Seaside Nights
Seaside Embrace
Seaside Lovers
Seaside Whispers

THE RYDERS

Seized by Love
Claimed by Love
Chased by Love
Rescued by Love
Swept into Love

SEXY STAND-ALONE ROMANCE

Tru Blue

Truly, Madly, Whiskey

BILLIONAIRES AFTER DARK SERIES

Wild Boys After Dark

Bad Boys After Dark

Logan
Heath
Jackson
Cooper

Mick
Dylan
Carson
Brett

HARBORSIDE NIGHTS SERIES

Includes characters from the Love in Bloom series

Catching Cassidy
Discovering Delilah
Tempting Tristan

STAND-ALONE NOVELS

Chasing Amanda (mystery/suspense)
Come Back to Me (mystery/suspense)
Have No Shame (historical fiction/romance)
Love, Lies & Mystery (three-book bundle)
Megan's Way (literary fiction)
Traces of Kara (psychological thriller)
Where Petals Fall (suspense)

ONLY *for* YOU

MELISSA FOSTER

Montlake
Romance

Published by Montlake Romance, Seattle

www.apub.com

Amazon, the Amazon logo, and Montlake Romance are trademarks of Amazon.com, Inc., or its affiliates.

ISBN-13: 9781542049016
ISBN-10: 1542049016

Cover design by Letitia Hasser

Printed in the United States of America

For Lisa Bardonski and Lisa Filipe

CHAPTER ONE

BRIDGETTE DALTON FLEW through the front doors of Chopstix, wincing at the sight of the owner, Li, holding up her bag of Chinese food. *I am officially becoming the worst mother on earth.* Someone who fed her son takeout three times in one week was not the type of mother she aspired to be.

She flashed a harried smile. "Thanks, Li. No offense, but hopefully I won't see you for a while."

"I packed an extra spring roll for Louie. Tell him Uncle Li misses him." He waved as Bridgette rushed toward the door.

"Will do! Thank you." *Uncle Li.* Okay, maybe she wasn't the *worst* mother on earth. She'd done at least a few things right, like moving back to her close-knit hometown of Sweetwater, New York, after the death of her husband five years ago. She and Louie had more family here than they could ever hope for.

She set the bag on the passenger seat with the other groceries she'd picked up, wishing there was a restaurant that offered takeout lasagna. At least then she'd be feeding her son his favorite meal, even if it was made by someone else. Pushing away her mommy guilt, she hightailed it over to her parents' new house.

It was strange not to be picking up Louie from her childhood home, which her parents had recently sold to her older sister Willow and Willow's fiancé, Zane, but she was happy the house was staying in the family. She flew through the front door, instantly calmed by the scents of family, love, and home-cooked meals.

"Mom!" Louie sprang to his feet and sprinted toward Bridgette, sending the action figures he was playing with scattering to the floor.

She scooped him up, and he clung to her like a monkey to a tree. He was getting heavy, but she'd never admit it. She was in no hurry for her little boy to grow up, although there was no escaping it. Louie was starting kindergarten next month. She brushed his mop of brown hair away from his eyes and kissed his cheek. "Sorry I'm late, sweetie. But I brought Chinese food, and Uncle Li sent you an extra spring roll."

Louie cupped his hand around his mouth and whispered, "Grandma Roxie gave me cookies!" Then, louder, he said, "I'm not supposed to tell you. I told her we don't keep secrets, and she said—"

"She said it was okay for grandmothers and grandsons to have a few secrets," Bridgette's mother said as she came out of the kitchen carrying a small grocery bag. Her springy blonde curls framed her smiling face. Roxie Dalton believed childhood should include mischief and mayhem, which was probably why Bridgette had been as rebellious as they came when she was a teenager.

"You know," her mother said to Louie, "there was a time when your mama was a great secret keeper." She tickled his belly, and he wiggled out of Bridgette's arms.

"Clean up your toys, honey, so we can go home." Bridgette melted at Louie's mischievous smile, which looked so much like his wild and handsome father's. There had been a time when that smile had caused as much pain as it had joy, but over the years the black sea that she'd been drowning in had abated, leaving a sacred cove of good memories.

"Mom," Bridgette said quietly, "I wish you wouldn't tell him I kept secrets." She *had* once been a master at keeping her own secrets, but she'd put aside her wild-child ways after losing her husband and was doing everything she could to focus on bringing up Louie in a safe and stable environment. The only secrets she kept nowadays were the ones her three sisters shared with her. After all, she needed to set a good example for Louie.

Her mother shrugged. "Life is full of secrets, honey. It's not such a bad thing that he knows you were a normal girl, but I will stop. Let's talk about you for a minute. You're racing around so much these days. I wish you would hire someone to help you. Even just a part-time person could free you up so you're not leaving late so often."

Bridgette had run her flower shop, the Secret Garden, with only sporadic seasonal help since opening it three and a half years ago, but her business had grown so much, it was getting difficult to manage alone.

"I'm trying. It's the end-of-summer rush. Things should slow soon, and then I'll be able to breathe again and think about hiring."

"Well, maybe this will help ease some stress until then." Her mother handed her the bag she was holding.

Bridgette peeked inside, seeing two bottles of her mother's home-made jasmine massage oil, and tried to hide her annoyance. Roxie sold homemade fragrances, scented oils, lotions, and soaps in shops around town, and she claimed to put love potions in some, though she rarely offered up which ones contained her supposed magic. Bridgette had a houseful of the deliciously scented gifts, and she knew *exactly* what her mother was up to. Ever since the mysterious, gruff, too-sexy-for-his-shirt Bodhi Booker had moved in next door to Bridgette, her mother and three older sisters had been on a matchmaking mission. Her overprotective brother, Ben, was the only one who wasn't pushing him on her.

She handed the bag back to her mother with an emphatic "No, thank you."

"Oh, honey. Just give it a try." Roxie pushed the bag back to her. "Maybe it's time to let a little lovin' in."

"*Please* don't talk to me about sex, Mom. It's weird." She took the bag just to get her mother off her back, intending to stuff it in the back of a closet where she wouldn't be tempted to even think about it. She'd built a stable life for herself and Louie, and she owned a thriving business. She was happy without the distractions of a man. *Mostly* happy, anyway. Just the sight of Bodhi Booker made all her best, and lonely, parts want to come out to play again, reminding her of exactly what she'd been missing out on.

Her mother leaned in closer and lowered her voice. "I'm the one who caught you behind Dutch's Pub with Robby Macamoy when you were sixteen. It's no secret that people need intimacy. Or as you told me that night, 'Human touch is important to a person's psyche.'"

"I can't believe you remember what I said."

Roxie tapped her temple. "Mothers never forget. You'll see."

She glanced at Louie, who was busy picking up his toys, and knew it was true. She remembered his first *everything*. Between her son, her close-knit family, and living in a town small enough that everyone knew when a person sneezed, Bridgette should *not* be lonely. But she hadn't been held or touched by a man since she'd lost Jerry. Five years, it turned out, was enough time to grieve *and* heal. She'd lived without him for more than twice the number of years they had shared, and she couldn't deny that watching Willow and Zane fall deeply in love over the past few months, so consumed with each other they practically finished each other's sentences, had made her long for the same type of special connection.

But Bodhi Booker and his piercing dark eyes was not the answer, even if the sparks between them could have blown up the place when they'd first met at Willow's bakery a few weeks before he'd moved in. Everything about him was tough, from his serious expression and chiseled jawline to the keep-your-distance vibe he emitted. No matter how sweet she was to him—neighborly sweet, not please-let-me-lick-those-incredible-abs-you-keep-flashing sweet—he'd barely said more than two words to her. And when he had, they were clipped or rough. She shouldn't be intrigued by that sort of man, but that didn't stop her from turning into a hot mess of hungry hormones around him.

With Louie safely strapped into his booster seat, she drove the few blocks home to their cozy little bungalow, thinking about those hungry hormones. They'd been at peace for so long, she'd wondered if they still worked. And every time they came to life around Bodhi, she felt the sexy, rebellious part of herself she'd buried for so long—and she missed that, too. After losing Jerry, she'd poured herself into filling Louie's home with so much love there would be no room for missing the father he had never really known. She'd gardened her broken heart out, creating lush, bountiful flower beds throughout the property, full of new life that needed nurturing and could not be ignored. Louie gave her purpose. The gardens gave her hope. Seeing the beautiful roses clinging to the white picket fence and the arched trellis over the walkway made her happy and reminded her that she was keeping the wilder parts of herself hidden for good reason. That very good, very cute reason climbed from his booster seat.

As she gathered the grocery bags, she heard the rumble of a truck pulling into the driveway next door, followed by a deep *"Woof!"*

Her pulse accelerated, and she tried to ignore her body flaming to life at the chance to catch a glimpse of Bodhi. The man had muscles upon muscles. *Big, hard* muscles that made her wonder how big and hard the rest of his parts were.

Don't look. Do not look.

"Dahlia!" Louie darted past to see the badass brooder's Great Dane.

Shoot. "Louie, don't bother them—" Bridgette turned as Dahlia barreled into her, sending her bags crashing to the ground. Before she could catch her breath, the dog was nose deep in Chinese food.

Louie laughed hysterically as Dahlia lapped up their dinner. "She was hungry!"

5

Bridgette glared at Bodhi as he stalked toward them, broad shoulders squared, chiseled jaw tight. His eyes heated up with every step, reminding her of a penned bull ready for a wild ride.

That reckless, carefree girl inside her began tugging on her boots. *No, no, no.*

She tried to look away, but it was futile. He had her rapt attention. And she had *his*.

Or maybe that was wishful thinking.

"Dahlia!" Bodhi reached for the dog's collar, pulling her away from his sexy-as-sin new neighbor's meal. Bridgette Dalton had been starring in his late-night fantasies since the day they'd met a few weeks earlier in the local bakery. She had a smile that lit up a room and a voice he could listen to all day long—but he'd like to hear it crying out his name in a fit of passion.

She also had the most adorable kid he'd ever met.

For a guy like Bodhi, Bridgette was the epitome of *off-limits*.

"Sorry," he said curtly. He was in town only to fix up the house he'd bought for his mother while he awaited his orders for his next assignment. As a covert-operations rescue specialist, he never knew exactly when he'd be called in, or if he'd make it home alive. And he certainly didn't need an irate husband on his ass if he did. It was probably a good thing he was returning home to New York City in two weeks to report to mandatory training. A daily dose of hot-as-sin temptation would surely screw with his focus.

Bridgette crossed her arms and narrowed her beautiful green eyes, throwing virtual daggers in his direction. At least that was how she probably wanted it to come across, but she was so frigging adorable in her short skirt and sleeveless sweater, it was hard to take all that anger seriously. Although that didn't make him feel any less of an ass for what Dahlia had done.

"You might as well let her eat the Chinese food," Bridgette said as she began picking up the groceries.

"It isn't good for her," he said, too harshly. Keeping his emotions in check should *not* be more difficult than strategizing a mission. Until meeting Bridgette he'd never had trouble keeping his mind off women, never mind having any emotions worth hiding. But all it took was one word, one glance from her alluring green eyes, and he was toast.

He picked up the egg carton. Half the eggs were broken, the milk was spilling across the pavement, and—

She snagged a box of panty liners from his fingertips, and her cheeks flushed. "It's okay," she said a little shakily. "I don't need help."

Spending several years in the Special Forces and four years working for Darkbird, a civilian company hired to carry out the most dangerous covert rescue missions, he'd been through some awful shit. But hearing that little tremor in her voice did something funky to his stomach a war zone never had. He forced himself to focus on the groceries and not the urge to thread his fingers into her thick, luxurious hair, which was about a hundred shades of brown and blonde, and kiss her until that harried look fell away.

He picked up a romance novel from among the mess and wiped milk off the cover. "*Everywhere and Every Way*? I've rea—" Aw hell, now he sounded like a wimp. A friend had turned him on to romance novels when he'd needed an escape from the death and destruction he experienced on the job. That particular novel was funny as hell. He'd devoured it, and several more since, though he wasn't about to share that bit of intel.

He cleared his throat and set the book aside. "I've seen it in the grocery store."

Her eyes flicked up, and she leaned her elbow on her knee with a curious smile. "Most guys wouldn't notice."

"I notice everything." *Like the erratic pulse beating at the base of your neck, the darkening of your eyes, the spike in temperature between us, and the way you're clutching that bag of peas so hard it's ready to pop.*

Her eyes shifted nervously to Louie, sitting cross-legged beside Dahlia, and his lust-addled brain snapped back to reality. What the hell was he doing? He had nothing long-term to offer a woman. And even if he did, he didn't know what Bridgette's deal was. He hadn't seen a man around, but that didn't mean there wasn't one.

"Looks like it's PB and J tonight," she said quietly.

Bodhi gave Dahlia a way-to-go look. The pup wrinkled her brow and cocked her head, watching him with sad eyes, as if she knew she had been naughty. He'd loved Dahlia from the moment he'd rescued her from the pound, but she was definitely not always the most well-behaved pooch. With a whimper, Dahlia stretched her giant paws out in front of her and rested her chin on her legs. He stifled the urge to love her up, knowing it would send the wrong message. He fucking hated tough love.

Bridgette glanced at Dahlia, and her expression softened. "You picked an interesting name for her."

"She'd been abused before I adopted her. I think Dahlia fits her perfectly. She's remained kind despite being tested in every way." He petted Dahlia's head, remembering the day he'd first seen her in the pound, rail thin with frightened eyes. She'd cowered from his touch, but she'd survived, and he'd poured as much love into her as he could ever since. His mother took care of her when he went on missions, and Dahlia was as comfortable with her as she was with him.

He concentrated on the task at hand and not the pouty pup beside him or the incredible woman in front of him, who was looking at him like she was trying to figure him out. He picked up a can of whipped cream and a container of strawberries, and his mind raced straight to a list of Bridgette's body parts he'd like to eat them off. He gritted his teeth as he set the items in one of the bags and grabbed a bottle. Massage oil. *Jesus.* His mind went deeper into the gutter.

She snagged it from his hands, her eyes darkening as she licked her lips.

Lust seared through him, coiling hot and tight in the pit of his stomach. He needed to look away, to break their connection, but he was having a hell of a time finding his "Off" button when she was repeatedly pushing on, on, *on.*

He needed to get ahold of himself. It'd been a long time since a woman had affected him like this.

"Can Bodhi and Dahlia eat dinner with us?" Louie asked.

Bridgette's lips parted on a sexy sigh, and her eyes—*damn*, those angelic green eyes—turned to liquid heat.

Combustible. That's what this was between them.

Unstoppable.

He couldn't afford unstoppable.

She snapped her mouth shut, and he imagined prying her sweet lips open with his tongue. *Fuck.*

That could not happen.

"No," came out fast and hard—from both of them.

CHAPTER TWO

WHILE LOUIE SET up a command station with his action figures in the playroom, Bridgette put away what was left of her groceries, hoping to distract herself from thoughts of Bodhi. When that didn't work, she searched the pantry for peanut butter to make Louie's dinner. Her phone vibrated with a text, and she snagged it from the counter. Her sister Piper's name flashed on the screen, and she read the text. *I booked a table at Dutch's for Willow and Zane's engagement party Friday night. Can you get a sitter so Mom and Dad can come?*

Dutch's was a local pub, and it would be packed Friday night. Perfect. She needed a night out to de-stress, although her sisters would probably use it as another chance to push her to get back in the dating game. *That's what margaritas are for.*

She typed a response and sent it off. *Yup. I'll line up a sleepover with one of his friends. What can I do to help?*

She grabbed the toiletries she'd bought, embarrassed anew at the thought of Bodhi's big hand holding the box of panty liners. Disappearing into thin air would have been ideal right then.

"Louie, I'm going to run a few things upstairs," she called out on her way up.

She put everything away and sat on the edge of her bed, pondering the man whose eyes went dark as midnight nearly every time he looked at her. A thrill tickled up her spine, and thoughts of Jerry brought a thread of guilt. They'd had a great relationship and a hot and exhilarating sex life. Touring with his band had added extra excitement to their lives, as they were always looking for a place to slip away and be alone. But they'd never gotten past the wild-crazy-sex stage to the sensual, lovingly intense experiences Willow talked about having with Zane. Sometimes Bridgette wondered if she and Jerry would have ever slowed down enough to get there. Their lives had seemed jet-propelled from the moment they'd met. They'd toured and attended after-parties even while she was pregnant, although Bridgette had steered clear of alcohol. She'd stopped attending the parties late in her pregnancy and had never resumed after Louie was born, but she and the baby had continued traveling with Jerry. While she longed for the same deep connection she and Jerry had shared, she wasn't sure she was capable of ever truly falling in love again.

Her phone vibrated with another text from Piper. She read it as she headed downstairs. *I've got it all taken care of. Wear something sexy and leave your mom panties at home. >snort<*

Bridgette laughed but didn't bother responding, because Piper loved having the last word. Piper was two and a half years older than Bridgette was, and was her toughest, though most petite, sister. She packed a lot of mouthiness and bravado into her five-two, hundred-and-ten-pound body. When Bridgette had quit college at nineteen to marry Jerry, Piper told him that if he hurt her, she would hunt him down like his worst nightmare and he'd never be able to play the drums again.

That was Piper to a T.

Unfortunately, even Piper's best intentions couldn't stop Jerry's car from running the red light and putting him in the path of the truck that ended his life.

A knock at the door startled her. Through the screen she saw Mike Gladnor, a local teen who worked as a delivery boy for several restaurants.

She pushed open the door. "Hi, Mike."

He held up a bag from Chopstix. "Dinner."

"I didn't order dinner." She looked at the receipt, which had Bodhi's name on it. *Guess our ruined dinner made you hungry.* "I think you want the house next door."

"Nope. He ordered it for you."

Maybe he's not so gruff after all.

"He even asked that we throw in a few extra fortune cookies," Mike added. "He said you'd had some bad luck earlier today."

"Bad luck" was one way of putting it. Although it had given her a chance to look at Bodhi up close and personal again, filling her fantasy bank for later.

Louie came out of the playroom and ran to the door. "Hi, Mike! Did you bring us dinner? Mom was going to make peanut butter and jelly."

"Hey, buddy." Mike gave Louie a high five while Bridgette grabbed her purse.

She gave Mike a tip and carried the bags to the kitchen table, wishing she had Bodhi's phone number so she could text him to say thank you. Louie ran back into the playroom.

"Louie?" She followed him into the playroom, where his action figures were set up all around his play castle. "Aren't you hungry?"

"Can I play for a few more minutes first?"

"Sure. Bodhi sent us dinner. I'm going to run over and thank him. Would you like to come and then play?"

"Can I stay here?"

"How about if you play on the porch where I can watch you?"

He gathered an armful of action figures and carried them out to the porch.

She thanked her lucky stars that Louie was so amiable. Like any typical little boy, he had his stubborn and tired moments, but they seemed few and far between these days.

"I'll be back in a few minutes." Butterflies took flight in her stomach as she crossed the yard toward Bodhi's house. She could do this without weak knees. It was just a quick thank-you. Or maybe she should invite him to eat with them. That was the neighborly thing to do, wasn't it? Surely she could stop lusting after him for one measly hour.

She climbed the front steps and peeked over at Louie, who was engrossed in his toys. She lifted her hand to knock, taking a moment to go over what she would say. *Hi. Thank you for sending dinner over. That was so nice of you. Would you like to eat with us?* Pleased with the casual tone of her invitation, she knocked at the door. Dahlia barked and heavy footsteps approached, sending her nerves into a tizzy.

The door swung open, and her jaw dropped. *Oh no. No, no, no.* Bodhi's dark hair was soaked, his skin glistening wet. There was no saving her. Her gaze slid south, following a drip of water from the hard ridge of his pecs down his bumpy roller-coaster abs, to the dark-blue towel around his waist. And—*oh Lord, no*—her gaze traveled lower still, to the prominent outline of that other body part she'd been wondering about.

Um. Yeah. Big. Mighty big.

"Hey," he said in a clipped tone, snapping her from her trance. He made a signal with his hand, and Dahlia plopped down beside him.

"I . . . um . . ." She couldn't think past all the hotness in front of her.

He chuckled and reached out, lifting her chin with one finger, so she had no choice but to soak in his wolfish grin and panty-melting eyes.

"Sorry." She shook her head, but like metal to magnet, her gaze locked on his body *again*. It took all her concentration to force her eyes up and push her voice out. "Thank you for dinner. Would you like to eat me?"

He scrubbed a hand down his face, and she realized what she'd said.

"Oh shit! *Dinner.* Would you like to have *dinner?* With us. Me and Louie. Oh God. I'm sorry." She turned to leave, and he grabbed her arm, pulling her back. Heat radiated from his body, filling the space between them.

"Bridgette," he said calmly, his gaze serious. "Take a breath."

She breathed deeply, feeling her cheeks burn.

"That's a girl," he said without a hint of patronizing. "Better?"

"A little." His hand was searing fingerprints into her skin. "You shouldn't answer the door like that."

"You were pounding on my door. I thought it was important."

"I wasn't pounding." *Was I?* She had no idea, but she was pretty proud of herself for looking him in the eyes instead of . . . "You can let go of my arm now."

"Are you going to run away?"

"I wasn't running away. I was escaping mortification. There's a difference."

He cocked a brow, and she laughed, earning a slight *almost* smile from Bodhi.

"Thank you for dinner. It was very nice of you, and unnecessary. Would you like to join us?" She glanced at Louie, glad he hadn't come with her and witnessed her spiral into Lustville.

"Thanks, but I have plans tonight."

"Oh. Of course. Sorry."

A red Jeep pulled into the driveway, and he released her arm, the muscles in his jaw working overtime.

"Well, thanks again." Bridgette headed back to her house, trying to ignore the green-eyed monster perched on her shoulder as a beautiful blonde stepped from the Jeep and walked directly into Bodhi's arms.

Early the next morning, Bodhi lifted a forkful of egg-white omelet and stopped midair, remembering Dahlia had ruined more than just Bridgette and Louie's dinner.

"Problem?" Shira looked up from the documents she was studying.

"Yeah." He set the fork down. "I have to go to the grocery store." He should have gone last night, but he'd had to take a cold shower after the run-in with Bridgette in her hot little skirt. And then Shira had shown up, and they'd spent hours going over minutes from the most recent board meeting for the charity he'd started for grieving military families, Hearts for Heroes. They'd worked so late, he'd insisted she stay over rather than drive two hours back to the city when she was exhausted.

"That does sound like a problem." She rolled her eyes and pushed the document across the table. "You missed a signature on this last night."

Shira was a brilliant accountant, a badass martial artist, and a loyal friend since childhood, who had been there for him when his father had been killed while on a tour of duty. She was also the president of the Hearts for Heroes foundation.

She pointed at him, moving her finger in a circle. "What's going on in that bullheaded brain of yours? You've been sidetracked since I caught you banging the hot chick next door."

He gave her a deadpan stare. "Bridgette," he said flatly. "And you know I wasn't banging her. She's got a kid, for God's sake, and for all I know she's married. Not to mention that she's going to be my mother's neighbor." He signed the document and shoveled his food into his mouth. "You know me better than that."

She crossed her arms and sat back, watching him intently. "You're right. I do, which is why I'm asking. She's the one you've been all distracted by, and probably fantasizing about, since you settled on the house, isn't she?"

He never should have told Shira about his inability to get the sweet, sexy woman from the bakery out of his mind. He continued eating, ignoring her question.

"Look," Shira said sternly. "This is me you're talking to. I know you never hook up with women anywhere near home, and honestly, I don't think you hook up at all anymore. You're wound so tight I'm waiting for you to blow."

Grinding his teeth against how well Shira knew him, he got up to clean his dishes. "Your point?"

She joined him by the sink and grabbed a dish towel to dry the plate he'd washed. "Maybe it's time to loosen up and find a girlfriend."

"We're not discussing this." For the millionth time. They finished the dishes in silence. He patted his thigh, and Dahlia popped off her dog bed and followed them into the living room, which was littered with tarps, ladders, cans of paint, and a plethora of tools.

"This place looks like a war zone."

"What do you know about war zones?" He cocked a smile. This was a much safer topic than where she'd been heading.

"You're not sidetracking me." Narrowing her hazel eyes, she said, "I wasn't saying you need to get married. But you live in this fucked-up world in your head. You think no woman deserves to be stuck at home waiting for you."

There wasn't another person on earth he'd allow to speak to him that way, but he respected the hell out of Shira and knew she was saying it out of love.

"You've got ten seconds to make your point, Shira, and then I've got shit to do."

"I have to leave in eight seconds, so calm down. People get killed every day driving to work, walking across the street, slipping in the shower. Give. Yourself. A break. You leave me behind and you don't see me crying about it."

They'd had this conversation so many times he could recite it in his sleep. He loved Shira like a sister, and he knew she worried about him when he went on missions. But there was a difference between their relationship and a relationship with a lover. Maybe that wasn't a fair way to think about things, but friends chose each other, and while losing them was difficult, losing a lover, someone with whom you were so connected that you carried the other with you at all times, was different. Lovers—*real* lovers, two people whose lives had become

16

one—might make that initial choice to have a relationship, but they only had so much control over their emotions. He knew from watching his mother's devastation after they'd lost his father that when people fell in love, their hearts guided them and made the bigger commitment. He could protect himself from that and, in doing so, protect any woman from being hurt because of his career.

"You done?" he asked sternly.

Her gaze slid down his bare chest, and she nodded. "Yeah. But don't torture the woman. Put a shirt on before you walk outside. She's only human."

He laughed as he grabbed her bag and walked her out to her Jeep. "Maybe I like torturing her." The fact that he'd never felt a thing when Shira looked at his body and he'd nearly combusted when Bridgette did was not lost on him.

"I wish I could believe that. The trouble is, I know you too well. The look in your eyes as she walked away last night was not the look of a guy who had no interest. The more you flaunt those magazine-worthy muscles, the more she'll want you. The more she wants you, the further withdrawn you'll become. You believe you're protecting yourself. Or her. Or both. But you're really torturing yourself, Bodhi."

"You think you know me." He played it off as a tease, but she was spot-on, as always, and it bugged him that he was so transparent.

"Like a pain-in-the-ass brother from another mother." She hugged him and touched his cheek. "You need a shave—oh, and sugar. I used the last of yours in my coffee. Sorry." She flashed her you-love-me-anyway smile. "Do yourself a favor. Find out if your hottie next door is married, and if not . . ." She shrugged and climbed into her Jeep. "You deserve to be happy in more than just your line of work."

He watched Shira drive away and turned to go inside, catching sight of Bridgette standing beside her car watching him. Her cheeks flamed. He lifted his chin in a silent greeting, but it was too late. She'd already turned away.

CHAPTER THREE

"I HAVE A sleepover tomorrow night!" Louie announced Thursday morning when they arrived at the bakery. The Secret Garden adjoined Willow's bakery, Sweetie Pie. Most mornings Bridgette and at least a few of her siblings met at the bakery before work, and Roxie picked up Louie there each morning.

Piper sat on a counter eating what was probably her third doughnut. It was a wonder she still fit into her size 2 jeans, the way she scarfed down goodies. Willow was wrist deep kneading dough, her blonde hair tied back in a thick braid that hung nearly to her waist.

"A sleepover?" Roxie said. "How fun."

"Uh-huh," Louie agreed. "Mom said I can have a blueberry scone today, Auntie Willow."

Willow flashed a curious smile at Bridgette. "Mommy did, did she? A *scone*. Interesting." For as long as Willow had been baking, she'd connected people with baked goods. She'd even created a special dessert named after Zane, before he'd become her fiancé. *Loverboys. The perfect mix of pleasurable, memorable, and guilt inducing.*

Today Bridgette understood why her sister made those connections. Bodhi was a definite *scone*. Hard on the outside and probably scrumptious on the inside.

"Scone." Piper shook her head. "I haven't needed a scone in forever. But coupling a scone and a child-free Friday night? That might be interesting."

"Hold your tongue until little ears leave, please." Bridgette put a scone and a handful of napkins in a bag, handed them to Louie, and gave him a hug and kiss. "I won't be late tonight. Promise."

Piper slid off the counter in front of Louie and pointed to her cheek. "Plant one on Auntie Piper."

Louie giggled as he kissed her.

"Thanks, cutie-pop." Piper hoisted herself back up on the counter.

"Come on, little man," Roxie said. "We'll eat that in the car, and if you're good, after our deliveries we'll go to the park." Her mother loved taking Louie with her to deliver her products to the local retailers who sold them. They'd fawned over him from the time he was a baby. On the way out the door, Roxie looked over her shoulder and said, "Scone? I was sure my oils would at least make this a cinnamon bun morning! I'll have to try harder."

Bridgette groaned and grabbed a hard-crusted pastry, chomping into it as the door closed behind them.

Willow set the dough she was kneading in a pan and washed her hands, drying them on a towel she pulled from the back pocket of her cutoffs. "What did I miss?"

"Rough night with Mr. Muscles?" Piper asked.

Bridgette paced. "Why does everyone think my moods suddenly revolve around *him*?"

Bridgette and Piper exchanged a knowing smile.

"Maybe because he's been the only thing to ruffle your feathers in the last few years besides a certain mini-man's terrible twos." Piper took another bite of her doughnut. "And that wasn't the same kind of ruffling."

Bridgette rolled her eyes.

"Am I wrong?" Piper grabbed the towel from Willow and snapped it at Bridgette.

"No, but it's annoying. I'm not looking to get involved with anyone. My life is crazy enough right now. But I *look* at him and I turn into this . . ."

"Horndog?" Willow suggested.

"Sex kitten?" Piper added.

"Why isn't Talia here when I need her? She'd say something like *curious woman.*" Talia, her most reserved sister, was a professor at a nearby college and always had the tamest outlook and suggestions. But she rarely had time to join them before work.

With a heavy sigh, Bridgette relented. "Fine. Yes to Willow. No to Piper. I'm anything *but* a sex kitten, and it wouldn't matter if I were. Some gorgeous blonde spent the night at his house last night after I made a complete ass out of myself." She fessed up to their grocery and towel fiascoes. "I was perfectly fine before he walked his big, sexy ass into this bakery and opened some long-forgotten door or something. I don't know what is wrong with me."

"What's wrong with you," Piper said as she hopped off the counter, smiling like the cat that ate the canary, "is that you are finally back in the game. You want to play his skin flute! Chomp his cock rocket! Let him bang the bouquet!"

Laughing, Bridgette held her hands up. "Stop already. No! *Maybe.* I don't know. You guys are such bad influences."

"It's been years since you've been with a man, Bridge," Willow reminded her. "We're *realistic* influences."

"I'm personally a little worried," Piper said with a serious tone. "If you don't use that coochie, who knows what could happen. It could dry up. Close up. Fall out. Grow *teeth.*"

"You're a freak." Bridgette laughed. "People abstain all the time. And did you *not* hear me say a gorgeous blonde *slept* at his house?"

"Since when have you been afraid of competition?" Willow asked.

"It's not a competition. I'm not that reckless anymore. I have Louie to consider, and besides, I don't know this guy from Adam!"

"Then why are we *sconing?*" Willow set the tray in the oven.

"Because!" Bridgette huffed. "I don't know! I've never had trouble having a conversation with a man. And this rugged, stoic, hot-ass guy says two words to me and I ask him if he wants to *eat me*?" She threw her hands up in the air.

Piper and Willow burst into laughter.

"And the blonde?" Bridgette said. "Seriously, you guys? How can I be jealous over a guy I've barely spoken to? A guy who probably has more women at his beck and call than any man ever should? What *is* that?"

"Lust, baby!" Piper exclaimed. "The most amazing feeling in the world."

"What part of 'I'm a mother' do you not understand?" Bridgette leaned against the counter and folded her arms over her chest. "I can't be lusting after my neighbor." *Or anyone else, for that matter.* But if she said that, her sisters would push even harder, and she didn't really believe it. She was still a woman, even if she was a mother and a widow. There was nothing wrong with being interested in a man, even if it scared her. But a neighbor? That opened the door for too many complications if things went bad.

"I have a little boy who needs me to be sane, rational, and stable," she said with an air of confidence.

"And well fucked," Piper added.

"Piper!" Bridgette glared at her. "That's not helping."

Willow moved in front of Bridgette with a serious expression. "Bridge. You're not a nineteen-year-old kid anymore, and you're the best mother I know."

"Don't let Mom hear that," Piper chimed in.

"Seriously." Willow's eyes never left Bridgette's. "I know we've been pushing you to date, but now it's not us. It's your own body, *your* own mind, telling you what you want. That means something."

"Yeah, that I'm an idiot. *Gorgeous blonde*, remember?" She began pacing again. "I know what I have to do. My brain just got a little side-tracked and hung up on the chase or something. It's been a long time, and just because I'm attracted to him doesn't mean I must have him. I need to focus on work and Louie, get back to being responsible, take charge, and forget the foolishness."

"Take charge. That's one way to play him," Piper said. "Guys like confidence."

"Not that way," Bridgette said. "Besides, I'm sure you'll read any guy I want to sleep with the riot act and scare him off anyway."

"You're probably right," Piper agreed. "You're better off without a quick roll in the hay with this guy. Because I would have to give him a piece of my mind, and the last time I did that, Willow got engaged. That's not what you need in your life. You're definitely better off with a battery-operated boyfriend."

"Exactly," Bridgette said. "Wait. What?"

"Did you just take credit for my engagement?" Willow asked.

Piper grabbed another doughnut and headed for the door. "Just stating a fact. Later, girls."

"I better get to work, too," Bridgette said, and walked out of the kitchen and into the bakery, heading for her shop. She wanted to surprise Louie tonight by doing something fun with him, which should also help distract her from her neighbor and his Jeep girl.

"Are you sure you're okay?" Willow asked. "Do you want to talk about it?"

"No, thanks. I know what I have to do, and if I'm going to get out of work on time, I need to get started." She unhooked the chain hanging across the archway between the two businesses with the hand-painted sign that read, WE'RE BUSY PLANTING SECRETS. PLEASE COME BACK TOMORROW, and threw herself into work, hoping to forget the man who had gotten under her skin.

After painting the two upstairs bedrooms and installing a new sink in the bathroom, Bodhi went for a run. In addition to working on the house, he was still learning his way around town, and he enjoyed his late-afternoon workouts. He'd first heard about Sweetwater through his friend Aurelia, who worked at his favorite bookstore in the city. She was also the one who had turned him on to romance novels a few years ago. She'd told him about a series set in a small town that had reminded her of Sweetwater, her hometown. A quick Google search painted Sweetwater as a charming small town built at the foothills of the Silver Mountains, with cobblestone streets, old-fashioned storefronts, and seasonal festivals held around Sugar Lake. After visiting the area with his mother, they'd agreed the quaint small town would be an ideal location in which she could eventually retire. He'd purchased the home a month later.

He jogged down the sidewalk toward the lake. Having grown up in the city, waking to glorious views of the mountains and Sugar Lake was a welcome change. He turned onto Main Street, running parallel to the lake and fairgrounds. A banner announcing the upcoming Peach Festival was strung over the road. The bakery came into view, and he wondered if Bridgette was working. Shirtless and sweaty was probably not their preferred state of dress, so he peered through the window.

"Checking out my sister?"

Bodhi snapped to attention at the sound of Bridgette's voice, and *holy hell* was she beautiful in an off-the-shoulder white blouse and jeans that fit like a second skin. She was holding a potted plant and looking at him like he was a Peeping Tom, which bugged the hell out of him.

"I wasn't checking out your . . . Wait. Your *sister*? You both work at the bakery?"

Her lips curved up in a smirky smile. "Let's circle back to you peering through the window at Willow. I'm pretty sure your overnight guest wouldn't like knowing her man was checking out the hot blonde in the bakery."

"*Christ,*" he uttered and wiped the sweat from his brow. Maybe it was safer if she thought he was a pig who had slept with Shira and then checked out her sister. But she was pushing all his buttons, and he couldn't resist pushing hers right back. He closed the distance between them, taking immense pleasure in the morphing of her smirk into a much hungrier expression.

She tightened her grip on the planter, her eyes drifting down his bare torso.

Oh yeah, this was torture all right.

She squared her shoulders, and her gaze darted up to his, as if she'd caught herself staring.

"Let's start over." The dead-calm tone he used when commanding his team came out of habit. "Hello, Bridgette. Do you and . . . *Willow* . . . both work at the bakery?"

"Hello, Bodhi," she said with an impressive amount of snark. She lifted her chin, glowering at him. "Willow owns the bakery, and I own the flower shop. But you're out of luck. She's engaged."

He clenched his jaw, lifted the planter from her hands, and set it on the ground, allowing him to step closer and invade her personal space. This pretty little filly was going to learn not to doubt his word. "I said I wasn't checking her out, and I *only* say what I mean."

"Then that makes two of us," she said sharply.

He felt a smile tugging at his lips. "Is that so?"

She crossed her arms, tipping her chin higher. She was a sexy little thing, a solid nine or ten inches shorter than he was, with confidence he admired. Confidence that turned him on. He had the urge to lift her up until they were eye to eye and take the kiss he'd been dreaming about. *And then some . . .*

"Always," she said without as much as a single blink.

"I'll remember that next time I'm in my towel and you ask if I want to eat—"

"Oh God! No!" She whipped her head from side to side, as if she were afraid someone might have heard him.

He chuckled and leaned in closer, inhaling the enticing scent of sinfully sexy Bridgette caught off guard, and said, "Now I know where to find you."

Casually picking up the planter, he handed it to her. "Pretty soon it'll be too cool for the peace lilies to be outdoors."

Surprise registered in her eyes.

"See you around, neighbor." He jogged across the street to finish his run along the lake and hopefully burn off the heat coursing through his veins.

Six miles, one long-ass gym workout, and a cold shower later, he still had Bridgette on his mind. He walked up the stone path to her front door later that evening, wrestling with knocking and leaving the bag of groceries he'd bought her on the porch like a kid pulling a prank. That would be a hell of a lot safer than coming face-to-face with the woman who laced his every thought. But he'd been raised to do the right thing. At least that was what he told himself as he knocked.

"Who is it?" she called from behind the closed door.

No peephole? Earlier in the week he'd noticed a missing board on Louie's playset. If there was a man in her life, he needed to be more attentive to those sorts of things.

"Booker." He winced. Once military, always military. "Bodhi. I brought you groceries."

"Bodhi? Um. Can you open the door, please? My hands are sticky."

He tried to ignore the sexy images *that* brought to mind and pushed the door open. Bridgette's hands were covered in lumpy green slime, and there were pieces of it on her T-shirt and hot little shorts, her forearms, cheek, and one bare thigh. Why on earth was that so sexy?

"Hi," she said shyly.

That shyness was new, and frigging adorable. "Hi. Sorry to interrupt. I wanted to replace the groceries Dahlia ruined."

"Mom!" Louie called from down the hall.

"Coming, baby," she called to Louie.

He'd noticed how often she played with Louie in the yard, and seeing her all slimed up warmed him inside. In the city he rarely saw women doing anything with their children other than catching cabs, dragging them in and out of stores, and eating at restaurants. Maybe that was just the difference between small-town and city life, or maybe it was that he'd never paid close attention to any woman until now.

"Sorry." She flashed that killer smile again. "You really didn't have to do that."

Not knowing how to answer that other than *I wanted to*, he shrugged. "Want me to set them in your kitchen?"

"Would you mind?"

He followed her down the center hall, trying not to watch the seductive sway of her hips. When had he become such a letch? He turned his attention to the pictures hanging on the wall, slowing to get a better look. The first appeared to be a preschool photo of Louie, with a forced toothy grin. The next was Louie as an adorable toddler sitting in the grass, and the third, as an infant, cradled in his mother's arms. The pit of Bodhi's stomach sank as he took in the rest of the picture. Bridgette was snuggled up against a handsome, longish-haired guy who looked vaguely familiar, though he couldn't place him. That didn't matter. There was a man in her life, and he had no business being in her house.

"You can set them on the counter," Bridgette said.

"Bodhi! Want to play slime with us? We made it." Louie beamed proudly, stretching the gooey, lumpy slime into a stringy mess.

"Hey, little dude. I'd better not."

"What's the matter?" Bridgette walked toward him wiggling her green fingers. "Afraid of a little slime?"

Afraid of wanting to kiss another man's woman. "No, I've got to . . . uh . . . take Dahlia for a walk."

"I want to walk Dahlia!" Louie yelled.

26

"No," came out too fast. He quickly added, "You're busy with your mom. Maybe you can walk her another time." He started to leave, and turned back, unable to leave unsafe stones in their path. "You should have your husband put a peephole in that door, for safety. And Louie's playset is missing a slat. He's probably got it on his honey-do list, but I thought I'd mention it." *Honey-do list? Ramble much? Get out of here.*

Bridgette pressed her lips together, a haunted expression descending over her face, and just as quickly it disappeared. "It's just me and Louie," she said in a small voice that made him want to hold her. "But I can get my dad or my sister to fix those things."

Interest piqued, Bodhi debated playing with the slime after all. But he'd already used Dahlia as an excuse to leave.

"What's a honey-do list?" Louie asked.

"Just a list of things to do around the house," Bridgette answered.

"Bodhi can help us!" Louie blinked big, hopeful eyes in his direction. "I could help, too. We saw you fixing your back door. Remember, Mom? You were watching him that day when you kept forgetting to throw me the ball?"

Interesting . . .

Her cheeks flushed, and something inside him switched on. He *wanted* to help them, to make sure they were safe. But trying to keep his emotional distance felt more dangerous than stealthily invading other countries. That was a battle he wasn't sure he could handle.

"I think Bodhi has enough on his hands right now," Bridgette said.

If he opened his mouth to speak, he'd tell her she was wrong. He could handle the work on his mother's house and Bridgette's repairs, and still make love to every inch of her body all night long.

He. Was. Screwed.

With a reluctant nod of agreement, he left the way he'd come. *Wanting* Bridgette Dalton.

CHAPTER FOUR

FRIDAY WAS A madhouse at the flower shop. Bridgette didn't have five minutes to breathe. She was thankful that her mother had been willing to watch the shop long enough for her to bring Louie to his sleepover. Bridgette might have been relying on fast food and looking forward to a night out with her sisters, but that didn't mean Louie wasn't her priority. She needed his sweet hugs and kisses to hold her over until she'd see him the next morning, but mostly, she didn't want him to feel that having only one parent meant he came second to her other responsibilities. Her mind was scattered enough these days by the big, beefy guy living next door. But Louie had given him an in last night, and Bodhi had been quick to turn him down. A little too quick. He'd also skillfully evaded responding to her comment about the blonde in the Jeep yesterday afternoon.

And yet here she was, pulling into her driveway later that evening, running late to get ready for Willow's engagement party, and instead of worrying about that, she was thinking about Bodhi. How did he know about peace lilies? And his dog's name? *She's remained kind despite being tested in every way.* Could his explanation have been a coincidence? Or did he know that was one of the meanings behind the dahlia flower? Her mind drifted to his hard, sweaty body in those revealing running shorts and the dark look in his eyes when he'd taken the planter from her hands and stepped close enough that his *maleness* had invaded her every sense.

Tingling with the memory, she threw her car door open. The sound of a chain saw drew her attention to Bodhi's side yard, where he was precariously perched high up in a tree, severing a dead limb. Even from that distance, she could see the definition of his triceps and biceps as he manhandled the machine. His powerful thighs flexed beneath him. Good Lord, was there anything the man could not do? The chain saw roared, and the limb fell to the ground. A satisfied smile lifted his lips. The air seemed to vibrate even after he turned off the chain saw. He wiped his brow, then absently swiped at his chest. Bridgette's fingers curled with the urge to feel his hot, sweaty muscles and see his lips curl into a wanting grin because of *her* touch. She imagined him climbing down from the tree and onto *her*, his piercing eyes and commanding, steady voice telling her they'd make the most of Louie's night out.

Dahlia barked from behind the fence, startling her from her fantasy. She was practically panting, and Bodhi's serious eyes blazed a path to hers. She lifted a shaky hand hip height in an embarrassed wave, hoping she didn't look as turned on as she felt, and made a beeline for her front door.

It was time for desperate measures.

Willow was right. After all these years, her body had come alive again, and she needed to do something about it. Thank goodness her brother, Ben, was picking her up tonight. Maybe she could drink Bodhi off her mind.

She tried not to think about Bodhi as she showered, but if there was one thing she'd learned since he'd moved in, it was that if she didn't take care of the hungry bunny between her legs, she'd be horny all night. She stood beneath the warm spray and closed her eyes, her mind sifting through images of that delicious man, on the sidewalk, crouched in her driveway, in the tree. Her hands moved down her belly, becoming his in her mind. His thick fingers slid between her legs, adeptly finding all the right spots. His voice whispered through her mind. *Now I know where to find you.* God, that voice . . . *Yes. Find me. Make me come for you.* Five years of self-gratification made her an expert, and Bodhi's image quickly sent her soaring. She gripped the tile for stability as her body pulsed, and "Bodhi" sailed from her lips like a prayer.

She dried off and heard her phone ringing. *Darn it.* She'd left it downstairs with her purse. Wrapped in a towel, she hurried down the steps. She'd left the front door open for Ben, and cool air swept over her legs, breezing in through the screen door. She hurried into the kitchen, arriving just as her phone stopped ringing. *Ugh.* As she filled a glass with water, her phone vibrated with a text from Piper. She read it as she took a sip. *Where are you? Ben tried to call you, too. He's running late. Remember to dress hot. No mom panties!*

Her sister had no idea what they were in for tonight. Bridgette was going to dress sexier than she had in years. If nothing else, a night of shameless flirting should clear her mind of Bodhi. Maybe then her body would calm down, and she could return to being a normal, sensible neighbor.

She set her glass down and typed a response as she headed for the stairs. *Sexy panties. Check! See you soon.* She lifted her eyes from her phone and started at the sight of Bodhi standing on the other side of the screen door, wearing only his shorts and boots. Her traitorous body threw a celebration, making her hot and bothered again. Seriously? Now she needed another shower. A *cold* one.

"Hi. Um, sorry," he said, and turned his face away. "I just came by to borrow some sugar."

"Sugar?" Adrenaline pounded like a drum in her ears.

He lifted an empty mug, his eyes gliding back to hers. "For coffee. I forgot to pick some up at the store and—" He waved at his body, which she realized was covered in sawdust. An incredible, deep laugh fell from his lips. "What is it about us and towels? Sorry. I'll clean up and go to the store."

The mother in her said to let him go, but the passionate *woman* he'd unleashed reared her wild head and pushed the door open. "Get in here. I have sugar."

The house seemed to close in around them as he followed her into the kitchen. She heard every footstep, every breath, felt his powerful presence keeping his distance as she reached for the sugar in the top cabinet.

He cursed under his breath. "Let me." His hand swallowed her wrist as he lowered it. "You reach up like that, and I'm going to get one hell of a show."

He kept hold of her, standing so close she could smell his musky male scent. If she leaned forward, she could taste him. Now, there was an idea.

A bad one.

Neighbor. Neighbor. Neighbor.

He watched her intently as he set the sugar bowl on the counter. His gaze moved to his hand, and he released her wrist. She instantly missed the heat of his touch, though the inferno raging between them had her palms sweating.

Needing something to do with her hands besides touching *him*, she opened the top of the container. "How sweet do you like?"

His eyes smoldered. "*Very. Sweet* and *hot.*"

Oh Lord. She began scooping sugar into his mug, and he grabbed her hand, stopping her. He was *handsy*. She'd forgotten how much she loved *handsy*.

"Too much?" she asked breathlessly.

He shook his head, eyes locked on hers.

She swallowed hard. She was a mother and had gone through childbirth. She could handle anything. Including this fast-burning wick of dynamite between them.

"Bodhi?"

His massive chest rose and fell with each heavy breath. "Bridgette."

"We seem to have a problem." *Oh God.* Did she really say that out loud? That's what being a mother did to a woman. Wasn't she always teaching Louie to use his words and not to be afraid to express himself? She had a bone to pick with her own mother for teaching her those things.

He cocked his head, his eyes narrowing. The man didn't need a voice, because heaven help her, she wanted to experience a *horizontal* conversation with him. No words necessary.

But right now words *were* necessary. "We can't be near each other without—"

"I know." His jaw twitched, and he looked at his hand, still clutching hers.

"'Kay" was all she could manage.

Her phone vibrated, and she started. He remained still as a statue.

"That's my . . . I'm late . . . Ben's coming."

With a curt nod, he grabbed his mug and headed for the door. "Thanks for the sugar."

Bridgette's breath rushed from her lungs. She hadn't realized she was trembling. Or damp between her legs. Oh man, one cold shower coming up . . .

No amount of exercise could break the spell a certain sexy blonde had cast on Bodhi. He'd been *this close* to claiming that pretty mouth of hers, but the name *Ben* had snapped his idiot brain into submission. He'd gone for a run, worked out harder than he had in ages, and taken a frigid shower. But the thought of Bridgette and another man had him tied in knots. After today's scorching encounter, he wasn't about to sit around wondering what they were doing. He needed a diversion.

He gave Dahlia a kiss on her snout, locked up the house, and headed for the local pub by the marina. He'd met the owner, Harley

Dutch, when he and his mother had first visited Sweetwater, and had been surprised to learn that Harley had moved from New York City to help his family out when his father had fallen ill. Four years later he was still there. Harley had pretty much sold them on Sweetwater.

The parking lot was packed, reminding him it was the start of a weekend. Days of the week hadn't meant much to Bodhi in years. In his line of work, he showed up when he was needed and didn't think about days, nights, or anything other than the mission until it was over. Time in between assignments could be a few weeks or a few months. He always prayed for the latter, hoping those serving their country were safe.

He pulled open the heavy wooden door, greeted by the din of the dimly lit bar. He made his way through a crowd of couples bumping and grinding to a fast beat. Women smiled at him, trying to hook the big fish. At six three, with a body made for war, he stood out in a crowd. As a badass twentysomething, he'd loved the attention. But at thirty-four, he liked his privacy. Unfortunately, sitting next door to the empty house of the woman he wanted in his bed led to frustration. Tonight, distraction won out over privacy.

He leaned on the end of the bar and flagged down the burly bar owner.

Harley flashed a friendly smile. "The usual?"

"Sounds good. Thanks." Bodhi wasn't a big drinker, but Harley had turned him on to a locally brewed beer that hit the spot.

"Things are busy tonight. I'll put it on your tab." Harley set a bottle down in front of him. "How are the renovations going?"

"Coming along. There's a lot to do, but I'll get there." He took a swig of his drink as Harley went to help another customer. A brunette at the other end of the bar was eyeing him seductively. If only he were an asshole, he could pick up a random chick and bang the thoughts of Bridgette out of his system. But he'd sowed those oats, and he had no desire to be that guy again.

"Bodhi?"

He turned at the sound of a familiar voice, and it took him a second to place Aurelia outside the bookstore, and in Sweetwater instead of New York City. Her short black dress threw him off, too. Every time he'd seen her she'd been wearing jeans and Converse. "I didn't recognize you without a book in your hand. How's it going?"

She tucked her long brown hair behind her ear. "I'm great, thanks. So, you really did it? You came to check out the town for your mother?"

"Actually, I bought her a place up the road. I'm just here fixing it up. Do you come back home often?"

"About once a month, but tonight is my friend Willow's engagement party. You should come meet everyone."

His thought skidded as *Willow* connected dots to *Bridgette* in his mind. Aurelia pointed to a table in the back, where Bridgette sat with her hand on a guy's shoulder, talking to someone farther down the table. What were the frigging chances he'd end up at the same place as Bridgette and her date?

"That's okay." *I've had enough torture for one day.* "I think I'll pass."

"Oh, come on." She grabbed his arm and pulled, like a gnat trying to drag an elephant.

The song changed, and all the girls around the table pushed to their feet, bringing Bridgette into full view. *Christ*, she was beautiful, wearing some sort of barely there black silk blouse with spaghetti straps and a plunging neckline. Her legs looked a mile long in a short white skirt and a pair of strappy black heels. Aurelia was talking, but Bodhi had tunnel vision, and everything other than Bridgette dragging the tall, dark-haired guy to the dance floor was white noise. Bridgette wrapped her arms around the dude's neck, smiling up at him with adoring eyes, and Bodhi's pulse spiked.

He became aware of his feet moving and forced himself to break his stare as Aurelia tugged him toward the dance floor.

"Aurelia, I'm really not looking for—"

She set her hands on his shoulders. "Relax. I'm not trying to pick you up. I just want to dance. Everyone has someone to dance with except me."

"There are plenty of other guys in here who would probably kill to dance with you."

"Yup. You got that right," she said with a cheeky smile. "But I'm hot off the heels of a stormy relationship and not looking to get involved with anyone. I'm just here for the party anyway. I haven't moved back. But one day soon I'm coming back for good and combining my grandmother's old bookstore with Willow's bakery."

"Sorry about the relationship, but that sounds like a great idea," he said, trying to focus on her and not Bridgette and her date, who were dancing closer to them by the second.

"I think it will be. We're making plans. Thanks for dancing with me."

"So, I'm your safe bet?" he teased. "Dance with me and guys leave you alone?"

He stole another glance at Bridgette, who seemed oblivious to his presence. If only he could be of hers. He was drawn to her like a moth to a flame, wondering what that guy had that he didn't. *A career that doesn't include possible death every time he reports to work.*

"Pretty much," Aurelia said. "You're like the Incredible Hulk with all these muscles. Nobody will dare hit on me now."

"Glad to be of service."

Bridgette laughed, and he wanted to know what the guy had said to earn the sweet sound.

"Why are you so tense?" Aurelia followed his gaze over her shoulder. "Ah. Bridgette. She has that effect on guys. She's gorgeous, isn't she?"

"Sorry." He forced his attention back to Aurelia. "I didn't mean to stare. That was rude."

"No, it's not. It's not like I'm your date. Besides, how can you resist?" She glanced over her shoulder again. "Hey, Bridge."

Aw, hell.

Bridgette turned with a wide smile, which instantly faded. Her brows knitted, her eyes darting curiously—*jealously?*—between Bodhi and Aurelia.

Bodhi tried to refrain from being a dick, but "Nice to see you with clothes on" came out anyway. He'd probably get struck by lightning for saying it, but he wasn't above pushing a few buttons of the woman he knew wanted him as much as he wanted her.

"Wait, you know each other?" Aurelia asked.

Bridgette's cheeks flamed. "Yeah, this is him. The neighbor I told you about." Her eyes narrowed seductively as she said, "I think I prefer you in the towel. Are you following me?"

"This is the neighbor?" The guy she was with held out a hand. "Ben Dalton, and you are . . . ?"

Dalton? Oh, fuck. She'd said it was just her and Louie. Maybe she was only separated, not divorced. Squaring his shoulders, he met Ben's gaze, manning up to step down. "Bodhi Booker, and I'm *not* following your wife."

CHAPTER FIVE

"WIFE?" BEN LAUGHED. "Dude, I don't have a wife." His eyes turned serious. "Bridgette's my sister."

Bridgette couldn't stifle her smile at the lost look on Bodhi's face.

"I'm sorry. I just assumed when you said *Dalton* . . ."

Ben glared at him. "Should we talk about you two seeing each other in various stages of undress?"

"No, we should not," Bridgette snapped, wondering if Bodhi knew Aurelia or if he'd just picked her up. Aurelia Stark had been raised by her grandparents, who had owned the only bookstore in Sweetwater for more than forty years. She'd gone to school with Willow and had moved away after college.

"Come on, Benny." Aurelia dragged him away.

Bodhi's gaze bored into Bridgette as wordless seconds ticked by like a hundred fuses nearing explosion. His arm swept around her, bringing her against his magnificently hard frame. One large, strong hand splayed across her lower back, and the other threaded into her hair, like he owned her. And *oh*, how she *wanted* to be owned by him. Just for a night. A very steamy, sexy night that she could relive a trillion times over. It was such a bad idea, lusting over her neighbor. She was almost glad that somewhere in the back of her lust-addled brain she remembered he had been dancing with Aurelia, and jealousy gripped her.

"Did I mess up your nightly hookup?" She felt his entire body flex against her.

He remained silent for a long moment, pressed so close not even air could fit between them.

"I don't hook up," he said in a low, rough voice.

"Aurelia . . . ?"

The muscles in his jaw jumped. "She's a friend from New York City, where I live. She dragged me to the dance floor while I was busy watching *you*."

He guided her hands around his neck as the weight of his confession sank in. Feeling his warm skin beneath her fingers for the first time sent adrenaline rushing through her. The back of his neck was smooth save for a few thin, bumpy lines. *Scars.* He made a very male sound of appreciation, a cross between a groan and a grunt, and it was a surprisingly huge turn-on. The two drinks she'd had lessened her inhibitions, and she was glad for the high. She told herself she deserved it as she touched the back of his neck again, hoping to earn another wanton sound.

The song "River" by Bishop Briggs came on, and Bodhi picked up the erotic beat seamlessly. She closed her eyes, giving herself over to the music, reveling in the feel of his hard heat against her belly. She matched the pulse of his hips, enjoying the graze of his powerful chest and his ragged inhalations. She'd kept this sensual part of herself suppressed for so long, it was freeing to get lost in the music, lost in *him*. His body moved with fluidity *and* virility, reminding her of a powerful boa constrictor seducing its prey. *Oh, yeah, baby, wrap around me and squeeze me tight.*

He pressed his scruffy jaw to her cheek. It had been so long since she'd felt the scratch of a man's whiskers, the hard press of his chest, her whole body lit up from the inside out.

"You were right," he said beside her ear. "We *definitely* have a problem."

Oh Lord. She hadn't been this turned on since Jerry. She should say something, anything, but her mind was too swept up in him to speak.

"I can't stop thinking about you," he said heatedly.

His warm breath slid over her skin, sinking into her pores and taking his confession with it.

"You're not *mine*, but seeing you with another guy . . ."

She shuddered at the intense way he said *mine*.

His lips grazed along her cheek, and she held her breath, anticipation building inside her. When his lips brushed lightly over hers, her whole body rose, trying to capture the kiss, but he drew back, a full-on battle raging in his eyes.

"We should talk," he said firmly.

Man, she had it bad. She would have ended that sentence with *kiss*.

"Your sister's party . . . ?" He searched her eyes with a serious expression.

"Over," she said quickly. "We've been here for hours. Most everyone has already left."

The edges of his mouth tipped up, softening the inherent command in his granitelike features.

"I just need to say goodbye," she added.

For a beat, neither of them moved. Was he already mourning the impending distance between them, as she was? She slid her hand down his arm, slowing to enjoy the feel of each muscle as it reacted to her touch. She'd been dreaming of touching him since the first night they'd met, and he was even more magnificent than she'd imagined.

She wrapped her hand around his long fingers, and his eyes heated, never wavering from hers. She'd never met a man so intense. Her nerves were on fire as she led him toward the table where some of her family members were talking. Awareness of the significance of her decision, of the signals she was sending, slammed into her, and she slowed to catch her breath. Was she ready for this?

He put a finger beneath her chin and lifted, as he'd done at his front door, gazing thoughtfully down at her. "Would you rather I leave?"

She shook her head. "No. I'm just . . . I'm good." And she was. She'd needed that pause to acknowledge and accept what she was feeling. She was nervous, but she wanted this. She wanted *him*. Her smile came genuinely, and earned her one in return. "Come on."

She became more nervous as they approached the table. Willow was practically sitting in Zane's lap as they mooned over each other. Piper and Talia were scoping out some guy across the room, and Ben was in a heated discussion with Aurelia. She shouldn't be nervous. This was her *normal*.

Except normal didn't usually include holding hands with a man she wanted to strip naked and devour. *Oh boy . . .*

"Well, well, well. If it isn't the naked neighbor." Mischief danced in Piper's eyes as she pushed to her feet and strutted around the table in her skinny jeans and slinky little blouse. She set her hands on her hips, running an assessing eye over Bodhi.

His jaw clenched.

"Bodhi, this is my sister Piper. She works in construction and is around guys all day, which means she has absolutely no filter. Please take her with a grain of salt."

He flashed a cocky grin. "For the record, I had a towel on."

"For the record," Piper said, "she wished you didn't."

"Piper!" Talia called across the table. She sounded, and looked, like the astute professor she was, with her long dark hair secured at the base of her neck and wearing a pretty white blouse and a black pencil skirt.

Bodhi's expression turned serious again. "I'm pretty sure Louie wouldn't have appreciated that."

She swallowed hard. Did he know that watching out for her son was better than foreplay? "You knew Louie was outside?"

"As I said"—Bodhi leaned closer and lowered his voice—"I notice *everything*."

Can you tell my nerves are on fire, too?

"Being attuned to your surroundings is an admirable quality," Talia said. "I'm Talia, by the way. Also one of Bridgette's sisters."

Bodhi nodded. "Nice to meet you."

Zane stood and reached over the table to shake Bodhi's hand. "Willow and I were leaving the bakery the night you and Bridgette met. I'm Zane Walker, Willow's fiancé." Zane had grown up in Sweetwater. He was Ben's best friend, and had always been close with their family. Before Willow had gone away to college, she'd secretly asked Zane to *help* her lose her virginity. Ten years later, Zane had needed to clean up his bad-boy reputation, and he'd asked Willow to be his fake fiancée. It hadn't taken long for their love to rekindle, ten times stronger than it had been years earlier. They were proof that true love could appear out of nowhere and overcome anything.

"Walker." Bodhi's brows drew into a serious slant. "You're an actor?"

"Was," Zane answered. Looking at Willow adoringly, he said, "Screenplay writer now." He turned his attention to Bodhi. "Bridgette said you were checking Willow out the other day. I'm cool with that. Just don't get handsy with my woman or I'll have to have you killed."

Willow laughed. "He's kidding about the killing part."

"And I was kidding about the checking-out part," Bridgette insisted. "Gosh, you guys. Way to scare him off."

"Aren't you glad you met me, Bodhi? Now you have a famous friend and the Dalton clan to drive you bonkers." Aurelia rose to her feet and tugged at Ben's shirt. "Get your butt up and drive me home, Benny boy. You guys wore me out."

"You and Ben?" Bridgette asked skeptically. "*What* have I missed?"

Aurelia rolled her eyes. "Please. He's my chauffeur. I walked here, but I'm too tired to walk home."

Piper tapped Bodhi's shoulder, and he leaned in close to hear something Bridgette couldn't. She wondered what type of hell Piper was giving him now.

Ben hugged Willow. "Congratulations, sis." He nodded at Zane. "Congrats, bro."

That sparked the end of their gathering, as everyone got ready to leave. Bodhi stepped closer to Bridgette, placing a hand possessively on her lower back. Heat blazed through the thin material of her blouse, making her want to be in his arms again. *Now.*

"Bridge? You okay? Need a ride?" Ben asked.

She glanced at Bodhi, who looked like he was just as ready to be alone with her as she was with him. "I think I'm good, thanks."

Ben pulled Bridgette's phone from his pocket and handed it to her. She'd forgotten he had it.

"Piper? Need a ride?" Ben asked.

Piper pointed to the bar, where Harley was watching her like a hawk. "I think I'm going to hang around and harass Harley."

After a round of goodbyes that took far too long, Bridgette and Bodhi were finally alone—in a bar full of people.

"Would you like me to hold your phone?" Bodhi's gaze trailed over her body. "Do you have house keys?"

"I have a key hidden at home so I don't have to carry one." She slipped the phone into the back pocket of his jeans. "Thank you."

He leaned in close. "I need to give you a lesson in safety for the single woman."

"Is it a hands-on lesson?"

His eyes went volcanic. "What time do you need to be back for Louie?"

Chalk another one up for best foreplay ever. How many men would think of Louie first and not the inferno raging between them? "He's spending the night at a friend's house."

He hauled her onto the dance floor, and there was no calming the dizzying currents racing through her.

♥ ♥ ♥

Bodhi was stuck somewhere between paradise and hell. Meeting Bridgette's family and friends had given him enough time to think things through, but he didn't like the answer he'd come up with. He knew he shouldn't be leading her on, or wondering if she kissed like a tigress or a kitten, or what she had on underneath that slinky little outfit. But every glance, every brush of her warm, soft skin, made him want *more*, and for the first time in his life, he wanted to do the wrong thing and risk getting burned.

Gone was the shy woman he'd seen earlier. Holding his gaze with a glimmer of fierce possession, Bridgette mouthed angsty lyrics about paradise and war zones, dancing like rhythm ran through her veins. The tempo climbed fast and frantic, exploding into a storm of vibrations. Bridgette tossed her head back, her long hair sweeping over her shoulders, her breasts brushing against Bodhi's chest. The beat faded to a dull hum that wound around them, drawing them closer. His hands moved along the dip of her waist, and hers came to rest on his chest. When she set her beautiful green eyes on him, the rest of the world spun away, and he lowered his mouth toward hers.

The second before their lips touched, he tangled his hand in her hair, holding their kiss at bay. "Bridgette . . . I'm not . . . I can't . . ." He had no words. How could he tell her he wasn't looking for a relationship when he wanted her this badly?

"Unless you're married, just kiss me."

He caught sight of Piper in his peripheral vision, awakening his brain and reminding him that despite feeling like they were the only two people who existed in the crowded bar, they were far from alone. *Fuck.* With an arm around her waist, he headed for the door.

"Where are we going?" she asked as he hurried outside and around the side of the building.

"I'm *not* married."

"Then why . . . ?"

43

He drew her against him, and holy fuck did she feel good. "Because I don't want you to be the talk of the town tomorrow."

"Oh . . ." Her lips curved up.

He tucked a lock of hair behind her ear and brushed his lips over hers, trying to slow himself down long enough to do the right thing. "Bridgette?"

"Yeah."

"I need my mouth on you."

"Yes," came out like a plea.

He tightened his hold on her, hoping it might keep her from blowing him off when he said what he had to. She was trembling, and for the second time that night he wished he could be an asshole and not reveal his truth. But he wasn't an asshole, and Bridgette deserved honesty. "As badly as I want you, you've got a son. You need someone who will be around. I'm only here for a couple weeks, and my job . . . I never know when I'll be around. I can't make promises for more than tonight."

Her arms circled his neck, and those delicate fingers brushed over his skin, sending shocks of heat straight to his core. "Bodhi?"

"Hm?"

"I hear you, and I have a lot of questions, but can you please just kiss me before I lose my frigging mi—"

Her words were smothered by the hard press of his lips, and *sweet baby Jesus*, he devoured her succulent mouth, crushing her to him. Her body was warm and soft. She made a sexy sound of surrender, melting against him and somehow kissing him harder at the same time. He wanted to savor this kiss, to memorize the feel of her. His hands moved along the dip at the base of her spine, and she arched forward, pressing deliciously against him. Lust pooled deep within him, bubbling up with every swipe of their tongues. She was torture and pleasure, sweet and sinful, and he never wanted to let her go. He couldn't remember *ever* kissing a woman like this, and when she gripped the base of his skull and held on tight, he deepened the kiss with such force she stumbled backward and hit the building.

Fear of hurting her rose above all else, and he tore his mouth away. "Are you okay?"

Her cheeks were flushed, her swollen lips curved up in the sexiest smile he'd ever seen. "God, yes."

She pulled him into another kiss, and it took all his self-control not to lift her into his arms and wind those gorgeous legs around his waist. He angled her head, plundering and sweeping his tongue over every crevice, like he wanted to do to the rest of her body. His hands moved down her bare thighs, then up, lingering at the edge of her skirt.

"Christ, Bridge," he said between kisses. "You're too sexy."

She smiled against his lips, and he took her in a demanding kiss, grinding his rock-hard cock against her. She moaned into his mouth, and that sexy plea did him in. He clutched her ass, holding her tighter, letting her feel every inch of what she was doing to him.

"Bodhi," she said in one long breath.

Fuck, came out before he could stop it, and then all hell broke loose with his *verbal* control. "I knew one kiss would never be enough. I want to strip you naked, drop to my knees, and pleasure you until you feel me licking you in your sleep."

"Ohmygod," rushed from her lungs. She clung to his chest, her fingers digging into his skin through his shirt. "You don't say much, but boy, you do know when to use your words."

He kissed her again, cringing for his crudeness. "I'm sorry. It's been a really long time since I've done anything like this."

"I'm sure I have you beat."

His lips came down softly on her cheek and traced the line of her jaw. "I've been dying to do this."

He sealed his mouth over the base of her neck, pressing his tongue against that frantic pulse that had taunted him since he'd first set eyes on her.

She whimpered, holding his head in place. "Don't stop. Oh God." She bowed off the wall. "It's been so long. That feels good."

He sucked and licked and kissed and tasted, until she was writhing, moaning, digging her fingers into his skull. He needed *more*, and he wasn't about to take it here where anyone could see her.

He reluctantly tore his mouth away, both of them breathless.

Framing her face with his hands, he kissed her over and over again, unable to tear himself away completely. "What do you say we get out of here?"

CHAPTER SIX

BRIDGETTE'S THOUGHTS RACED every second of the short drive home. She tried to think rationally and slow herself down. But her body was acting like it was the Fourth of July, and every rational thought was shot down by how badly she wanted Bodhi. The fact that he was her *neighbor* should at least give her pause, for Louie's sake if nothing else. But as she watched him stalk around the truck, impossibly handsome and powerful, his taste lingering in her mouth, *neighbor* didn't hold the significance it probably should. Her body clearly thought she was not only ready to get back in the game, but it was anxious to play.

He opened her door and with one swift move turned her toward him, planting his hands on either side of the doorframe, his face a mask of serious restraint. "I meant what I said," he warned. "If you're looking for more than tonight, we end here."

Why was his bluntness such a turn-on? "I'm not *looking* for any-thing. This—*you*—are unexpected."

He glanced at her house, then his, and found her eyes again with genuine tenderness that would have knocked her legs out from under her had she not been sitting down.

"Bridge . . ."

She reached up and touched his cheeks, riveted by his compassion. "Unexpected doesn't mean *bad idea*."

"I need to know we're both going into this with our eyes open. No dreams of finding a happily ever after. You need to be sure, because I don't want to hurt you or Louie."

She was soaking up every dose of compassion he unknowingly doled out. Louie was her world, and Bodhi inherently knew that in ways other guys who had asked her out hadn't. They'd seen Louie as a roadblock, someone to work around. He saw Louie as the person who mattered most. Although Bodhi wasn't asking her out. He was asking about something far more important, something of more value than just her time. *Do I want to give myself over to you for only one night?*

Her answer didn't take any thought. "I'm nervous, but I'm as *sure* as I have ever been."

His arm circled around her waist, tugging her forward, and he captured her mouth with the force of a tsunami. She couldn't even say she'd forgotten how great kissing could be, because kissing Bodhi was nothing like kissing any other man. It was a full-body experience, and she felt it from her spinning mind to the very tips of her toes. He drew back, their lips parting for only a second before he returned for more, time and time again.

"Can't do this here," he said fervently, and lifted her out of the truck. His arm locked around her waist and then fell away. "Neighbors."

What a thrill it was to be with a man who thought of her before himself. She might not have dated since losing Jerry, but she kept up on the dating scene with her sisters, and she knew there were a lot of jerks out there. But she missed his touch, so she reminded him, "Did you not notice that the closest neighbor is about two acres down the road from your house? They can't see us."

"Maybe you shouldn't have reminded me. It opens way too many doors," he said with more than a hint of wickedness. He unlocked the front door, and Dahlia practically leapt into his arms.

"Hi, baby." He loved her up, then motioned with his hand, and Dahlia sank to all fours, panting at Bridgette.

Bridgette petted her. "You're a sweet girl, aren't you? Except when you're busy knocking people's groceries out of their hands."

Dahlia barked, and Bodhi groaned.

"I was only teasing," she assured him. "I love dogs, but I'm not home enough to take care of one."

"I know what that's like." He patted his thigh and headed through the living room. Dahlia trotted beside him and happily went out the back door.

Bridgette took in the mass of tarps, paint cans, brushes, ladders, and other tools on the floor. A comfortable-looking couch sat between two end tables, a few paperbacks were stacked on one, and a hammer lay on the other. Across the room were a dog bed, a stepladder, and more paint cans.

"Excuse the mess," Bodhi said, closing the distance between them.

"Toys in my living room, tarps in yours. We all have our messes."

"I'm freshening the place up for my mother, and wasn't expecting company."

He settled his hands on her hips, and her pulse quickened. "Your mother?"

"Yes. I bought the house for her to retire in. She sold her flower shop and is closing on her condo and moving here in November. Until then it'll be a place for her to get away from the rat race of New York City. I'm only here for two weeks, fixing it up for her. Then I'll go back to the city."

Trying to process what he'd said while standing a kiss away from him was like trying to do algebra in her head. *Or at all.* "That's why you knew about peace lilies."

"I think I was born with two green thumbs. I spent more hours working at her shop than I spent at home all through high school." He cradled her face in his hands with a dark look in his eyes. "Would you like to talk about my mother?"

She shook her head and went up on her toes as he captured her mouth in a smoldering kiss. How would she ever get enough of these kisses? She wanted to disappear into them, to be devoured until morning. He fisted his hand in her hair, sending a shock of heat between her legs. She clung to his shoulders, wanting—*needing*—to be closer, to feel his weight on her.

"God, your mouth," he said against her lips.

God, your voice! His roughness rumbled through her chest. He lifted her into his arms, guiding her legs around his thick waist, never breaking their kiss. Dahlia barked at the back door. Bridgette smiled. Bodhi sighed.

"It's okay." She kissed one corner of his mouth. "Let her in." She kissed the other side. "She's your baby. She depends on you."

He carried her to the back door. "You're some kind of saint."

"You can put me down."

His eyes narrowed with an authoritative air that left no room for negotiation. *Good.* She was totally into this Neanderthal, grunting hunk of a man.

Bodhi pulled the door open and gestured to Dahlia. The pup whimpered and sank down to her butt, looking up at him with sad eyes.

"She's not used to sharing me."

The pit of Bridgette's stomach knotted as she remembered the girl in the Jeep. What was she doing? She didn't really know anything about Bodhi. How could she put herself on the line like this? She knew better, but she wanted him. *Desperately.*

"Except with the blonde in the Jeep," she said softly, trying to wiggle free.

He tightened his hold on her. "Shira runs the charity I founded, Hearts for Heroes."

"You founded a charity?"

He nodded and said, "Shira is my closest friend, and I would never, *ever* sleep with her."

"Oh." She winced, feeling bad for assuming. She wanted to ask about the charity, but at the moment it seemed the less pressing of the two things he'd mentioned. "I assumed . . ."

"As I did with your brother." He cracked a smile. "I think we need to talk."

They needed to talk, but now that she knew she'd wrongly assumed he'd slept with Shira . . .

"I really wish you'd said *kiss*."

He chuckled and carried her over to the couch with Dahlia on his heels.

"You could change your mind," she suggested. "Try it. We need to *kiss*. It's easy—you just swap your four letters for mine."

He set her on the couch and sank down beside her. Dahlia nosed between his legs, pushing her big head toward his chest. He took the pup's face in his hands as he'd done to Bridgette. "I love you, but you need to lie down."

Melt. Melt. Melt. She tried to remember what the saying was about how a man treats his dog. Or maybe it was his mother. She looked around at the tarps and paint, and realized she was safe. Bodhi obviously treated both just fine.

He kissed the top of Dahlia's head. "Bed."

Dahlia seemed to frown as she lumbered off to the cushion across the room.

Bodhi stretched his arm across the back of the couch, settling his hand on Bridgette's shoulder, and turned so his whole body faced her. He laced their fingers together in another unexpected moment of tenderness. "Hi, beautiful."

She felt herself smiling, but her insides were whirling. "Hi."

"Let's get a few things out of the way. I am not the kind of guy who sleeps with random women."

"Aren't I a random woman?"

He shook his head. "Am I a random guy?"

She thought about that for a minute. She'd spent weeks secretly lusting after him, and in the week since he'd moved in, she'd learned a few things about him. Mainly that he looked amazing without his shirt on and had the power to weaken her knees with a single glance. But other important things, too, like knowing he was there to help his mother and that he took extra care thinking about Louie.

"Not random, no," she answered. "You're more than that."

He cocked a brow.

"Point taken," she admitted. "I don't sleep around, either. Honestly, I haven't been with a guy in years."

"Years? You don't have to make yourself out to be innocent. You're a sexy, smart woman. I imagine you've had plenty of boyfriends."

"Not for a very long time." She focused on his thumb, rubbing slow circles on her hand as she mustered the courage to tell him the truth. When she met his gaze, genuine interest looked back at her. "I was married."

"I assumed so," he said.

"I . . . *we* lost Jerry, my husband, to a car accident when Louie was four months old."

He squeezed her shoulder. "I'm sorry. That must have been awful."

She nodded, not wanting to get lost in a dark conversation. "It was. Jerry was the drummer for the band Sunderbolt."

"That's why he looked familiar when I saw the picture in your hallway."

"That's my Jerry." She smiled, and then her expression turned sorrowful.

"Were you married long?"

"Not that long. I was a rebellious nineteen-year-old when we met backstage at a concert, and he was as wild as they came. Like with you and me, sparks flew from the very first moment I saw him. I quit college, against my family's wishes, and we got married. We spent most of the next two years on the road, touring. He was leaving an after-party when it happened. He ran a red light, and a truck hit him." She swallowed past her thickening throat. "The media was all over me and Louie, so I laid low for a few months, changed our names back to Dalton, and started a new life here, near my family."

He lifted her chin with their joined hands, sorrow brimming in his eyes. "There are no words . . ."

"I don't need them. We're okay. We weren't for a while, but my family made sure we found our way."

"You're lucky to be close to your family, and you're clearly an excellent mother. Louie seems happy and well adjusted."

"Thank you. He's my heart and soul."

"That's evident in everything you do. I admire the strength it takes to be a single mother, and I don't want whatever this is between us to interfere with that."

What happened to Mr. Silent Brooder? She liked this sensitive side of him, and understood now why he kept it so well hidden. She'd seen lots of women gawking over him at the bar, and they'd fawn over him even more if they had any idea how thoughtful he was.

"Thank you. I don't want to turn tonight into a total downer, but you should know where I'm coming from. I haven't been with a man since I lost Jerry. I haven't even wanted to, and then you showed up in the bakery, and suddenly I'm like a groupie. I can't get enough of you."

He smiled. "That makes two of us. I haven't had a relationship since I was in college. My work is too dangerous to leave anyone at home waiting for me."

"What is it that you do?"

"I was Special Forces. Now I work for a civilian operation and handle covert rescue missions, and when I'm not away on an assignment, I help train others."

"Wow. That's impressive, and it explains your rough and rugged demeanor."

"You've got to be hard and be able to keep from getting emotionally involved to do what I do. I've seen too many worst-case scenarios play out not to be vigilant."

"I can see that. And by the looks of things, you're also a mama's boy, seeing as you bought her a house in our sweet little town. What about your father? Are you close to him, too?"

His expression hardened. "We lost him when I was eight."

"I'm sorry." She ached for him. "You must miss him very much."

"Not a day goes by that I don't. What about you and Jerry? You must miss him, too. Real love never leaves you."

She wasn't expecting such a bold question, or such an insightful comment. Usually people danced around the topic of her husband. But Bodhi obviously wasn't an insecure guy who needed to feel like he was the only man she'd ever set her eyes on. He seemed as grounded in reality, and as deeply rooted in family, as she was.

"You have no idea how nice it is to hear you say that," she admitted. "Most guys don't understand that just because a person is gone doesn't mean your love dies with them. We had a wild, crazy love, and I don't know if I'll ever love anyone in the same way I loved Jerry, but I hope one day I'll fall in love as deeply, even if it's different."

"I'm sure you will. Honestly, I'm surprised some guy hasn't already swept you off your feet."

"I wasn't exactly *sweepable*. Like I said, before you I never gave any guy a second thought. But time does heal all wounds. At first I thought about Jerry every minute. I saw him in Louie's facial expressions. I would have sworn I heard him playing the drums in the wind. The heart's a funny thing. It doesn't like to let go. But over time Louie became his own person, and now I see only glimpses of Jerry in him. And I don't know when or how, but at some point I went from being Jerry's widow to being Bridgette Dalton, mother, florist, sister, friend . . ."

She gazed into his eyes, feeling lighter with her confession, and foolish, because she'd just lost her chance at making out with the only man who had sparked her body to life in years. "Not exactly the hookup you thought you were getting, huh? You must want to run in the opposite direction now."

Maybe her confession would make a typical guy do exactly what she worried about, but Bodhi had never been typical. "I'm a rescuer, remember? My instinct is to take you in my arms and never let you go. To make yours and Louie's lives as full, and safe, and happy as they can possibly be. But I can't offer you that, and I won't even try."

She straightened her spine, and a forced smile appeared on her beautiful face. "I'm not looking for that, but I understand it's too much. I have a lot of baggage."

"First, please don't refer to what you've gone through as baggage. I know you didn't mean it negatively, but your past and Louie are a part of you, and anyone who would see Louie, your husband, or your past as baggage isn't worth a second look." That earned a genuine smile. "But you don't need rescuing, Bridgette. I was raised by a single mother. I know the strength and devotion it takes. Your parenting abilities make you all that much *more* attractive."

He pulled her closer. "With my career, I can't make any commitments, or even promise you tomorrow. They can call me in at any time and I'll have to drop everything and leave. And as I said, I'm going back to the city in two weeks. But I'm here now, and no part of me wants to run away."

"Bodhi," she whispered wantingly.

"I love hearing you say my name. But you need to make it clear if you want this, because once I get my mouth on you, I'm not going to stop. And I'll never forgive myself if I misread you."

She gripped his thigh, her fingers curling around his muscles. "You make me feel more than I have in years. Even if tonight is all we have,

I don't want to miss it. Kiss me, Bodhi. Kiss me, and don't stop until you have no kisses left to give."

He wasted no time drawing her closer and urgently claiming her mouth. He deepened the kiss, passion and greed driving him to take more as she groped his arms and neck, back and head. He caressed her thigh, following her curves over her hip and beneath her shirt, feeling the heat of her skin and craving so much more. His thumb grazed her bare breast, whipping his insides into a flurry of heat and desire. He palmed her breast, and she moaned. He pressed a series of feathery kisses along her lips as he brushed his thumb over her taut nipple. She shuddered against him, and the sexiest sighing, needful sound fell from her lips.

"I need more of you, beautiful." He lifted the hem of her shirt, and she bit her lower lip, giving him the sweetest, most vulnerable look.

"Hurry," she whispered.

Thank fucking God. He tore her blouse over her head and tossed it onto the other side of the couch. "Christ, you're gorgeous."

She tugged at his shirt, and he tore it off and dropped it to the floor, kissing her as she groped him. He kissed her neck, working his way down and teasing over her breast with kisses and slow licks. She dug her fingers into his hair, arching and moaning as he sealed his mouth over her breast and sucked *hard*.

"Ah," she cried. "*So* good. Geez—"

He teased and taunted, and gave her other breast the same sensual attention. She rocked her hips, and he pushed his hand beneath her skirt, seeking silk or lace—and finding the sexiest bare hip he could have ever imagined. His fingertips grazed the thin strap of a thong, ripping a greedy sound from his lungs.

"Expecting mom panties?" she said heatedly.

"I don't know what mom panties are, but I'm sure you'd look amazing in them."

She laughed, and he kissed her again, deep and possessively.

"We need more room." He rose to his feet with her in his arms and her legs circling his waist. He carried her downstairs with Dahlia on their heels and headed toward the bedroom.

"I'm getting a little addicted to the feel of your legs around me."

"Good."

"Bed," he said to Dahlia. The pup obediently lay down on her cushion.

"I thought that command was meant for me," Bridgette said.

"Disappointed?"

"Wouldn't you like to know?" She touched her lips to his. "Why are we downstairs? Isn't the master bedroom upstairs?"

"There's no way I'm going to do all the dirty things I want to do to you in the bed my mother is going to be sleeping in."

"I like you, Bodhi Booker," she said breathily. "You're thoughtful even when you're hot and bothered."

"You haven't *seen* hot and bothered." He toed off his shoes and set her on her feet in the dark bedroom. "You have no idea how many fantasies I've had about you in my bedroom."

"Maybe as many as I've had about you?" She dragged her finger down the center of his chest all the way to the button on his jeans.

He'd fought his desires for weeks, and now she was here, his for the night. He wanted to savor her, to cherish this night and make it one she would never forget. He took her face in his hands and gazed into her eyes. "You're messing with my head, beautiful."

He gathered her hair over one shoulder and kissed the skin he'd exposed, following the sleek ridge of her shoulder, down her arm, memorizing the feel of her trembling against his lips. He lifted her hand and pressed a kiss to the center of her palm. Her breath rushed from her lungs.

"Mm. My beautiful girl likes that." With a hand on her hip, he moved behind her, kissing the back of her shoulder, along the nape of her neck, and grazed his teeth over the shell of her ear. She reached behind her, gripping his thighs, and he began to sway. There was no music, no sounds in the room beside her seductive moans as their bodies moved to a secret beat.

He reached around her, filling his hands with her breasts, teasing the taut peaks between his finger and thumb.

"Bodhi," she panted out.

He sank his teeth into the curve of her neck and sucked.

"Oh. My. Lord."

He unzipped her skirt, bathing her neck and shoulders in kisses. Her skirt fell to her feet, and she leaned her head back against his chest with another needful sound. He quickly stepped out of his jeans and tugged off his socks, leaving on only his briefs. He brushed his cock sensually against her ass, and she met each slow grind with one of her own. He loved hearing her ragged breathing turn shallow as his hand moved down her belly and beneath her thong.

"Yes," she said.

His fingers moved over her damp curls, to the slick heat between her legs. She rocked against his hand. He dragged his tongue along her neck and whispered heatedly in her ear, "You feel so good, baby. I'm going to make you come so many times, you won't remember what the word *need* means."

He kissed a path down her spine and used his teeth and hand to remove her thong, leaving her in only her high heels. Dragging his hand over her hips, he moved in front of her. Her eyes were closed, her lips parted. He lowered his mouth to hers and traced her lips with his tongue. She panted harder, and he did it again, loving the flush of her skin, the taste of her desire. He cradled her face with one hand, kissing her deeply as his other hand sought the tight heat between her legs. It didn't take long to learn her pleasure points. Her shallow breathing and sultry noises gave them away with each stroke of his fingers.

"Come for me." He claimed her mouth again as he took her up, up, up and over the edge.

"Bodhi—"

Her body pulsed hot and tight. She was beyond sexy, standing next to the bed in her high heels, her thighs slick with her arousal, breathing heavily. And he was nowhere near done.

He continued his pursuit of driving her out of her mind, kissing the swell of her breasts, circling the tight peaks with his tongue. She clung to his shoulders, her body trembling.

"Still with me, beautiful girl?"

"Yes," she whispered.

"Cold?" He kissed his way down the center of her belly.

"Hot. So *hot.*"

When he reached the juncture of her thighs, he held her hips and pressed a kiss to her curls, inhaling the intoxicating scent of her arousal. When he took his first taste of her, she made a breathy sound that slithered beneath his skin, all the way down to his eager cock.

"So sweet, beautiful girl."

He licked and tasted, teasing until she was so wet and needy he couldn't resist devouring her sex. She rocked against his mouth, and when he teased his fingers over her most sensitive area, she held her breath. Her thighs flexed, and she tugged his hair to the point of pain, but he didn't relent. He thrust his tongue in deep, wanting to feel her lose control.

"Oh God. Yes. Don't stop. Bodhi—"

Her pleas and indiscernible noises filled the room as she shattered against his mouth. He stayed with her through the very last shudder of her climax, and when her body went slack, he carried her to the bed and took off her heels.

He held her as her breathing calmed. She blinked up at him with the hazy eyes of a sated lover, and he lowered his mouth to hers, testing her boundaries. He still tasted of her arousal, but she kissed him hungrily, bowing off the mattress. She palmed him through his briefs, squeezing tight enough to make him lose his mind.

"One night will never be enough, Bridgette," he said between kisses. "I know."

They kissed again, a slow, exploratory kiss that went on and on. Her hand moved tight and hot along his shaft, and when she slipped her hand inside his briefs, he groaned again, breaking the kiss.

"*Christ.* Eight months, Bridge. That's how long it's been for me. I'm not going to last if you do that."

Her eyes flamed, and she scooted lower on the bed, tugging at his briefs. "You realize that makes you all the more appealing."

"Because if you put your sexy mouth on me I'll come?"

She laughed and touched her lips to his stomach. "No, because it'll be a challenge to get you aroused again *after* you come."

"Oh, like that's going to be a problem with you lying naked beneath me?" He lifted her up beside him, and she squealed with delight. Her golden hair swept across the pillow. "Your smile kills me."

"What does this do?" She wiggled her hips beneath him.

"Definitely *doesn't* kill me." He pinned her hands to the mattress as he lowered his face near hers. "I can't remember the last time I smiled this much."

"Eight months ago. *Duh!*" Laughter burst from her lungs, and he kissed her hard, turning those giggles into hot, hungry moans.

A phone rang, and they stilled, eyes wide open.

"Louie," she said at the same time he said, "Louie?"

CHAPTER SEVEN

BRIDGETTE WRESTLED WITH guilt as she washed up and dressed after learning that Louie had a bellyache and had just thrown up. She'd been having the most magnificent night she'd had in years when she should have been with her son.

"I'll drive you over," Bodhi said for the second time.

"Bodhi, I appreciate the offer, but it'll just raise questions that he doesn't need to think about." She'd been a single mother long enough to handle a puking kid, but she loved that he'd offered to help.

He took her by the shoulders with a serious look in his eyes. He was back to Bodhi, *neighbor*, with an undercurrent of something more.

"He knows I'm your neighbor, and he's . . . five?"

"Yes."

"Then hopefully his mind isn't attuned to the nuances of adult romance yet. All he's thinking about is being in Mommy's arms. If he throws up on the way home, you'll have to pull over to help him. Besides the fact that he could choke in the car, it's not safe for the two of you to be alone on the side of the road this late at night."

She stumbled over his thoughtfulness. "It's Sweetwater. It's not like anything's going to happen."

"Bridgette," he said firmly. "I'm sure you had a few drinks tonight, right?"

"Yes, but—"

"I'm driving you. No one will know there's something between us."

"Something . . . ?" *Something secret?* That was a horrible thought, but it was what she needed when it came to Louie.

"All anyone will see are two friends. The fact that we happen to be more—at least tonight—doesn't have to be common knowledge. I care about you and Louie, and I'll be here for you while I can."

Why did it sting to hear him say this would be kept between them, when it was exactly what she wanted? She wasn't even sure it *was* what she wanted, but it was what she needed where Louie was concerned.

"Come on." He took her hand and headed upstairs.

"Bodhi, when he's sick, he's really clingy and whiny. He won't want you anywhere around him. He won't even let my mother take care of him."

He gave her a deadpan look as they crossed the yard toward her house. "Where are your keys?"

"I keep a house key under the potted plant out back."

"Not anymore you don't."

He proceeded to lecture her on safety while they retrieved her keys. If any other man had tried to tell her what to do, she'd probably have told him that she'd do *what* she wanted, *when* she wanted. But it didn't feel like Bodhi was trying to control her. She knew this was the rescuer in him coming out. The man who had seen worst-case scenarios and tried his best to help others avoid them.

They picked up Louie, and he threw up twice on the short drive home. Bridgette was thankful Bodhi was there, enabling her to sit in the backseat with Louie.

"I'll carry him up. He's half your size." Bodhi reached for Louie before she even finished unlatching his seat belt.

"He's really particular about—" She was silenced by the sight of her son reaching for Bodhi. He rested his head on Bodhi's shoulder, looking impossibly safe and small in his arms. Her heart had been working overtime around Bodhi, but this . . .

"Can you unlock the door?" He handed her the keys. "I'll clean up the car after he's tucked in."

"*I'll* clean the puke off the floor after he's asleep. You've done enough."

He gave her that don't-argue-over-this look again, and some part of her that was buried way below the proud mama she'd grown to be didn't want to argue. That part of her reveled in his insistence, accepting his thoughtfulness for what it was and not seeing it as a slight to her abilities.

Forty minutes later, with Louie cleaned up, tanked up on children's Tylenol to bring down his fever, and sound asleep, she headed downstairs. She found Bodhi pacing the kitchen floor and heard her washing machine running.

"I threw his dirty clothes in the laundry, and the car's clean." He crossed his arms, his eyes drop-dead serious again. "Who fills in when you can't work?"

"Um." She hadn't even thought about tomorrow yet. Her mind was still catching up on tonight's events. "No one right now. I'm looking for help at the shop, but I've been too busy to interview."

"I'll take care of it tomorrow. Just give me a key and tell me what needs to be done. I'm sure I've done it all at my mother's shop."

"Bodhi." Her head was spinning. "You've got enough on your plate, and you've done more than you should have already."

He gathered her in his arms and tipped her chin up, a motion that had already become familiar. "You can't leave that sick little boy with a sitter."

"He'll be fine. My mother will come over."

"You said he won't put up with anyone but you when he's sick."

He really had listened to every word she'd said. She should accept his offer, but she was already *too* drawn to him. Accepting his offer would only make him harder to resist. "For a guy who doesn't want a relationship, you're acting very boyfriendish."

He ground his teeth together and went back to pacing, leaving her to regret the comment she hadn't meant to say out loud.

"I'm sorry," she said, and he stopped pacing. "I didn't mean that the way it sounded. We're really fine."

He nodded curtly. "I hope he feels better soon. Remember to lock up after I leave."

Her footsteps echoed in the silence after she locked the door behind him.

Later that night Bridgette stood in Louie's doorway seeking solace to help camouflage her discomfort and trying to bury the emotions Bodhi had unearthed. She felt horrible for shutting him down when he was trying to be helpful. But she couldn't allow herself to get attached to Bodhi any more than she could allow her son to. She'd made the right decision, even if it felt like she'd pushed away the best thing that had happened to her in years.

And I thought he was the one with the walls.

CHAPTER EIGHT

WHILE THE REST of Sweetwater slept, Bodhi painted the rec room and repaired the shelves in the pantry. If Bridgette continued to get under his skin, he'd have his mother's house renovated in no time. He'd been so frustrated over how the night had ended, he'd finally fallen into bed around four in the morning. But the sheets had smelled like Bridgette, and when he'd finally dozed off, she'd invaded his dreams.

After too little sleep, he'd seen her leave for work this morning, and she'd looked exhausted. He wondered how many times Louie had been up last night. He wished she'd taken him up on his offer to watch the flower shop. He knew what it was like to be the sick kid of a single parent and to be stuck at home with a sitter. Granted, a grandmother was different from a sitter, but still. She'd made it clear that Louie didn't do well with anyone but her when he was sick. He respected the hell out of her for doing what she had to do for her business and her family. She'd probably made the right choice. What the hell did he know?

Later that afternoon as he washed out his paintbrushes, he was still bothered by the way last night had ended.

Dahlia whined.

"What?" The dog was too attuned to his moods.

She pawed at him. He turned off the water and knelt to love her up. She covered his face with sloppy kisses. After last night they might be the only kisses he got for a while. He gritted his teeth against that reality.

"What do you think, Dahl?"

"*Woof!*"

"Yeah, no shit. I know I told her I can't have a relationship, but we *connected* last night, and then I blew it by pushing myself into her life where I didn't belong." He stood and paced, thinking about what she'd said. *For a guy who doesn't want a relationship, you're acting very boyfriendish.* He should forget about last night and go back to being neighbors who rarely spoke. It was safer that way. But every time he thought about the pain in her eyes after she'd said it, he felt like a jerk. She was right. He was putting himself out there in ways he had no business doing.

He went back to cleaning out the brushes, but all he saw was Louie's little face flushed from a fever. He could still feel his limp body on his shoulder.

Dahlia whined again.

He kissed her on the head. "She blew me off, Dahl. What was up with that?"

"*Woof.*"

"You know what? The hell with this wallowing shit." He headed for the door.

Dahlia whined.

"Don't worry. I'm not getting all wrapped up in her. I'm just letting her know I'm still around." It was a bald-faced lie, and what made it worse was that he was lying to his *dog*.

A little while later he found out just how little he knew about five-year-olds as he walked through the children's section of Everything and More, a small department store, looking for a gift for Louie. He had no idea if Louie could read, much less what would interest him. He tossed three comic books into the basket and added two books called *Where the Wild Things Are* and *Splat the Cat*. He put *Where the Wild Things Are* back on the shelf because the monsters on the cover looked a little scary, and tossed in a few packs of baseball cards, a stuffed dog that looked like

Dahlia, and a couple of toy pirates. On the way out, he stopped in the sporting goods department to see what else he could find, and picked up a pair of long-distance walkie-talkies.

He stopped at the grocery store to pick up Gatorade and crackers in case Bridgette didn't have any for Louie, and a few other things he needed. He wasn't trying to be *boyfriendish*. He was just trying to brighten the kid's day. There was nothing wrong with that. They were neighbors, and damn it, they'd had a connection, even if she'd pushed him away with her I-can-handle-it-and-don't-need-you attitude.

By the time he left the store, he was wound as tight as a fishing reel. He probably should *not* stop at the Secret Garden until he had time to calm down, but he didn't like how he and Bridgette had left things, and he needed her to know he was still around.

He grabbed the ten-pound bag of sugar he'd bought at the grocery store and headed into the bright and cheery shop. Every surface was covered with gorgeous flowers, throwing him back in time to when he'd worked in his mother's shop. He'd loved every second of it, regardless of the kids who had called him a pussy for working there. Slamming one bigmouthed asshole against a locker had shut them all up. Nobody dissed his mother's business. He supposed if life had been different, he might have continued working there instead of going into the military. But his father had lost his life because of a rescue gone wrong, and he'd known from that moment on what he had to do. If it were up to him, no other family would lose a loved one because of a botched rescue mission.

He spotted Bridgette talking with a tall brunette by the counter and stalked toward her. Did she always have to look so gorgeous? There wasn't a woman on earth who could make skinny jeans and a white T-shirt look sexier. Her hair hung in loose waves around her face, and his fingers itched to feel those silky strands wound around them again. Hell, he'd give anything to just hold her in his arms one more time.

She looked over as he approached, surprise rising in her eyes. "Um, excuse me for just one second," she said to the woman.

Bodhi set the bag down at the other end of the counter.

"Bodhi?" Bridgette said. "What's this?"

"Sugar. In case I need it."

She smiled, and it warmed him to the bone. *I'm not about to let my stubborn girl forget about me.* He scowled at the thought. She wasn't *his*, and couldn't be even if he wanted her to. He wouldn't do that to her or to Louie.

With a curt nod, he headed out to the car before he said something stupid.

Half an hour later, with Dahlia by his side, Bodhi stood in Bridgette's living room with Roxie Dalton, Bridgette's exuberant mother, watching Louie work his way, very slowly, through the presents Bodhi had brought. The poor little guy barely had the energy to pet Dahlia, who had parked herself beside the couch where Louie was tucked beneath a blanket.

Bodhi quickly assessed Louie's pallor and the glassiness of his eyes. "Is he getting enough fluids?"

"As much as I can get him to drink, right, sweetie?" Roxie brushed Louie's hair from his forehead and pressed a kiss there. "At least his fever is staying down. I think the yarrow tea bath I gave him helped."

"Look, Grandma Roxie, baseball cards." A weak smile lifted his lips as he turned to Bodhi. "I collect them, like my dad did. He's dead."

Roxie touched Louie's shoulder, pity hovering in her eyes.

Bodhi knelt beside the couch with a heavy heart. Dahlia licked his face, earning a giggle from Louie.

"My father's gone, too."

"Are you sad?" Louie asked.

"Sometimes," Bodhi said honestly. "Are you?"

"No. I don't remember him. But I think sometimes Mommy is sad."

Bodhi had seen that last night, even though Bridgette had tried to hide it. He glanced at Roxie, unsure of how much he should say, but there were no answers in her eyes. Only compassion.

"Luckily," he said, "your mom has you, and that makes her *very* happy. I'd love to see your card collection someday. My father collected coins. I never got into them, but my mother has them all."

"If my mom lets me show you my cards, do you think your mom will let me see your father's coins?" Louie asked.

"Yeah, buddy. I'm sure she will." He made a mental note to borrow the collection from his mother. Hoping to give Louie an incentive to drink more fluids, he took a bottle of Gatorade out of the bag and said, "You know, baseball players drink a lot of Gatorade. Do you like Gatorade?"

Louie nodded. A new glimmer of light shone in his eyes.

"Maybe you could be like them and drink a bottle this afternoon." He winked at Roxie, who mouthed, *Thank you.*

"I will. I'm going to play for the Yankees when I grow up."

"I bet you'll be their best player ever." He broke the seal on the Gatorade, then screwed the top back on and set it on the coffee table. "Let me show you what else I brought." Bodhi opened the walkie-talkies. "These work for miles."

"Can I call you on them?" Louie asked.

"If your mom says it's okay, sure." He showed both Louie and Roxie how to operate them.

"Can you hook it to your pants like G.I. Joe?" Louie asked.

"Maybe I should leave it here so you can use it with your mom."

"I can call her on the phone," Louie insisted. "Please?"

Bodhi glanced at Roxie, who nodded. "Okay, little dude. But you need permission from your grandmother or your mother before using it, okay?"

After they played with the walkie-talkies, Roxie walked Bodhi to the door. "It was really sweet of you to bring Louie all those gifts.

Bridgette told me you drove her to pick him up last night. It's been a long time since she's had a friend like you. Thank you."

"Happy to help." He was surprised Bridgette had mentioned him. "There's a paperback in the bag for Bridgette."

"I'll be sure she gets it. She also mentioned that you're fixing up the house next door for your mother. I assume, like most hardworking men, your hands could use a little attention, and I have just the thing." She dug around in a box sitting by the stairs and handed him a jar. "Think of this as a thank-you gift for all you've done."

Dahlia nosed the container, trying to get a whiff. Bodhi read the label. CLARY SAGE & CINNAMON LOTION BY ROXIE. He wondered if she had any idea that clary sage was known for its aphrodisiac qualities, and whether she believed in the tales that cinnamon promoted warmth and spice in a relationship. Then he remembered she'd given Louie a yarrow tea bath and realized she probably did know those things.

"You made this? Thank you. It's an interesting combination."

"Oh, honey." She waved her hand. "I made that and about every other lotion, oil, fragrance, or soap in this town worth its salt. I put a little extra love in every batch. I'll bring something special for your mother when she settles in. I'm sure she'll love it here. Sweetwater has a way of growing on a person. Once the people here work their way into your heart, it's impossible to leave."

The glimmer of mischief in her eyes reminded him of Bridgette. He'd just seen her in the flower shop. Was it possible to miss her already?

"Before I forget," Roxie said, "would you mind leaving me your number? It's always good to have a neighbor's number handy."

"Sure."

She grabbed a paper and pen, and while he jotted down his information, she said, "Half the town is talking about you and Bridgette dancing together last night."

His gut fisted, hoping no one had seen them kissing. The last thing he wanted was for Bridgette to be the center of gossip. He handed Roxie the paper and pen. "She's an incredible woman. A wonderful neighbor."

"Yes, she is. She was once a feisty little gal, my Bridgette. Maybe you can bring that out in her again."

What did Bridgette tell you? "Roxie, I'm only here for a little while. I'm not looking to get involved in that way."

"Yes, Bridgette mentioned that to me as well." She glanced at Louie, who was drinking the Gatorade, and said, "I understand. But some towns are harder to leave than others."

Bridgette lay on her bed Saturday night, staring up at the ceiling and trying to figure out what to do about Bodhi. She'd been shocked when he'd brought the sugar into the flower shop and dropped it in his big, brooding fashion without so much as a simple conversation. But to come home and find out he'd bought presents for Louie and had spoken to him about Jerry and his own father? The man was a walking contradiction—and his phone number was like the apple in the Garden of Eden. Leave it to her mother to meddle where she didn't belong. Roxie hadn't even told Bridgette that Bodhi had left his number, or that he'd left her a copy of *Any Time, Any Place*, the follow-up book to the one she'd bought at the grocery store. The pages were dog-eared, and the book was signed by the author to Bodhi. Bridgette had found both items on her bedside table, with a note from her mother. *Such a nice man. You should call and thank him for the gifts for Louie. Maybe invite him to dinner when Louie's better? After all, he's here by himself, and from what I hear, all the single women in town are hot on his trail.*

She rolled onto her side and picked up the novel, turning to the inscription. *Bodhi, I will never be able to thank you enough for everything you do for our country. Meeting you and knowing you enjoy my romances is truly an honor! Jen*

She flipped through the pages, trying to imagine Bodhi reading the book, and she felt herself smiling. She wished she'd gotten a look at the titles on the table beside his couch. She eyed the walkie-talkie he'd given Louie and set the book down beside it. Louie had called him to say good night, and Bodhi had been sweet to him. She'd hoped he'd at least tell Louie to say hello to her, but no such luck. *Good night, little dude. Feel better tomorrow, and remember to turn off the walkie-talkie so the batteries last.* She looked at his phone number again, debating calling him.

Butterflies took flight in her stomach, and she chickened out. She went to check on Louie, hoping to distract herself from thoughts of Bodhi. Her boy was fast asleep, clutching the stuffed dog Bodhi had given him. He'd named it Jeter, after his favorite baseball player. His fever was down, but he still wasn't himself. She tucked him in and went back to her room.

Unable to escape thoughts of Bodhi, she picked up the walkie-talkie, pressed the "Talk" button, and lay down on her bed, talking to dead air. "Listen here, Mr. Brooding Badass Booker. It's not okay to make out with a woman and then walk away in a huff because she calls you on your own rules." Feeling emboldened by getting this off her chest, she sprang off the bed and paced.

"And as for *sugar*? Well, I have something sweet for you, all right. You only got a taste of it last night. There's a lot more where that came from. But you're only here temporarily, and I have a little boy to protect, so there can't be any more sugary goodness for you, Mr. Rule Maker." She gazed out the window into the darkness and touched her forehead to the cool glass as the longing inside her expanded and her emotions continued to pour out. "Which is a shame, because it's been a really long time since I've felt anything this big. This powerful and good. And I want to feel more of it. The worst part of all of this is that after five years without so much as a single butterfly in my stomach, you awakened a part of me that I wasn't sure still existed. It's like someone's playing a horrible trick on me. 'Here, you can love one man, and then I'm going to take him from you forever. But don't worry, you'll get a taste of another man who makes you feel alive again. And then I'll take him away, too. Quicker this time, so you'll never know what could have been.'"

She set the walkie-talkie on the bedside table and poured some of the jasmine massage oil her mother had given her into her hand, then lay on the bed as she rubbed it soothingly into her skin, willing the heartache away.

CHAPTER NINE

SUNDAY SWEPT THROUGH Sweetwater with clouds and sporadic rain. The perfect day for Bridgette and Louie to lie low while he recuperated. His fever hadn't returned, and by midday he was back to his chatty self. Louie begged to go outside and play on the porch, but Bridgette knew that while her little boy thought he was ready to plow full speed ahead, he still needed to rest. But resting didn't have to be boring.

Using the bookshelves, coffee table, and couch as anchors, she made a fort out of sheets in the living room, like she and her siblings used to do, and filled it with his favorite toys. They spent the afternoon playing games inside their hideout. Every time she went into the kitchen, she thought of Bodhi standing beside her when he borrowed sugar. Those thoughts led to the image of him stalking into her flower shop with a big bag of sugar and stalking right back out. He was about as easy to read as hieroglyphics.

It's silly, she told Willow when she'd called earlier. *I can't miss someone I haven't even dated.* Willow had offered to come over, but Bridgette wanted to focus on Louie, and she knew if Willow was there, she'd talk about Bodhi every time he popped into her head. Which meant she'd never shut up.

After a dinner of chicken noodle soup, Bridgette set up Louie's favorite movie, *The Lion King*. He was moving at half speed, and she knew he'd probably fall asleep while they were watching.

"Can I call Bodhi on the walkie-talkie to see if he wants to watch the movie with us?" he asked on the tail end of a long yawn.

Bodhi's truck had been gone most of the day, but she'd heard him come home a little while ago. "He's so busy fixing up the house for his mother, how about if you just call to say good night and we invite him over another time?"

"Okay."

"But remember, honey, he might not always have his walkie-talkie on. Don't be upset if he doesn't answer."

"He'll answer," Louie said as he turned it on. He cuddled up against her as he spoke into the gadget. "Hello? Bodhi, it's Louie." He yawned again. "Are you there?"

"Ten-four, little dude. How are you feeling?"

Bridgette's pulse quickened.

"I'm better, but Mom wouldn't let me go outside to play. We made a fort and we're watching a movie. What did you do today?"

Bridgette winced. She felt like she was eavesdropping.

"I went to see my mother," Bodhi said.

Louie's eyes lit up. "Did you get the coin collection? Did your mom say I could see it?"

Coin collection?

Bodhi chuckled, and even through the static of the walkie-talkie it made Bridgette's body tingle.

"As a matter of fact, I did. It's okay on my end, but you'll need to ask your mother, okay?"

"Mom? Can I show Bodhi my baseball cards and see his father's coin collection? His dad's dead, too."

Bridgette's stomach lurched at his bluntness. She'd have to talk with him about that at some point, but not tonight. She kissed the top of Louie's head. "Sure, honey. We'll figure out a time."

"Tomorrow night? *Please?*" Louie begged.

"Honey, finish saying good night, and Bodhi and I will check our schedules and pick a time. Let's let him get back to whatever he was doing."

After reluctantly saying goodbye, Louie turned off the walkie-talkie, and they lay down to watch their movie. By seven o'clock he was fast asleep. Bridgette carried him upstairs and tucked him in, placing the walkie-talkie beside his bed so she wouldn't be tempted to use it.

She was washing their dinner dishes and listening to music when a knock on the front door sent her pulse into a panic. Hoping it was Bodhi, she ran into the powder room and glanced in the mirror. Her hair was a tousled and tangled mess, her sweatshirt had water spots on it, and she wore no makeup. *Ugh.* She looked like a mother who had been home with her recuperating boy all day. Another knock sounded, and she went to answer the door. She drew in a calming breath and smiled as she pulled the door open.

"Hi. I hope you don't mind that I didn't call first."

Disappointment swept through her, immediately followed by guilt. "Aurelia. Hi. Not at all. Come on in. Louie's down for the count. I could use the company."

"I can only stay a minute. I'm heading back to the city and wanted to say goodbye before I took off. My boss called, and two of my coworkers have the flu." She stepped inside looking fresh and energetic, like she'd stepped out of an Old Navy commercial. "Wow, that's an awesome fort."

"Louie wanted to go outside, so I made inside more fun." Bridgette filled her in on Louie's recovery. "I hate that I didn't get any time with you this trip. Maybe next time?"

"I'll be back in two weeks for the Peach Festival. Your sisters are making bets about you and Bodhi. So? Dish, baby."

Bridgette wrapped her arms around herself and shrugged. "I don't really know what's going on with us, but it's not like you think. He's only here temporarily, and I've got Louie. What about you and Ben?"

"You guys keep asking about us, and I can assure you, there's nothing there besides friendship. But Bodhi . . . ?" Aurelia grinned. "I don't know him all that well. I know he's hot and he's nice, but I swear he lives inside a brick silo. He's not exactly warm and fuzzy."

"Oh, he has a warm and fuzzy side." Bridgette felt her cheeks heat, and her eyes snapped to Aurelia's.

"I knew you two hooked up! He was staring at you like he wanted to throw you over his shoulder and carry you off to his dirty den."

Bridgette laughed. "I wouldn't have minded."

"I can see that. You know, women check him out all the time at the bookstore, but he never seems to notice. Of course, what woman in her right mind wouldn't look at a guy like him buying romance novels?"

"So, he *does* read them?" Pieces of Bodhi were falling into place. "I bought a romance book at the grocery store, and when he saw it, I swear he stopped short of saying he'd read it. And yesterday he dropped off the second book in the series, signed to him, by the author. I wondered if he'd read it, or if his mother had."

"That man is as addicted to romance as I am." Aurelia laughed. "He came into the store a few years ago all stone-faced. He said he had a stressful job and needed a book as an escape. I gave him all the typical guy books—military, horror, thrillers—but he wanted nothing to do with anything that dealt with dark topics. I jokingly handed him a romance, and he devoured it. He came back later in the week and bought the others in the series. You know," she said with a glimmer of mischief in her eyes, "that could actually work to your benefit. Romance authors know their sexy scenes. Hopefully he's studied them like how-to books."

"Trust me, Bodhi does *not* need help in that department." Her body heated with memories of his rough hands and talented mouth all over her.

"Then you need to take advantage of the time he's here and get your groove on, because not only was he looking at you like you were dinner, but you definitely had that look in your eyes like he was dessert." She hugged Bridgette. "I have to go before it gets too late. I'll see you in two weeks, and you can fill me in on just how good of a neighbor he really is."

Bridgette walked her out and waved from the porch as she drove away. It had stopped raining, but the air felt damp and heavy. She leaned against the railing, thinking about Louie and his friendship with Bodhi. She had to tread carefully there. Louie was too little to remember losing his father, and he'd had no exposure to anyone in his life leaving for good. Bodhi's leaving wasn't a question. It was a given.

She looked down the road at the familiar lights of the town, warmed by a sense of comfort and security. Movement caught her eye, and she saw a broad-shouldered figure running up the hill. *Bodhi.* Her pulse quickened as he slowed to a walk, pushing a hand through his short-cropped hair. He passed beneath the golden spray of the streetlight, his body glistening with sweat, or maybe the misty rain that had started up again. His gaze found hers, and she waved, glad to see a smile softening his features as he headed up the walkway. She stepped off the porch to greet him.

"I hear it's dangerous to be out alone after dark," she said, hoping to break the ice. He stepped so close she could smell his ruggedness. Even after a long run he smelled delicious.

"Hi, beautiful." He wiped his brow with his forearm, and she realized he was holding the walkie-talkie.

"You ran with the walkie-talkie?"

His lips quirked up in a small smile. "I leave it on all the time in case Louie wants to talk." He hooked it to the waist of his shorts.

Her mind raced back to last night. "Did you . . . ? Um. Did you run with it last night?"

"No."

She exhaled with relief.

"I didn't run last night." He held her gaze, stepping closer. "I was replacing the flooring in the bathroom."

She focused on the rising and falling of his chest, hoping he hadn't heard her confess to what she'd thought was dead air. "Oh."

He slid a finger beneath her chin, tipping her face up. The emotions warring in his eyes mimicked her own.

Music played softly from inside the house. A dim melody serenading what felt like their most critical moment. Bodhi was forced to make split-second, life-and-death decisions on every mission. Decisions that impacted the men on his team, the people they were sent to rescue, and like a domino effect, their family members back home. He was used to carrying that weight on his shoulders, and he was mindful of the responsibilities that came with every decision. What he did, or said, in the next sixty seconds carried the same weight. He knew what he should do—tell Bridgette the walkie-talkie *hadn't* been on last night, wish her and Louie well, and walk away.

But this wasn't war, and this wasn't a mission. This was even more complicated. He'd spent the last twenty-four hours thinking about every word Bridgette had said when they were together, and what she'd said when she didn't know he could hear her through the walkie-talkie. As he gazed into her eyes, he didn't want to cause her any more pain, but walking away would surely hurt both of them. Unsure which was the lesser of two evils—getting closer or breaking it off before either one of them had a chance to get in too deep—he erred on the side of honesty.

"You were right," he said. "It wasn't okay for me to walk away the other night the way I did, and I'm sorry."

"You heard everything I said." She swallowed hard. "I didn't think you'd have it on."

"I'm glad I did. At least I know I'm not in this alone." He paused, taking a pulse on the magnetic draw between them. Powerless to resist her, he took her hand in his. "I don't know how to do this, Bridgette. I can disarm a bomb, face down the enemy under the most extreme circumstances, and do a hundred other things most guys can't. But seeing you without wanting to take you in my arms?" He shook his head, grasping for the right words. "I don't think that's possible."

"I know the feeling." She stepped closer.

That simple movement told him she was standing on this jagged edge with him. He leaned down and brushed his lips over her cheek. "Is Louie awake?"

"He's sleeping." She leaned her head to the side, allowing him to place a kiss on the base of her neck, where he knew she loved them. Her fingers moved over his. "Your hand feels soft."

"Your mother gave me lotion."

Her eyes widened.

"Something wrong with using her lotions?"

She shook her head with a sweet smile that brought a rush of emotions.

"Should we go inside in case Louie wakes up?"

"Sure."

He placed his hand on the small of her back as they made their way up the porch steps.

"You're acting very boyfriendish," she teased.

"I told you it was hard not to touch you. Maybe you should scowl instead of smile."

She smiled even wider. "Maybe you should start wearing more clothes."

She stepped onto the porch, and he remained on a lower step, turning her in his arms and bringing them almost eye to eye. "A few weeks ago I didn't even know you existed. Now I can't go five minutes without thinking of you, or wondering how Louie is."

"He's sleeping with Jeter, the adorable stuffed dog you bought him."

Jeter. *That boy* . . .

"You know what I mean." He gathered her in his arms. "Talk to me, Bridge. I need to know what you want. The other night I thought we were on the same page, going into this with our eyes open. That we both agreed we could be the *here* and *now* for each other, and not anything more."

"We did."

"Then maybe I misread you. I'm not very good at this kind of thing, but it seemed like you were upset with me when I offered to cover for you at the flower shop. I wasn't trying to take over or push my way into your life. I just wanted to help so you could be with Louie. I was raised by a single mother, and I know how much you're balancing. I also know you don't *need* my help, but that doesn't change the fact that I wanted to give you the chance to be with Louie when he was sick. I'm sorry if I overstepped my bounds."

She put her arms around him, and she felt so good, the line between right and wrong blurred even more.

"I was upset," she admitted.

Hating that he'd upset her, he loosened his hold, and she tightened hers.

"I didn't think you were trying to take over." She touched her lips to his, and he wanted to disappear into her. "I was upset with myself."

"Yourself? Bridge—"

"Hear me out," she said softly. "I feel the connection and all the same worries that you do. The difference is, I've felt this way before, and I *know* what it means for me. If I had let you help me with the shop, then it would be even easier to open the next door, and the next."

He brushed his check over hers, breathing her in. "You and Louie are my biggest concern. I can't be close to you and not want more, but I'm having a hell of a time staying away."

"Aren't you worried about getting hurt?"

"Every time I go out in the field, I'm at risk of being killed. Maybe I'm numb to my own pain. I don't know. But the thought of you and Louie getting hurt scares the hell out of me." He drew back and gazed into her eyes. "I'm being selfish, Bridgette, because I want to spend whatever amount of time I have here with you. I want to take you on dates, with and without Louie. I want to hear you laugh, and hang out with you and your friends and family, and see you blush when they give you a hard time about us. I want to put the freaking peephole in your door and fix Louie's playset and—"

"And be our *here* and *now*?" She held him like she didn't want to let go.

He shifted his eyes away, but there was no looking away from the truth. "Selfishly, yes." He met her gaze. "I know it's not fair."

He brushed his mouth over hers. "Tell me to go home, Bridgette. Tell me to leave, because I'm not strong enough to walk away."

"No," she said emphatically, but it was the slight pout on her lips that snapped his control.

He pushed his hands into her hair, and their eyes met for half a second before his mouth descended upon hers, devouring her with the force of a starving man.

"How can I miss you this much?" he said between kisses. "How can I want you this much?"

Every kiss was hotter than the last, and when she went up on her toes, locking her hands behind his neck, he lifted her into his arms.

"I love how strong you are," she said as he carried her across the porch. "I think you should carry me everywhere."

She pressed her soft lips to every inch of his face as he opened the door and stepped inside. He turned toward the living room, stopping at the threshold when he saw sheets draped over the furniture.

Holding his shoulders, she kissed him again, and his thoughts spun away. Her mouth was hot and eager, and she felt like heaven in his arms. It took all his focus to pry his mouth away long enough to say, "Fort?"

"Kitchen."

He smothered her with another steamy kiss and followed the sound of music into the kitchen.

"What is it about us and your kitchen?" He set her on the counter and brought her up to the edge, going straight for her neck.

"I don't know," she panted out, grasping at his back. "But I like you in my kitchen."

She leaned into him, and he greedily claimed her mouth, touching her everywhere at once. When he brushed the sides of her breasts, she made a sexy, needful sound. Her hot little hands grabbed his ass, holding him tight against her center.

Cradling her face in his hands, he was drunk on her, and he knew he was in trouble. This was dangerous territory. Her son was right upstairs, and he was on the verge of taking everything he wanted. "I can't get enough of you, Bridgette."

The music competed with the sounds of their eager kisses and heated whispers.

"I like you hungry for me," she said with a challenge in her eyes.

He kissed her again, deep and sensual, slowing them down long enough for him to try to regain control. The song "Wanna Make You Love Me" came on the radio, and as the artist sang about wanting to buy a rose for the woman he loved, and be a better man for her, they were the exact sentiments he was feeling. He'd been determined not to be in this position, and for more than a decade he had maintained his steadfast belief in not getting involved. And in the span of a few days, Bridgette had broken right through every barrier. He should walk out that front door and never look back, but his body took control, and he lifted her off the counter and set her bare feet on the floor. She was so petite, so feminine and tempting, he wanted to wrap her up in a golden ribbon and protect her. But as she wound her arms around his neck and their bodies moved seamlessly from heated kisses to sensual dancing, he wanted more of this. More of *her*.

His hands sailed along the curve of her spine as their hips moved to a beat all their own. "I want to take you out on a real date, and I don't want to exclude Louie. We'll take him, too. But at some point I want to treat you like you deserve to be treated."

"You're dancing with me in my kitchen. This is the most romantic thing I've done in years."

"You haven't seen romance yet." He kissed her again, and she laughed. "Careful, beautiful. You'll hurt my ego, laughing at my kisses."

She pressed her lips to the center of his chest, sending heat racing south. "I adore your kisses. I laughed because Aurelia was here earlier."

"Here we go." He knew his affinity for romance would get out sooner or later, but he'd been hoping for *later*.

"I'm trying to picture you reading romance."

"How about you picture me reading your body instead?" He lifted her up again, and she laughed as he sank down to a chair with her straddling his lap.

"Do you actually *like* romance novels?" she asked. "Or do you have a stack that you write in, pretending the authors sign them, then give them out to unsuspecting single moms to get nookie points?"

He laughed. "Maybe I should try that."

She scowled.

"I don't usually give women the time of day. You're an exception to my every rule." He gathered her hair in one hand, hooked a finger in the collar of her sweatshirt, and pulled it aside, placing kisses along her shoulder. "I've seen horrible things. I like to keep things light between assignments." He tugged her collar down and pressed a kiss to the center of her breastbone. "No fake autographs. Just a need to disappear into something that ends with a happily ever after." *Something I can never have.*

"An escape," she said breathlessly.

He lifted the hem of her sweatshirt, tugged the cup of her bra down, brushed his mouth over her nipple until it pebbled, and took it in his mouth. She arched forward, clutching his head and writhing against his cock as he licked and sucked.

"Bodhi—"

The heated whisper brought his eyes up to hers.

"Don't stop," she pleaded.

He pushed his fingers beneath the fringe of her shorts, stroking her through her damp panties, and a groan tore from his lungs. He pushed her panties aside and sank his fingers into her tight heat.

She clawed at his skin, pleas pouring from her lungs like demands. *"Harder. There. Bodhi—"*

He claimed her mouth, swallowing her cries as she gave herself over to him completely. He slowed their kisses, competing with the frantic clenching of her sex, holding her at the peak, and enjoying every second of driving her out of her mind. They kissed until she went limp.

"Bodhi." She snuggled against his neck. "I've lost count, but I think I owe you a few orgasms."

He kissed her cheek, chuckling. "Babe, you don't owe me anything."

"If you were with a girl without a child, you could be in her bed right now."

"If I were with a *girl*, I'd be in jail. Don't you get it? I don't do this. I'm not the kind of guy who goes after single women to get off for a night." He touched his forehead to hers. "I want *you*, Bridgette. I like who you are with your son. You're protective, and loving, and you made a fort that took over your entire living room without making him clean it up before bedtime. You have your priorities straight, and at thirty-four, that's much more attractive to me than a quick roll on the mattress with someone who'll be in another guy's bed the next night."

"And knowing *that* makes you very hard to resist." She pressed her lips to his. "Do you think we can do this? I know people date without commitments all the time, but they don't have little boys around twenty-four-seven. I don't think we should let him see us holding hands or anything."

He nodded, hoping like hell he could keep up his half of the bargain. "We'll be careful."

She closed her eyes, resting her cheek on his shoulder, and he soaked in their closeness. As much as he hated to leave, he knew he had to. "I'd better go. If I don't, I'm going to kiss you again, and then I'll never leave."

"I wish you could stay," she whispered.

His chest constricted. He knew she was just swept up in the moment, making it that much more difficult for him to rein in his own rampant desires.

"I know you can't, but . . ." She gazed into his eyes, and a world of longing stared back at him. "I would never wish Louie wasn't with me, but I'd give anything to have a whole night alone with you."

"We'll make plans when Louie's all better." He kissed her tenderly. "Louie's your *here*, *now*, and *forever*. He needs to come first."

CHAPTER TEN

BRIDGETTE SLEPT THROUGH the alarm Monday morning, sending her into a panic. She raced through her shower and getting Louie's breakfast ready. Louie spilled cereal all over his clothes, and all over Jeter, which caused a torrent of tears.

"It's okay, honey. You run upstairs and get changed, and I'll get him cleaned right up." As her little man hurried up the stairs, she washed the stuffed animal in the sink, trying to picture Bodhi's reaction to this morning's mayhem. His morning chaos probably consisted of which to do first—turn on the coffeemaker or let Dahlia outside.

A knock sounded at the door, and she hurried to answer it, but Louie got there first. Her insides melted at the sight of Bodhi crouched in front of her boy with their foreheads almost touching. Louie had changed into a long-sleeved T-shirt with YANKEES emblazoned across the chest, a pair of shorts, and his favorite old, one-size-too-small blue rain boots he refused to throw away. He put his arms around Bodhi's neck, and Bodhi rose to his feet, scooping up Louie with one arm and holding an empty mug in the other hand. Bodhi's gaze trailed down Bridgette's pink sweater, over her white miniskirt, all the way down to her strappy white sandals. An appreciative smile broke through his serious expression.

"Morning, beautif—*Bridgette*. I just came by to borrow some sugar and heard about the cereal tragedy."

His presence was like the calm at the eye of her morning storm. *Just what I needed.* "It was only a little spill. But Jeter's all cleaned up. Grandma Roxie can put him in the dryer when she picks up Louie."

"See that?" Bodhi said to her little boy, who was beaming at his new buddy. "Your mom's got your back."

"What does that mean?" Louie asked, absently tracing the line of Bodhi's scruff with his finger.

"It means she loves you, and she's always watching out for you. Think she'll mind lending me some sugar for my coffee?"

"Nope." Louie wiggled out of his arms. "We have a huge bag of sugar in the pantry."

"Honey, run up and get your backpack with all the things you want to bring to Grandma and Grandpa's while I get Bodhi some sugar, okay?"

Louie darted up the stairs. Bridgette tugged Bodhi into the kitchen and around the corner, out of the line of vision from the hallway in case Louie came down. Bodhi backed her up against the wall, taking advantage of every second, and kissed her breathless.

"I didn't expect to get two seconds alone with you." His mouth came down over hers again, sending gusts of heat swirling through her.

At the sound of Louie's footsteps on the stairs, Bodhi pushed back, while she tried to remain erect on Jell-O legs.

"Did you get your sugar?" Louie asked.

"I did, little dude, and it was even sweeter than I'd hoped."

Louie smiled up at Bodhi and said, "Mommy has your back, too."

Bodhi's eyes darkened. He ran a hand through his hair and gave Louie a serious nod. One glance at the enticing bulge in his jeans told Bridgette she wasn't the only one still reeling from their kisses.

♥ ♥ ♥

"So, you're fuck buddies?" Piper followed Bridgette to the back of the flower shop late Monday afternoon as Bridgette prepared to meet with a couple to discuss floral arrangements for their wedding.

"Do you see any hard hats in here? How about being a little less crude?" Piper had come directly from a job site. Clearly her mind was still stuck in man-mode.

Bridgette pulled several thick binders from a shelf and carried them to the table by the windows, thinking about being in Bodhi's arms last night.

"Sorry, Bridge. I forget you've been brainwashed by years of mommying. I do love that he came over *and* left with an empty mug."

"He might have left with an empty mug, but he did not leave *running on empty*."

Piper touched her arm, stopping her from fidgeting with the binders. "Seriously. Do I need to worry about you?"

"Why? We're not even sleeping together yet." Although she wanted to be. She headed toward the back of the store and grabbed a bouquet for the table. "I can handle this, Piper, and I'll be careful with Louie. He won't know there's anything more than friendship between us."

"I joke about you getting down and dirty, but in all seriousness, are you sure you can do this without getting attached?" Piper arched a finely manicured brow. "The guy lives next door, which means easy access to nighttime rendezvous, and he cleaned puke off the floor of your car. That's got to do something to your mommy hormones."

Bridgette set the vase on the table. "Isn't it crazy that I can get turned on by a guy cleaning up puke? That was truly one of the hottest things he could have done."

"Yeah. Gross. I think I might wait until I'm totally over hot sex to have kids."

"What makes you think you'll *ever* get over hot sex?" She looked at her tough-as-nails sister, knowing that beneath her steel armor was a sensitive soul. But it would take a hell of a tough man to break through her barriers. Bodhi had come off the same way, but he wasn't completely encased in a brick silo, as Aurelia had thought. *Bodhi and I aren't that different after all.* Her mind traveled back to Jerry, who *had been* very different from Bodhi.

"Why do you look like you're doing algebra in your head?" Piper asked.

Bridgette shrugged. "Just thinking how different Bodhi is from Jerry. Jerry was like my male counterpart. We were both wild. We never planned or thought things through. We just did whatever we wanted, around his touring schedule, of course. And he was always smiling and joking. Bodhi's careful and he's *always* thinking ahead, worrying over things. And his smiles come few and far between, like secrets I don't want to miss."

"And . . . ?" Piper flipped open a binder and began leafing through it.

"I don't know. It's just interesting that I've only ever felt completely swept up in two men, and they're complete opposites. And yet I feel like I was as similar to Jerry as I am to Bodhi, which is even weirder."

"Well, baby sister. Maybe that says more about you than them. Are you sure you can handle this? There's a lot of analyzing going on in that pretty little head of yours."

"*Pfft.* This is a piece of cake compared to dealing with a colicky baby or two-year-old tantrums. Sex with no commitments? I've totally got this. That's my thing, remember?" She was a big, fat liar. She'd been a wild child, going to too many parties, drinking with her friends, staying out all night, though she'd never slept around. But Willow was the only one who knew the truth about that part of her life. Piper took what she wanted, when she wanted it, without her emotions getting in the way. Maybe if she could convince Piper she could handle it, she could convince herself, too.

Piper smirked. "That *was* your thing, years ago. It hasn't been your thing for a very long time. Not that I don't think you deserve it. I just don't want you getting hurt."

"Not a chance." Bridgette put her hands on her hips, meeting Piper's concerned gaze. "We put all our cards on the table. I know he's leaving in a couple of weeks, and he knows I can't put Louie at risk of getting attached."

"Getting attached to what?" Willow asked as she came through the archway carrying a bakery box.

"Hey, Will," Piper said. "What's in the box?"

"Zane and I are going to a dinner meeting in the city about his screenplay." She opened the box. "I'm bringing these, but I have way too many. Take one."

Bridgette and Piper each grabbed a pastry.

"So . . . ?" Willow asked. "Attached?"

Piper turned an expectant gaze on Bridgette.

"Me and Bodhi," Bridgette answered. She'd filled in Willow before work about her talk with Bodhi. "She's worried I can't handle the friends-with-benefits thing."

"I sucked at it, obviously." Willow waved her engagement ring. "But Bridge has great willpower, and she has her priorities straight. She's careful. She's definitely got this. I was thinking, since you don't really have any time alone with Bodhi to take advantage of the *neighborly* things he is so generously offering, Zane and I would be happy to babysit. This coming weekend is crazy at the bakery, and the Peach Festival is next weekend, but maybe one day in between?"

Excitement whipped through Bridgette. Louie was feeling better this morning, and Roxie had taken him to the park to run off some energy. Bridgette had actually considered opening the shop late and showing up at Bodhi's house to seduce him. But sanity had taken over, and she'd come in to work like a responsible adult. Adulting sucked sometimes.

"I'd give anything for a night with Bodhi without worrying about being interrupted," Bridgette admitted. "I feel like we're teenagers dodging our parents, making out in fits and spurts. I don't need a lot of freedom. All I want is one night to fall asleep in his arms and wake up with him in the morning. Does that make me a terrible mother?"

"It makes you a twentysomething *woman*. But if I were in your position, I'd want one night to attack him," Piper said. "You can cuddle when Louie's watching television."

Bridgette rolled her eyes. If only it were that easy. "No, I can't. Louie's never seen me with a man." She'd been up half the night worrying over how to handle things around Louie. Could she keep her lips to herself around him when Bodhi was with them?

"None of us have since you moved back home," Piper reminded her.

"Yes, but you guys are adults. You're pulling for me to enjoy myself. Louie's impressionable. If he thinks Bodhi and I are a couple, it'll make it harder for him when Bodhi leaves."

Willow and Piper exchanged a look that Bridgette read too easily.

"You can fool a kid, but what about you?" Piper asked.

Oh, the tangled web of lies she was weaving. "I'm a mother. I can handle anything."

Bodhi finished painting the trim in the upstairs bedrooms and bathrooms Monday evening, cleaned up, and went for a run. It was after nine when he got back. Louie hadn't called on his walkie-talkie, and Bodhi imagined the newness of the gift had worn off. He could kick himself for not asking for Bridgette's phone number. After barging in unannounced that morning, he decided against showing up again this evening. But she was like a drug, and he wanted his next hit.

Badly.

He took a shower, and his phone rang as he dried off. Shira's name flashed on the screen. He tugged on his briefs and answered.

"Hey, you."

"Hi. How's life in Sweetwater? Do you miss the incessant noise of the city yet?"

"Not even a little. What's happening with you?"

He dressed as she caught him up with the latest events on the charity front. They were planning a fundraiser for the holidays, and as always, she had it under control.

"Who do you want to be seated with this year?" Shira asked.

Bridgette. "I don't know. Ask me in a few weeks."

He went down to the living room with Dahlia and sat on the couch, wishing Bridgette were there with him. Dahlia rested her chin on his leg, and he grabbed a paperback from the end table.

"A few weeks?" Shira asked.

"I've got mandatory training after I leave here."

"Unless you get called for an assignment," she reminded him.

"No shit." He didn't mean to sound harsh, but every day that passed brought him that much closer to leaving, and he didn't want to think about leaving—for training or for an assignment. "If I am called in, and if I make it back alive, *then* you can ask me who I want to sit with."

"If you get sent away, your lame ass better make it back or I swear I'll kill you a second time over."

He smiled. "Hey, Shira?"

"What?" she snapped. "You pissed me off. I hate it when you talk about not making it back."

"I'm sorry, but you know—"

"Booker? Shut. Up. I know the reality of your stupid job."

"Right. Sorry." He petted Dahlia. "I need a favor. Can you see about getting me four tickets to the Yankees game this weekend? And see if you can set up a call between me and the manager. I need a favor." The owners of the Yankees were major donors to Hearts for Heroes, and every year they offered up tickets to the games. Bodhi's mother, Alisha, was an avid Yankees fan, and he tried to take her to at least one or two games each year.

"I'm on it. Wait. Who's your plus two?"

"Wouldn't you like to know?" He sat back and thumbed through the book.

"You'll tell me soon enough. How're the renovations going? Will you be done before you come back?"

"Yeah. I should be fine. It's a cute town. Mom will like it here."

"Or maybe Bodhi likes Mom's neighbor?"

A text came through, and Bodhi lowered the phone to see who it was from. He didn't recognize the number, but it gave him a long enough pause to avoid answering Shira's question. "Sorry, Shira, but I've got to run."

"That's cool. I'll check into the tickets. And, Bodhi?"

"Yeah?"

"Don't think I didn't notice you avoided answering my question. I'm hoping you lifted your not-getting-involved rule and are enjoying some time with that cute blonde next door. But come on. Plus *two*? You, your mom, and hopefully blondie would be three. What does plus *two* for baseball mean?"

He chuckled. "It means her kid likes baseball."

Shira was silent for a long moment, and hell if he didn't know exactly what was going through her mind.

"Bodhi," she said with a serious tone. "You sure you know what you're doing?"

"Definitely not, but aren't you the one who encouraged me to relax and enjoy myself?"

"Yeah, but . . . a kid?"

Silence filled the airwaves. This was not a conversation he wanted to have, no matter how right she was.

After an uncomfortable end to their call, he read the waiting text— *Hi. What are you up to?*—and thumbed out a response. *Who is this?*

He opened the book and kicked his feet up on the coffee table. His phone vibrated with another text. *Your sugar supplier.*

The knot in his gut loosened as he sent a response. *About to start Charlotte Sterling. But I could sure use some sugar.*

Bridgette's text came through seconds later. *Who is this Charlotte chick? I'm not above taking a bitch down.*

He pushed to his feet, and Dahlia jumped to hers, following him into the kitchen as another text came through. *Not that we have that type of commitment or anything.*

"My ass we don't," he grumbled as he grabbed two glasses and the bottle of wine the Realtor had given him when he'd bought the house, and placed them in an empty box. "Let's go, Dahl." He grabbed the book, threw the blanket from the back of the couch over his shoulder, and headed out the door as he called Bridgette.

"Hi," she said shakily.

"Open your kitchen door."

CHAPTER ELEVEN

BODHI'S HARSH TONE made Bridgette's stomach twist. She'd kicked herself seconds after sending those last two texts. She sounded like a possessive girlfriend. She'd wanted to send a text telling him she was hoping for a kiss good night, but that seemed too needy. She walked through the kitchen and saw his hulking figure bent at the waist as he placed something on the ground. Her nerves took flight as she opened the door.

Dahlia trotted to the porch as Bodhi rose to his full height, broad and powerful against the night sky. He stalked toward her, amping up her pulse with each determined step. He didn't stop until he was nearly standing upon her. He hauled her against him and took her in a punishingly intense kiss that rang through her veins. She pushed up on her toes, wanting more, and used his shoulders for leverage as she futilely tried to climb him like a mountain. He smiled against her lips and lifted her into his arms. His mouth was like an ocean of heat and desire, and she wanted to sail away to the far reaches of the world and disappear into it.

Dahlia whined, and Bodhi tore his mouth away, his gaze blazing through Bridgette. He opened his mouth to speak, and she silenced him with hers. When he broke their connection again, his eyes were dark as night.

"We have that kind of goddamn commitment," he seethed.

"But we're just friends with benefits," came out teasingly, as if she'd gone five years without a man and she'd want to keep her options open, when really, she ached over the idea of sharing him. Unable to hide her true feelings, her next words were somber. "Here and now."

"My here and now doesn't include any other women, and yours sure as hell better not include other men. You can call it whatever you want, but you get with another man, and we become *past tense*."

Lord, this man was raking her over the best kind of coals. She didn't know if she should claw for purchase and hold on tight, or skitter away before she got burned. It didn't matter which her *mind* chose, because Bridgette believed in following her heart, just as she had with Jerry, and Bodhi had already claimed a piece of it.

"How's this playing out, Bridgette?" His face was as serious as if he were negotiating world peace. "The ball's in your court."

He was *so* serious her mind should not go straight to the gutter. But it did, and a giggle bubbled out before she could stop it. "The *balls* aren't near enough to my *court*, but I prefer that we remain exclusive partners while you're here in town."

A warm smile pushed all his stoniness away.

She ran her finger along his jaw and traced his lower lip, further softening her broody man. "You like to break rules as much as you enjoy making them."

"You make me crazy, Bridge." He took her in another toe-curling kiss. "Utterly *mad*," he whispered.

"Since we're exclusive, can I ask who Charlotte Sterling is?" she asked as he carried her off the porch to a blanket he'd set out on the grass.

"An erotic romance writer. If you're nice, maybe I'll share her books with you."

"I'd rather create our own erotic scenes." She touched her lips to his, and Dahlia bounded over, nudging her head between them.

"Lie down," Bodhi said, and Dahlia lay on the blanket, her big head resting on her legs and her brown eyes trained on her man.

"Good girl." He lowered Bridgette's bare feet to the blanket. They sat side by side, and Dahlia inched up until her front paws were touching Bodhi's legs. He loved her up. "I hope you don't mind that I brought her, but I want her to get used to seeing us together. Otherwise she'll whine every time we touch."

"I don't mind, but you know we can't do this in front of Louie, so most of the time she won't be in danger of the green-eyed monster taking over."

"I know. I'm sorry about showing up this morning, too. I should have waited and visited you at the shop." He pulled her closer. "But I just wanted to see you, even if only long enough to say good morning."

"I'm glad you did. We had a crazy morning, and you made it better."

He glanced at the open door. "Do you have a way to hear Louie in case he gets up?"

"I have a monitor from when he was a baby. I still use it when I'm downstairs, *just in case*. I must have left it in the living room." She started to get up, and he placed his hand over hers.

"I'll get it. You don't have shoes on." He pushed to his feet, and Dahlia's head popped up, eyes wide. "Stay, baby."

Bridgette petted Dahlia while they watched Bodhi disappear inside. "You could have warned me," she whispered. "Was that why you knocked my groceries out of my hands? Were you trying to tell me to stay away because he was addicting? Or were you trying to get me to pay attention? Breaking the ice like some kind of four-legged wingman?"

Bodhi stepped off the porch with a serious expression. "You two conspiring?"

"We girls have to stick together."

He sat down and set the monitor to the side.

"Thank you for always thinking of Louie. You can't imagine how much that means to me."

He glanced at Dahlia. "Thanks for looking after my girl."

"It's hardly the same."

"It's totally the same. Come here." He pulled her down so they were lying next to each other. "That's better. You were too far away. I brought wine. Would you like some?"

"Maybe after I get some Bodhi time."

"Good answer." He kissed her again. "Was Louie okay today?"

"Yeah, he's all better. He wants to show you his baseball cards."

"Tomorrow," he said. "Does that work?"

"Perfectly."

"I'll come over and fix his playset, too. Louie can help."

"You don't have to do that." She told herself she should have some sort of boundaries between Bodhi and Louie, but this was what friends did. They helped each other out. That didn't have to mean anything more.

"I want to. Besides, he seemed excited to help."

"What is it about boys and tools?"

"What is it about me and you?" Bodhi's hands slid along her hip. "I've been thinking. I want to take you out alone, but since that might take some time to coordinate, I'd like to take you and Louie to the city for a Yankees game this weekend."

"Are you serious?" She hadn't been to the city since before Louie was born, when Jerry's band was touring, and Louie had never been.

"Yes. I want to do something special with both of you."

Every shred of restraint she had on her emotions tugged free. She would be careful about letting Louie see her true feelings for Bodhi because she had to, but she wasn't about to deny them. She wanted to share Louie's first visit to the city, and his first time seeing the Yankees play, with Bodhi more than she wanted her next breath. "Louie would *love* that. Are you sure? I mean, can you get tickets? And what about Dahlia?"

"I'm pretty sure I can get tickets, but don't mention it to Louie until I get confirmation. I figured we'd leave Saturday after you get off work, and take Dahlia with us. I thought we could grab dinner and see a Broadway show that's appropriate for kids if Louie's up for it. We can stay at my place for the night, then go to the game Sunday and come back afterward."

"That sounds amazing." She threw her arms around his neck. "Thank you, but are you sure? Louie can be a handful."

"Don't thank me yet, and yes, I'm sure. I need to get the tickets, and we'll have to take your car. There's not enough room in my truck for the three of us and Dahlia."

The excitement bubbling up inside her was quickly tamped down with reality. Bodhi had been very careful with Louie, but she felt compelled to clarify their sleeping arrangements. "But we can't sleep together with Louie there. Do you have enough room at your place? He and I can stay at a hotel."

"Bridgette," he said sternly, "you are *not* staying at a hotel. Do you really think I'd assume you and I were sharing a room when we can't even hold hands in front of Louie?"

"No, but . . . It's the mom in me coming out."

"I get it." His expression remained serious. "Have a little faith in me," he said, a tad softer. "You'll take my room, Louie can sleep in the guest room, and I'll sleep on the couch."

"I'm not going to make you sleep on the couch. I'll share a bed with Louie. He's the size of a peanut."

"However you want to do it is fine with me, but there's one catch. My mother's a die-hard Yankees fan, and if I don't take her to the game, she'll disown me. Think you can handle meeting her?"

She swallowed hard. "Your mother? That sounds more serious than *here* and *now*."

"I know it does, but that's not my intent. She honestly is a huge Yankees fan, and I want to do something special for Louie. Is it wrong to want our short time together to be full of moments none of us will ever forget?"

For Louie, it would be fine. But for her . . . ?

"No," she said, made happy by his desire to do something so thoughtful, and scared by what it did to her emotions. "It's not too much, and I can't wait to meet your mother. But I'm not sure Louie can sit through an entire game. Will she be okay if I have to leave early with him to let him run around in the parking lot or something?"

"Babe." He pressed his lips to hers and lowered her down to her back, gazing at her with so much emotion, she never wanted to move. "She raised me, remember? And she loves kids."

"Can you do me one tiny favor?"

"That depends. Does it involve anything illegal?"

She laughed. "No."

"Anything *dirty*?"

She could think of a whole lot of dirty things she could ask him to do. "Maybe as *payment* for the favor."

"You're killing me." He took her in another blissful kiss. "Anything you need."

"Can you be a little bit of a jerk from now on?" She couldn't even pretend she really wanted him to, and when his smile turned to a scowl, she added, "Just so Louie and I don't totally fall for you."

"Babe, you're not going to fall for me, because you know how this ends. We both do." The warning in his voice was softened by the regret in his eyes.

It was good to know she wasn't the only one struggling with their relationship limitations.

"And once we explain to Louie that I don't live in Sweetwater, he won't expect me to stick around forever. I'll be like any other friend who passes through town."

When it came to protecting Louie, his confidence returned, putting her worries about her son to rest. If only it could do the same for her.

"When we're in New York, we'll explain it to him. Okay? Then he'll see where I live, so he'll have a picture in his mind, and it will all fit together for him. I'm not going to let him get hurt," he assured her. "But if it's too much, just tell me. We don't have to go to the city."

"Part of me thinks it's too much, but a bigger part thinks you're the most generous man on earth, and I want us both to experience as much of you as we can."

He showered her with kisses, covering every speck of exposed skin from her hands to her neck. She'd never been so thankful for a private backyard before in her life. He skipped over her sweater and miniskirt and moved right down to her ankles, working his way up each leg, kissing and caressing until her entire body hummed with need. When he came down over her, his weight was magnificent, bearing down in all the right places. Even through their clothes, their heat was unstoppable. She bent her knees to accommodate the width of his hips, and her skirt bunched at the tops of her thighs.

"Bridgette," he said in a husky whisper.

He buried his face in her neck, both of them rocking and grinding, refusing to stop the illicit torture. He slid his hands beneath her ass, angling her hips so he could press harder against her center, and their mouths came together, fierce and hungry. She could barely breathe for the tingling sensations crawling up her thighs and the delectable friction wreaking havoc with her control. Just when she was ready to break their connection with the need for air, Bodhi breathed into her lungs, giving her the last of what she needed to abandon all thought.

Bodhi was hanging on to his sanity by a thread. He needed to put space between them, guzzle some wine, take a breather, or he was liable to take more than he should. He'd nearly detonated last night. A cold shower hadn't cut it. He'd needed a freaking ice bath.

"Babe." He sounded as desperate as he felt. "We've got to stop, or I'm going to strip you naked and have my way with you right here on the blanket."

She was gripping his arms like a security blanket. Her eyes narrowed, and she pushed at his chest. "Get up."

He rose to his feet, and Dahlia rose beside him.

"I feel guilty for asking this," she said. "But can you please put Dahlia in your house?"

"Sure. What's wrong?"

"Nothing. Can you just put her in your house and come back, please?"

He took her by the shoulders and realized she was trembling. "Bridge, talk to me. I'm sorry I got carried away."

"Ohmygod." She grabbed his shirt and yanked him down for a hard kiss. "Stop apologizing! Please, trust me. Just put her in the house and hurry back."

He was back in record time, cursing himself the whole way. She grabbed the baby monitor, and his hand, and hurried onto the porch steps. She reached for him, and he met her in a messy, urgent kiss and lifted her into his arms.

"You know me already," she said, smiling so wide it cut right through him.

"I know I love having you wrapped around me. And I love your laugh, and your smile, and I'd carry you across the state if you'd smile like that every second."

"I'll do better than that. Take me to the laundry room." She lowered her mouth to his neck as he carried her through the kitchen, making his whole body throb and taking his mind off the lingering question—*laundry room?*

He reached for the light, and she stopped him. "No lights. Just close the door."

"I like where this is headed."

"Louie can't hear us in here." She wiggled from his arms and pushed him against the dryer. "You've been so patient with me. Now it's my turn to make you feel good." She yanked his shirt up, smothering his stomach in hot, wet kisses.

Heat climbed up his torso at the unexpected pleasure as she licked and kissed and groped. "God, babe. That feels amazing."

She yanked the button of his jeans free.

"You don't need to do this." *But oh, fuck, I want you to.* "I can wait as long as we need to."

"Well, I can't." She gazed up at him in the darkness, raw passion brimming in her eyes. She was the hottest thing he'd ever seen. She unzipped his pants and yanked them down to his knees, briefs and all. His erection bobbed free.

He took her mouth with savage intensity, greedily sucking on her tongue and devouring the warmth that would soon surround him. She broke the kiss, leaving him gasping as she gathered her hair over her shoulder and crouched before him. She wrapped her fingers around his cock, and it twitched within her hot little hand. She dragged her tongue around the head, down the length of him, then up again, over and over, until his shaft glistened and throbbed. She lowered her mouth over the head, and his hips bucked at the first touch of her lips. He grabbed the sides of the dryer to keep from deep-throating her as she found her rhythm. *Holy shit, her rhythm.* She worked him so perfectly, fast and tight, with a hard suck when she reached the head. There was no holding back. He grabbed her hair, rocking into her mouth, deeper and deeper. She moaned around his cock, and it vibrated through him.

"Baby, I'm not going to last."

She opened her eyes, meeting his gaze and squeezing him tighter, sucking harder, and holy hell, seeing his sweet, careful girl enjoying every second of pleasuring him sent him right up to the verge of release.

"Bridgette—" A last-ditch warning.

She stroked him faster, and when she cupped his balls, heat shot down his spine and his hips pistoned forward as he found his release.

"Bridgette—" His climax gripped him with magnum force that went on and on.

He clung to her shoulders as the last of the aftershocks rumbled through him. Bridgette rose to her feet, her swollen lips glistening in the darkness. Her eyes were warm and sated as she stepped into his open arms and curled into the curve of his body.

"Bodhi," she said in a soft voice.

He tipped her chin up and kissed her. He didn't care that she tasted like him. She needed to feel what he felt for her—not just for what she'd done for him. He deepened the kiss, wishing he could take her upstairs and hold her in his arms as she fell asleep. He hadn't wanted that in so long, it should scare the hell out of him, but he had no desire to run away. Their ravenous kisses turned soft and sensual, and a contented sigh escaped her lips. Bridgette rested her head on his chest, and he embraced her, worrying about her in ways he'd promised himself he wouldn't. He wanted to tell her that he needed more than making out in the kitchen, laundry room, or backyard. He wanted breakfasts with spilled milk, starry nights, and baseball games. If he had a different career, he would tell her that they could never make their own erotic romance, because this was so much more real than fiction could ever be.

But those thoughts came too fast and broke all his rules. Instead, he said, "Beautiful girl. You came out of nowhere, and suddenly you're all I see."

CHAPTER TWELVE

BRIDGETTE SPENT TUESDAY floating on cloud nine. Bodhi had come by the flower shop in the morning to tell her he'd gotten the tickets to the Yankees game, and seeing him for those few minutes had made her whole day brighter. She was a little nervous about meeting his mother, but he'd explained her love of baseball so matter-of-factly, she was trying not to read too much into it. She picked up Louie on time and mentioned the trip to him during dinner. After a full five minutes of jumping up and down and cheering, he'd called Bodhi on the walkie-talkie to thank him. Now it was early evening, and as she stood on the back porch with Dahlia, who had suddenly become very attached to her, she watched the two of them fixing the playset.

Bodhi had bought a child-size tool belt for Louie, along with a set of plastic tools, and Louie wore it proudly. He watched Bodhi intently, mimicking his actions. He grabbed his plastic hammer, holding it exactly as Bodhi held his. Bodhi said something and placed the plastic hammer back in Louie's tool belt. Then he wrapped his big hand around Louie's and curled them both around his real hammer. Louie's eyes bloomed wide. Her little man turned a proud and excited gaze her way, and she warmed all over.

She watched them pound a nail. How could it be that neither her father nor Piper, who both worked with those tools on a daily basis, had ever shown Louie how to use a hammer? She knew it wasn't a fair question, but it made her realize that while Louie helped her dig holes, plant seeds, and build forts, there were some things she might never get around to showing him. Guy things. Things a father might usually take care of. She needed to pay more attention to those things.

They finished hammering, and Bodhi helped Louie take off his tool belt. He hoisted Louie in the air and set him on the swing, giving him a gentle push. Louie kicked his little feet, beaming with joy as he swung with Bodhi standing watch behind him.

Bodhi waved, and then his focus fell on her boy again. He was so good with Louie, it was as if he had been around children all his life. They swung for a little while, then Bodhi hoisted Louie into his arms, carrying his tool belt in his other hand, and said something that made her son grin from ear to ear. Her heart took notice for the umpteenth time. If only it were as easy for her to keep him in the friends-with-benefits category as she'd led her sisters to believe. But everything he did was thoughtful, or ovary exploding, like the way he was tickling Louie's belly as they stepped onto the porch. And the way Louie rested his head on Bodhi's shoulder, like he belonged there.

"Hey, beautif—*Bridgette*."

The regret in his eyes over the slip of his tongue was palpable. He set Louie's tool belt on the table and petted Dahlia, who was busy sniffing Louie's boots. It made Bridgette sad that they needed rules defining what was acceptable around her son, but she knew it was best for all of them.

"How'd it go?" she asked.

"We fixed it!" Louie exclaimed as Bodhi set him on the porch. "Bodhi is going to get his coin collection, and I'm going to get my baseball cards. Then we're going to watch a movie. Can we watch *Cars*?"

"Sure."

A boyish grin lifted Bodhi's lips, as if Louie had worn off on him, giving him a whole new look she'd never seen, and *boy* did she like it.

Louie went inside, and Bodhi reached for her hand. "Is that okay? The movie?"

"Yes, of course. I'm glad you're staying, but don't feel pressure to spend your evening with him. It's okay to say you're busy. You just spent almost an hour fixing the playset." She went up on her toes and kissed him.

His eyes shifted over her shoulder.

"I heard him go upstairs," she assured him, loving that he thought to check.

His warm lips touched hers, as tender and light as a summer breeze.

"He's the greatest boy, Bridge. He's polite and funny, and he wants to know *everything*. 'Why is the hammer so heavy? What happens if we miss the nail? Have you ever built a house?'" Bodhi said quietly, dishing out more torture for her overwhelmed emotions. "I'm sure you saw us talking, but the reason it took so long to fix the playset was that the first half hour was spent discussing our trip to New York. He's really excited. I'm glad we're going, and I'm happy to stay for the movie, unless you'd rather I didn't."

"I want you with us." *With me. On me. Inside me.*

Down, girl.

He kissed her again, crushing her to him the way he always did, making her feel safe and wanted.

Louie's feet hurried down the stairs, and they each took a step back.

"Slow down, honey," she called into the house.

"I'd better go get the coin collection." Bodhi blew her a kiss, and he and Dahlia headed back to his house.

Over the next hour, Louie and Bodhi bonded over baseball cards and coins, and Bridgette tried not to make too much out of how easy they were with each other. Bodhi had brought a book on coins that had been his father's, and as Louie asked questions, Bodhi referred to the book, explaining the answers in relatable terms. He was patient and thoughtful, though in true Bodhi style, he nodded curtly, and his expression remained serious as they inspected and discussed each item.

"See the corners on these two cards?" Bodhi held up one card with a frayed edge and one with sharp corners, explaining how cards were judged and valued and the importance of keeping them in good shape.

By the time Louie put on his pajamas and they turned on the movie, her little man could barely keep his eyes open. He curled up between Bodhi and Bridgette with his head resting on Bodhi's lap. While they watched the movie, Bodhi absently ran his hand along Louie's back, as Bridgette usually did. Half an hour later, Louie was fast asleep.

"You wore him out," Bridgette whispered, standing to carry Louie up to bed.

Bodhi's hand remained on Louie's back. "Would you mind if I carry him up?"

"I think he'd really like that."

Upstairs, Bodhi placed Jeter beside Louie and tucked them both in. He brushed a kiss to Louie's forehead and whispered, "Night, little dude."

Bridgette's knees weakened at the warmth and love he exuded. Aurelia was wrong. Bodhi had a warm and fuzzy side as big and present as his intimidating side, and she had a feeling she and Louie were two of the few people who were blessed with experiencing it. She pulled the door almost closed on the way out of Louie's room and took Bodhi's hand.

With her pulse racing, she led him down the hall to her bedroom, closing the door behind them.

Melissa Foster

Unexpected and hot as sin didn't begin to explain the thoughts racing through Bodhi's mind as Bridgette slipped her finger into the waist of his jeans, and gazed up at him with desire and a hint of nervousness. He was right there with her.

Her sweet perfume filled his senses as he took her hands in his and pressed them to his lips. "You're sure this is okay?"

A smile trembled over her lips. "As sure as I can be."

"Bridgette." Her name fell like a prayer as he lowered his mouth to hers, kissing her until that tremble disappeared and she went soft against him. "Do we need to hurry?"

She shook her head. "He never wakes up."

"What's our plan if he does? What if we're in the middle of making love and he comes in?"

She smiled and touched her forehead to his chest. "Thanks for that visual."

He tipped her chin up. "I promised never to hurt either of you. We need a plan, babe."

"Let's go with not freaking out, and hope for the best."

He knew short of not making love, that was about the best plan they'd come up with, and he wasn't about to walk away. He took off his shirt, needing to feel her hands on him, and kissed her as he unbuttoned her blouse. Her fingers were warm and soft against his skin as he kissed her breastbone, the warm cushion between her breasts, the center of her belly. He eased her top off her shoulders, kissing each one as the fabric fell to the floor.

She inhaled a shaky breath as he unhooked the center clasp of her bra and slid it off, baring her beautiful breasts. Wanting to remember everything about this night, he focused on the heat of her hands, the hunger in her eyes, and her shallow breathing as his mouth came down over hers. Her heart beat frantically against his chest as her body molded to the contour of his hard frame. His emotions burgeoned inside him, boring deeper as he worked the button and zipper of her shorts, and they puddled at her feet. He made quick work of toeing off his shoes and stripping down. He gathered her against him, her bare skin pressed against his arousal, sending heat pounding through him and knocking his brain into gear.

"Bridge, I wasn't expecting this. I don't have a condom."

Her cheeks flushed. "You can thank Willow for convincing me to go on birth control last year *just in case*."

Relief washed over him as he lifted her into his arms, drew her pretty pink covers back, and laid her on the bed. She reached for him, and he laced their hands together, placing a series of light, teasing kisses over her mouth and tasting his way down her body. She arched as he kissed and fondled her breast, slicking his tongue over the peak.

"Bodhi," she said heatedly. "You know that drives me crazy."

He grinned as he teased and taunted and sucked hard enough to bring her legs around his waist. Jesus, he wanted to drive into her in one swift motion, but that would have to wait. He intended to drive her out of her ever-loving mind first. She hadn't been made love to in years, and he'd *never* made love to a woman. He'd taken, he'd fucked, but he'd never *loved*. He didn't know if his raging emotions qualified as love, because he had nothing to compare them to, but he knew they were immensely bigger and more consuming than anything he'd ever felt before. Making love to Bridgette was not something he was going to race through.

Running his hands over every inch of her, he kissed and caressed, tasted and groped her ribs, her hips, her thighs. He adored her thighs, and took extra time loving them, making her quiver and plead. When his mouth finally hovered over her sex, his hot breath caused her to visibly tense up. He ran his tongue along her wetness, earning a sexy gasp. He spread his hands on her inner thighs, pressing her legs open and baring her most sensitive nerves for him to taunt and *claim*. He teased her with his tongue. She clutched at his hands and held on tight as he licked and tasted, slicked and sucked, making her tremble and pant, on the verge of release.

"Bodhi, *please*," she begged.

He kissed her inner thighs, slowly and teasingly, loving her with his mouth as he made his way up her body again. "I want you needy, baby, so when we finally make love, you can barely hold it together."

He took her hands in his, pressing them into the mattress, and nudged her legs open wider with his knees, aligning their bodies. The head of his cock pressed against her center, pulsing slowly, until it was slick and throbbing.

"I haven't done this in so long," she said softly. "I hope I don't disappoint you."

He touched his lips to hers, so full of her he could barely force words from his lungs. "Beautiful girl, you've already made me feel more than I ever have. There's no disappointing going on."

"What if I suck?" The tease in her eyes made him smile.

"You sucked impeccably well last night." That earned a sweet laugh. "I'm nervous, too. I've never done this with someone I cared so much about."

"Bodhi," she whispered, her gaze serious.

He read her silent warning—*we can't fall for each other*—and did what he knew best. He tucked that knowledge down deep where he didn't have to think about it, right beside the desire to know her hopes and dreams for her future. It was better if he didn't know. Then he couldn't try to make them come true.

"I know, beautiful," he said in answer to her silent warning. "But you need to understand that *nothing* could ever compare to what I feel for you right now."

"Show me, Bodhi," she whispered. "Don't tell me. *Show* me."

He gazed into her eyes as he sank into her tight heat, slowly filling her so completely, she held her breath.

"Breathe, baby," he whispered over her lips.

"You feel so good," rushed from her lungs.

We're made for each other.

He tucked that away, too, and wrapped her in his arms, kissing her as they found their rhythm. Every thrust sent waves of heat crashing over him. Never had he felt so connected and *whole*. His hands skimmed down Bridgette's sides, savoring the feel of her moving with him. He clutched her hips and drove in deeper, harder, consumed by their passion. She gasped. *Whimpered*. Her nails clawed at his back.

"Jesus, baby. You're . . . We're . . ."

"Perfect," she panted out.

He wanted to learn all her pleasure points, master them with his hands, his mouth, his *cock*. He wanted to be the man she called for when she was lonely or happy, when she needed help or just wanted to share her day. He wanted to love her into the morning and wake up with her safely tucked against him.

Holy hell. She'd completely shattered his defenses.

Every last one of them.

"There," she cried out. *"Oh God."*

He angled his hips with the need to possess her, quickened his pace, stroking over the spot that made her toes curl under and her gasps become fast and stilted.

"Bod—"

He smothered his name with his lips as her body pulsed hot and perfect around him. Heat raced down his spine, up his legs, exploding in a firestorm of shuddering ecstasy.

They lay tangled together as their bodies came down from the clouds. Bodhi held her tight as she dozed off. Minutes passed like hours, hours like days, while a war raged in Bodhi's mind. He lay listening for Louie's footsteps, for the creak of the floor, anything to indicate he'd overstayed his welcome. He needed to leave, but he'd give anything to stay right there and fall asleep holding Bridgette. Nothing could top waking up with her in his arms. Except knowing he'd be there for her the next time she needed him—and that was a promise he couldn't make.

She made a contented sound in her sleep, and Bodhi kissed her temple, reluctantly giving in to his responsibility. "Bridge? Babe?"

"Hm?" She snuggled in deeper.

"I have to go before Louie gets up."

Her eyes opened, and a pout formed on her lips. "One more second?"

Snuggle. Snuggle.

Torture. Torture.

"Babe, if Louie gets up, I'll never forgive myself for waiting so long."

"Me either." She clung to his arms, keeping them securely around her. "Get out of here. Geez, you're great at doling out orgasms, but you suck at leaving."

She flashed a cheesy smile, and they both laughed.

He kissed her shoulder, wanting desperately to stay, and whispered, "Louie," as a reminder to them both.

"Fine." She released him, then quickly grabbed his arms again. "Same time tomorrow night?"

He swept her beneath him and rubbed his nose over her cheek. "What am I, your booty call?"

"Hey, a booty call. That's a great idea."

"I can't leave when you're so unbelievably cute. Can't you be bitchy or something?"

She wiggled her hips. "I can be *or something.*"

"*Christ*, Bridge. That's not helpful." He sat up on the edge of the bed, elbows on knees, trying to calm down his revved-up body and wrap his mind around the powerful emotions telling him to make love to her again. "For the record, I frigging hate leaving you." He reluctantly pushed to his feet and pulled on his briefs.

"I know. Hand me your shirt?"

"My *shirt*?" He tossed it to her.

She pulled it over her head and slid off the bed. His shirt tumbled down her thighs. "Perfect."

He drew her into his arms and went for her neck, making her squirm and giggle and making *him* want to stay even more. "Wearing my shirt is very *girlfriendish*."

"Don't fool yourself," she said with another sweet laugh. "I've totally got this friends-with-benefits thing down."

"Me, too." It was a flat-out lie. He needed chains and a padlock to even come close to reining in his emotions. He stepped into his jeans and ran a hand through his hair, trying to trick himself into believing he *wasn't* aware of every breath Bridgette took as she wrapped her arms around her middle, one knee bent, her hair falling sexily over one eye as she watched him dress.

"Get over here." He hauled her against him again, his chest constricting for the millionth time. "I'll get out of here so you can get some sleep."

"Thanks for the big O." She kissed the center of his chin. "See? No emotions. All sex and booty-call talk."

Her feigned casual-sex talk couldn't hide the longing in her eyes. "Bridgette," he said in the most serious voice he could muster. "Kidding aside, can I see you tomorrow night?"

She nodded.

"And the night after?" He should stop there, but there was no way he was going to. "And every damn night until I go back to the city at the end of next week?"

Sadness rose in her eyes. "At the end of next week?" she said in a small voice. "How did the time go so fast?"

"I have training a week from Sunday." Several painful silent seconds ticked by. "Bridge, we still have time. It's only Tuesday." He pressed a kiss to her forehead. "Tell me you'll spend every evening with me until I leave. Please give us that time."

"I will. But let's not talk about you leaving. I want to enjoy our time, so when you do eventually leave, we have nothing but happy memories." She hugged him and rested her cheek against his chest. "And then I'm going to pretend you'll live happily ever after under the lights of the Big Apple, and never risk your life again."

CHAPTER THIRTEEN

"I CAN'T HIRE that girl," Bridgette said to Talia. She was arranging the second of three centerpieces for a last-minute order from the owner of a local restaurant. It was Thursday afternoon, and she was late picking up Louie *again*. Talia had stopped by on her way home to help Bridgette work her way through the applications she'd been ignoring. "I know too much about her, and yes, that's judgmental. But she sleeps with every guy she can get her hands on. That's not the type of person I want around my family and customers."

"Bridge, you've nixed the last three applications because of personal reasons." Talia closed the laptop, giving Bridgette the have-I-taught-you-nothing look she'd honed over the years. "You need to throw caution to the wind, bite the bullet, and hire someone."

Bridgette sighed heavily and set the flower she was holding on the table. Hadn't she been throwing enough caution to the wind lately?

"Tell me something I don't know. Mom and Dad have plans tonight, and they're dropping off Louie on their way out because I had to fill this order from one of my biggest clients. My kid has eaten Chinese food so many times in the last two weeks that Li might as well adopt him, and other than five minutes when Bodhi came by to pick up my key this morning so he could install a peephole in my door, I haven't seen him since yesterday morning when he stopped by under the guise of borrowing sugar." *And I miss him desperately.*

"I couldn't even get near him, because Dad bought Louie a pack of baseball cards, and Louie wanted to show them to Bodhi before we left. And then last night I was so exhausted I fell asleep watching a movie with Louie, and I didn't see Bodhi's text until two o'clock this morning. So, my dear sister, we are in agreement. I need to hire someone *yesterday*, because I'm stuck here having serious *Bodhi* withdrawals wrapped in mommy guilt. And I appreciate you helping me with the applications, but if I hire someone I don't trust, I'll spend just as much time worrying about what they're doing as I would doing the work myself. Then I can add 'babysitting staff' to my list of stressors."

"That's true," Talia conceded. "Just listening to you makes me tired. You're doing too much, Bridgette. I don't remember you being this busy before."

"I know. A growing business is a blessing and a curse."

"What about putting an ad in a paper in the surrounding areas and hiring someone from a bigger town? Maybe you'll get lucky and find someone who's relocating. Or you could ask Aurelia to help out until she and Willow finalize their plans for the bakery and bookstore. Piper said it'll take a while to get their renovations done once they start, and Aurelia's smart as a whip. I'm sure you'd have to train her, which would take some time, but at least you would have time to cook dinners for Louie *and* hopefully you won't be so tired, so you'll be able to see Bodhi after Louie goes to bed."

"You always come up with creative ideas." Bridgette went back to arranging the flowers. "I'll think about it. But Bodhi's leaving at the end of next week, and I probably won't have time to hire someone quick enough to free up time for us. Also, Louie doesn't know there's anything between us. We have to be careful around him."

"But you'll see Bodhi after he leaves, right? Long-distance relation-ships work."

"It's not like that between us," she said solemnly, aching at the reality that their time together was quickly coming to an end.

"The man is putting in a peephole and taking you and your son to New York," Talia said. "How can it not be like that?"

She didn't want to discuss this, and she wasn't prepared to talk about why it had to be that way. Bodhi had been clear that his life was on the line with every mission. Talking about it would only make her sad. Instead she said, "I know you aren't into the whole friends-with-benefits idea, but that's where it ends."

The bell over the door chimed, and Louie and their parents walked in.

"Auntie Talia!" Louie plowed into her legs.

"Hey, pumpkin." Talia tucked her long dark hair behind her ear and crouched next to him. "Did you have fun with Grandma and Grandpa?"

"Uh-huh. We're going to New York City with Bodhi to see a baseball game on Saturday, and Grandpa said if I catch a foul ball he'll buy a special case to put it in. I hope I catch one."

"That sounds like a very special trip." Talia glanced at Bridgette. "I hope you catch one, too."

"It's going to be fun," Louie said. "Bodhi's mom loves the Yankees, and she's going with us."

"She is, is she?" Talia arched a brow. "That sounds . . ."

"Serious?" Roxie offered. She looked pretty in a dark-blue crinkle-cotton skirt and blouse.

"I was going to say *fun*," Talia said, eyeing Louie.

"It will be fun!" Louie wrapped his fingers around the edge of the counter and peered over it to where Bridgette was working. "Pretty flowers, Mommy."

"Thanks, honey." Bridgette blew him a kiss. "Just a few more minutes, okay?"

"Serious can be fun," Roxie said. "Just ask your very serious father."

Their father kissed Talia's cheek. "Hi, beautiful." Then he joined Bridgette and kissed her, too. "Hi, princess."

Dan Dalton was the quiet strength of their family. From his short-cropped hair to his pressed shirt and pants, he was conservative and careful, like Talia. And beneath that retired-professor facade was a heart as big as they came.

"Hi, Dad. Sorry to make you guys stop on your way out. The order came in late, and the restaurant is one of my biggest clients. I couldn't say no." Bridgette had always been close to her father. Despite making his disappointment clear to her when she'd quit college to marry Jerry, he'd never held it against her, and he'd loved Jerry as if he were his own flesh and blood. For that she would always be grateful.

"It's not a problem," he assured her.

The bell above the door chimed again, and Bridgette kicked herself for not remembering to lock it. She stepped out from around the table and was surprised to see a man carrying a gorgeous vase overflowing with flowers.

"Hi," he said. "I'm looking for Bridgette Dalton."

"That's my mom!" Louie grabbed Bridgette's hand, dragging her toward the man.

"There must be a mistake," Bridgette said. "I don't order premade bouquets."

"This is the Secret Garden flower shop, right?" the guy asked.

"Yes, but—"

"Then I'm in the right place. Enjoy them." He handed her the vase and left.

She set the stunning bouquet on the table and looked for a card. "This has got to be a mistake. These aren't even flowers I'd typically arrange together."

"Well, if it's a mistake, I'll be happy to take them home," Talia said.

Bridgette opened and read the card.

Beautiful girl,
> Louie is your forget-me-not.
> Iris.
> You're a red camellia, my chrysanthemum.
> I love the yellow tulip.
> Your gardenia,
> B. B.

She stared at the message, trying to figure out what it could mean. She looked at her mother, who was peering over her shoulder with a look of understanding and awe in her eyes, and it came to her. The note was a coded message written in the secret language of flowers.

Beautiful girl,
> Louie is your true love, your memories.
>> Your friendship means so much to me.
>> You're a flame in my heart, my wonderful friend.
>> I love the sunshine in your smile.
> Your secret lover,
> Bodhi Booker

Louie pulled at her shirt. "Who are they from, Mommy?"

Bridgette's eyes flicked up to her mother, who was still leaning over her shoulder reading the card. Her mother smiled. Roxie was the reason Bridgette had become a florist. When Bridgette and Louie had first moved back to Sweetwater, they'd stayed with her parents. Bridgette had needed a way to work through her most private feelings without having to confess them to a counselor or family. Her mother had suggested that she help in the garden to keep her hands and mind busy. Over the course of two weeks, Roxie had shared her love of the secret language of flowers. She had a way of weaving information into normal conversation without pushing or prying or even forthright teaching. She had given Bridgette a safe way to channel her energy, and she'd opened up a secret language for Bridgette to let her innermost feelings out in a way not many people would understand.

As she gazed into her mother's eyes, she saw the same surprise she felt. Bodhi understood.

"Mom?" Louie said, tugging on her shirt. "Who are they from?"

She placed a hand on Louie's shoulder and said, "A very special friend."

"Looks like the lotion I gave him is working its magic," her mother said with a glimmer of hope in her eyes.

"Mom," Bridgette scolded, and lowered her voice. "Not that I believe in your love potions, but it can't be like that. Please don't get your hopes up." *I'm having enough trouble trying to keep mine in check.*

Bodhi looked out the front window, watching for Bridgette's car, as he spoke to his mother on the phone. "All I have left is painting the downstairs bedroom, but I'll get that done. You'll be all set by the time I leave for training."

"Thanks, honey. I'm excited to see you and your friends on Sunday."

He'd been careful not to share any personal details with his mother about his relationship with Bridgette. She'd been on his case for years to get into a safer line of work, and he didn't need the pressure of her using Bridgette and Louie as leverage. He'd gotten enough of that from Shira when she'd called earlier.

"And the three of you are staying at your place?"

"That's the plan." He'd already called his housekeeper and asked her to make up the guest room and stock the kitchen with kid-friendly foods. She had worked for him for the past three years, and she'd worked for his mother for three times as long. Her curiosity over his first houseguest had brought more questions than the dozen Louie had asked when they'd fixed the playset.

"If you and Bridgette would like to go out for an adult evening, I'd be happy to babysit."

His instinct was to jump at the chance, but he didn't know if Louie would be comfortable, and he and Bridgette would worry about him the whole time they were out. "Thanks, Mom, but it's probably easier if we stay together."

The sound of Bridgette's car drew his attention. Dahlia pressed her nose against the glass. After ending the call, he and Dahlia headed outside. Even though he'd already seen Bridgette when he'd picked up the key to her house earlier, his body thrummed with heat at the sight of her long legs, figure-hugging brown leather skirt, and low-cut white blouse. She trained her gorgeous eyes on him and smiled, sending his body into overdrive. It took all his control to resist taking her in his arms and kissing her.

"Hi, neighbor," she said with a sultry tone.

Dahlia licked Louie's entire face, earning lots of little-boy giggles. "Guess what, Bodhi? A special friend sent Mommy flowers."

"Is that right?" He arched a brow at Bridgette, who mouthed, *Thank you.*

"Uh-huh. They're in the car." Louie ran into the yard with Dahlia and rolled onto the grass.

Bridgette stepped closer, her back to Louie. She hooked her finger in the waist of Bodhi's pants. "Did you know I've never been given flowers before, except for my high school prom?"

"No, but I'm a little jealous of the dude who gave you those."

Her sweet, melodic laugh made her even harder to resist. He shoved his hands in his pockets to keep from touching her.

"I'm serious. I never knew what it felt like to receive flowers. I only know what it feels like to arrange them or grow them. Bodhi," she whispered, "I thought dancing in my kitchen was romantic, but today

I felt like a princess. And your note?" She put her hand over her chest, and her expression turned serious. "You probably shouldn't do things like that, because you made me all swoony, and swoony isn't a friends-with-benefits emotion."

He shifted his eyes away, feeling like she'd pulled the pin from a grenade. There was no place to take cover, and the worst part was, he'd brought this on himself. He'd stepped willingly into the middle of a battle he wasn't prepared for.

Knowing she was right, he said, "I'm sorry."

"Sorry?" Her brows knitted.

"I shouldn't have done it. I won't do things like that—"

"Wait. I don't want you to stop." She covered her mouth, eyes wide. "That sounded greedy." She dropped her hand, smiling again, and spoke in a fast whisper. "I meant it's hard to resist you already, and when you make me swoon, it's even harder. *Please* keep doing it. I love how you make me feel, and I know it's not forever, but I don't need forever. I like our here and now. I can deal with it."

"Thank God," he said loud enough for her ears only.

"Did your mother teach you the secret language of flowers?" she asked. "Or did you leave it up to the florist to figure it out for you?"

His eyes darted over her shoulder to Louie, who had his arms around Dahlia's neck, hugging her, tweaking Bodhi's heartstrings even more. "Babe, when it comes to you, there's no substitute for the real thing. I have a degree in horticulture, and my mother has rattled on about flowers my whole life. Their meanings come as easily as the ABCs."

"You have a degree in horticulture? There's probably a lot about you that I don't know."

"Here and now, beautiful." Where the words had once sounded right, now they came with regret. He wanted to take her in his arms and reassure her. Instead, he nodded toward her car. "Want help carrying anything inside?"

"Sure, thanks. I got takeout on the way home." She opened the car door and handed him the flowers. After grabbing the takeout bags, she said, "Don't judge my mothering skills by our meals."

"Look at your boy."

She turned loving eyes to Louie, and her lips curved up in that special smile meant only for a mother's son.

"How could anyone judge you as being anything other than an incredible mother?"

She blushed as they headed up to the porch with Louie and Dahlia on their heels.

"Look, Louie." She pointed to the peephole. "Now Mommy can look outside to see who's at the door without opening it."

"It's either Bodhi or Mike," Louie said, as if he were bored.

He glanced at Bridgette. *Mike?*

"The pizza delivery guy," she said with a laugh.

He unlocked the door, feeling like a jealous fool.

Bridgette stepped into the foyer and stopped, sniffing the air. Confusion mapped her forehead. "What is that smell?"

"It smells like a restaurant," Louie said, pushing past her with one arm around Dahlia.

Bridgette's eyes narrowed. "Bodhi . . . ?"

He shrugged and followed her into the kitchen. Louie and Dahlia headed for the playroom. Bridgette dropped the takeout bags on the table and went to the French doors, gazing out at the table on the porch, set with three place settings.

Bodhi set the house key and flowers on the table.

"Bodhi," she said, turning to face him. "What have you done?"

He led her out of sight from the hallway and gathered her in his arms. "You've been working so hard, I thought I'd make you and Louie dinner."

She sighed and touched his chest. "Bodhi."

"I know it's all too much, but this might be the only chance I'll ever get to feel like this. Just go with it, Bridge. Friend to friend."

"*Bodhi,*" she said just above a whisper. "I wasn't going to say it was too much. I was going to say that I was wrong about the flowers. *This* is the most romantic thing anyone has ever done for me."

He embraced her. "I'm just going with what I feel, because I want you to look back on our time together and know it was worth trusting me and sharing your incredible little boy with me."

"Bodhi," she whispered.

"Don't say anything. *Please.* Let's just have dinner, take the little dude and Dahlia for a walk down by the lake, and enjoy what time we've got left." He took a step away to try to regain control of his emotions. "I made lasagna."

He said, "Louie's favorite," at the same time she did.

"How did you know?" she asked.

"He told me when we were fixing the playset. That boy has got a long list of favorite things." He pulled the lasagna out of the oven.

She smiled. "Tell me about it."

"I made it at my place and brought it over so it would be here when you got home. There's salad in the fridge."

"You're like a triple threat. Hot, sweet behind all that badassness, *and* you can cook."

He stepped so close her body heat flooded him. His arm circled her waist, and he hugged her against him. "Careful using words like *sweet* that paint me as a pansy, or I'll have to prove to you just how manly I really am."

"Yes, please," she whispered.

He took her in a demanding, possessive kiss, blowing sweet out of the water and leaving no room for anything but *too fucking hot to breathe.* She came away breathless, and he cocked a brow.

"What were you saying, sweetheart?"

She touched her lips and reached for the counter, as if she needed it to remain erect. "Maybe," she whispered, "you should show me again."

And he did. He kissed her until she dug her nails into his skin, making a needy sound in the back of her throat.

"Louie," he said softly, and turned away to adjust his painful erection. He glanced over his shoulder as he took a tray of rolls out of the oven, and chuckled at the dreamy look in her eyes. "Louie also told me that you have a thing for sweet potato rolls, and he hates them."

She fidgeted with the ends of her hair, holding his gaze. "Yeah. I sure do like them. I like them a whole lot more than I should."

He stepped toward her, intent on getting one more kiss, but Louie and Dahlia came around the corner.

"I'm starving." Louie pulled out a chair at the table and climbed up.

The interruption was a blessing in disguise. He was becoming all too swept up in his beautiful girl.

He carried the lasagna over to Louie. "What do you think, little dude? Can you do some damage to this lasagna?"

"Lasagna!" His eyes widened. "Can we give the Chinese food to Dahlia?"

"She'll get a bellyache from Chinese food. How about if we ask your mom if you can feed Dahlia breakfast tomorrow before you go meet Grandma Roxie?"

"Can I, Mom?" Louie asked hopefully. "And can I go outside with Dahlia just for a minute before we eat?"

"Yes, and yes, but stay in the backyard."

"I will!" Louie bolted out the back door with Dahlia.

"I hope that was okay." Bodhi closed the distance between them. "I didn't mean to put you on the spot. I have no clue how to do what we're doing, and it's driving me up the wall."

"I disagree. You know *exactly* how to do whatever it is we're doing."

CHAPTER FOURTEEN

THE NEXT TWO days flew by, and before Bridgette knew it, it was Saturday afternoon, and they were on their way to New York City. She'd been so excited about their weekend away, she'd closed the flower shop early. Bodhi had bought tickets to see *The Lion King*, and Louie had watched the movie twice since they'd mentioned it. Louie chatted the whole first half of the almost two-hour drive. Bridgette worried that his incessant talking might grate on Bodhi's nerves, but Bodhi took it all in stride. Now Dahlia slept on the seat beside Louie, and Louie, having worn himself out, was fast asleep.

Bodhi reached for Bridgette's hand and pressed a kiss to the back of it. He held it until they hit stop-and-go traffic in the city, when Louie woke up like a bundle of energy ready to explode.

Louie peered out the window. "There's no grass here. Where will Dahlia go poop?"

Bodhi chuckled. "I'll show you when we take her for a walk."

The three of them had taken Dahlia for a walk along the lake Thursday and Friday evenings. Louie had found it hilarious that Bodhi had to pick up Dahlia's poop with a plastic bag, and he declared that he was never getting a dog of his own. Bodhi tried to teach him how to skip rocks in the water, and when that proved to be too difficult, Bodhi showed him how to toss a handful of pebbles into the water so they looked like rain. Louie had mastered that and then ran around the grass with Dahlia until he was so tuckered out, Bodhi had given him a shoulder ride home.

Bridgette wondered what Louie would think of this fast-paced concrete jungle, and she had to admit, she was curious to see how she'd feel about it, too, after all these years.

Gazing out at the busy sidewalks and looming buildings, she felt her nerves prickling. She glanced into the backseat at her curious boy. Dahlia was watching Louie as intently as Bodhi did. Bodhi drove with his jaw tight and his eyes serious. He looked over and smiled, then nodded curtly in that reassuring way he had, and set his focus back on the road. And just like that, her nerves calmed.

She watched couples holding hands as they hurried along the sidewalk, and single men and women walking so fast and determined she wondered what could be so important. The last time she was there, they'd been driven from the venue to the hotel and back in private cars with blacked-out windows. They'd partied and laughed and had a great time, but she realized she'd never seen any of the tourist sights. At the time, just the energy of the city had been alluring, and she'd seen it as the ultimate place to live. Now she couldn't imagine raising Louie there. She'd changed, and she would never know if it was because of Jerry's death, because Louie depended on her, or if she would have one day grown up to be the person she was now. But she knew two things for sure. Some part of her would always be in love with wild, reckless Jerry, and she was thankful for the heart's ability to heal—because she was falling hard for a very serious, extraordinarily special man, who would one day soon break it anew.

"It smells funny in here," Louie said as he climbed out of the car in the parking garage.

"Once we're out of the parking garage it'll smell better," Bridgette said. The air was thick with exhaust and traffic noises, and she found herself stepping closer to Bodhi and Louie.

"But it'll never smell like Sweetwater," Bodhi said.

He swung their bags over his shoulder with a look in his eyes Bridgette couldn't read. Was it a look of disappointment? Or was it a warning—reestablishing their line in the sand? She found herself hoping for the first.

He held Dahlia's leash in one hand and settled a hand protectively on Louie's shoulder. "I'll come down and get the other bag when I take Dahlia out."

"I can get it." Bridgette reached for the bag in the trunk, and he touched her arm, stopping her.

"It's okay," he said reassuringly, and firmly. "I'll grab it later."

Her mind sailed back in time, to when she'd traveled with Jerry. Handlers had taken care of their luggage, and they had been so young, they'd treated life like one big, carefree adventure. Then again, their world had been one party after the next, one city after another, where Bodhi's life was spent saving lives in the most dangerous places. She'd never seen herself as someone who needed taking care of, but she enjoyed the way Bodhi watched out for them. She had also come to adore his serious demeanor, treasuring every secret smile, stolen touch, and furtive glance.

As they waited for the elevators and she watched Louie's awe-filled gaze take in the upscale lobby, the true weight of their visit sank in. Bodhi was as private as a person could be, yet here they were, entering the most intimate aspect of his life, spending the night in his home. This was a huge step, even if neither one of them was willing to acknowledge it.

Two women and an elderly gentleman were also waiting for the elevator. The women scrolled through their phones, faces serious, dressed in high heels and professional outfits. The elderly man stared straight ahead.

Louie squeezed her hand and grabbed Bodhi's pants leg.

Bodhi took his hand with a warm and concerned gaze. "You okay?"

Louie nodded.

In the elevator, Dahlia sat beside Bodhi as if she knew she was home and was expected to behave differently than she did in their yard. Bodhi was right. Taking care of Dahlia wasn't so different from caring for a little boy. Love, patience, and routines were the foundation of both relationships.

A few minutes later, Bodhi opened the door to his condo and unleashed Dahlia. She ran inside sniffing everything in her path, and Louie followed her down a hallway.

"Louie—"

Bodhi touched her hand. "He's fine. I have nothing he can get into. Let me set the bags in the bedrooms, and I'll be right back."

As she stepped farther into his home, she thought about the keep-your-distance vibes Bodhi gave off to most everyone. He was anything but warm and fuzzy, yet his home exuded an air of warmth. Dark hardwood floors ran beneath a plush throw rug, comfortable-looking, well-loved leather couches, and a heavy, masculine dining room table. Shelves lined the wall to her left, filled with books and photographs, and across the room, glass doors led to a large balcony that appeared to have more furniture than the living room and dining room combined. Drawn by the sight of large marble planters overflowing with lush greenery and colorful flowers, she went to the balcony doors.

Bridgette's body flooded with awareness seconds before Bodhi touched her hip.

"Is Louie getting into things?"

"No," he assured her. "He's checking things out, looking out the windows, sitting on the beds. He's fine."

She turned toward him, struck again by his rugged handsomeness. As excited as she was for Louie to experience the Big Apple, she couldn't help wishing she could snuggle up on the balcony in Bodhi's arms and kiss him until morning. "I really like your place, and your balcony is beautiful. It's your own secret garden."

"Thanks. The city can be oppressive, and the outdoor living space and plants help me feel less like I'm living where there's no air." His fingers trailed lightly over hers. "I've never had anyone over before, besides Shira and my mother. Do you think this will be okay for you and Louie tonight?"

He pointed to a small kitchen just beyond the dining room. "I had my housekeeper buy food I thought you and Louie would like even though we're eating out tonight. Just in case he gets tired, or changes his mind and would rather stay in."

He'd thought of everything. "It's perfect."

She gazed into his eyes, wondering about all the unsaid things between them. What if he wasn't called in for an assignment for months after he left Sweetwater? She knew he had no way of knowing if that might happen, but that didn't stop the nagging question from lingering in her mind. Would he want to chance falling harder for each other and continue seeing each other if he knew he could, or was this really it? She'd agreed to this . . . *fling*? That felt ten types of wrong. This wasn't a fling. This was real, but so was the little boy in the other room. The boy who counted on her to make smart decisions for both of them. Now, if she could only convince herself that this *was* a fling, that would make reining in her emotions a lot easier.

Bodhi was used to plowing through chaos while acutely aware of his surroundings, but as they made their way along Times Square, the city felt different with Bridgette and Louie by his side. It was even more oppressive and stressful. The lack of green space had never bothered him before, but when they'd taken Dahlia for a walk, the difference between Dahlia and Louie running around Sugar Lake and their leashed existence in the city had irked him. Seeing Louie's face light up with every new discovery was as addicting as Bridgette's smile, but Bodhi was even more vigilant about the people and things around them. It was killing him not to scoop Louie into his arms, tuck Bridgette against his side, and keep them so close nothing could harm them.

"How come we don't take cabs at home?" Louie asked. He'd been fascinated with the whole idea of riding in a cab when they'd taken one on their way to Times Square.

"Because Sweetwater is a small town, and we can walk almost everywhere," Bridgette answered.

"Maybe I'll be a cabdriver when I grow up." Louie blinked up at Bodhi. "But I'm probably going to play for the Yankees."

Bodhi loved his confidence. "I think you'll be great at whatever you want to do."

"If I play for the Yankees, can I sleep at your house sometimes?" Louie asked.

Yes was on the tip of his tongue. In the hour they'd spent in the condo, his home already felt more alive than it ever had. They'd explained to Louie that Bodhi lived there and he was only in Sweetwater for another week. Louie had asked if Bodhi would still let him walk Dahlia when he came to visit his mother in her new house and if they could still watch a movie together sometimes. It had nearly killed him to agree when he had no idea how much of a future he'd have. He didn't know how he'd leave them at the end of next week, much less how he'd handle things when his mother eventually moved there. There was no way he'd be able to visit without wanting to be the only man in their lives. But Louie was oblivious to their turmoil, and he was glad for that.

He bought Louie a Yankees baseball cap and shirt to wear to the game tomorrow, and they went into every shop Bridgette and Louie wanted to. When they came to a jewelry store, Bridgette slowed to admire a display.

"I haven't seen you wear much jewelry," he said as she hoisted Louie up to look at the display. "What kind of jewelry do you like?"

She looked at him for a long, silent moment, and he heard warning signals going off. She must have, too, because she said, "I'm not that into jewelry," and continued walking down the street.

Louie wiggled out of her arms, taking up the space between them again. "Look at all the lights." He pointed at the glowing signs on the sides of the buildings. "Do they turn them off when they go to sleep?"

"Some do," Bodhi said.

They joined a crowd of people waiting to cross the street, and Bodhi moved so he had one hand on Louie and one on Bridgette's lower back. Bridgette flashed her killer smile, and it quickly smoldered.

Louie gasped and pointed to a food truck, jolting them out of their secret moment. "Pizza from a truck! Can we eat dinner there? Please?"

Bridgette and Bodhi exchanged a glance, and he shrugged, giving her the option.

"Please?" Louie begged. "We can eat while we walk down the street. We never do that. Please, Mom?"

"Absolutely," she said, knowing Bodhi wouldn't care if they skipped having dinner at a restaurant. "Every kid should eat pizza while they walk down the street at least once, right?"

Louie's excitement didn't waver while he ate and talked and walked, getting pizza sauce all over his cheeks and shirt. He was too adorable for words.

Bridgette cleaned him up and planted a kiss on his cheek. "Best dinner ever."

"Can we ride in one of those?" Louie pointed to a horse-drawn carriage.

"We have tickets to see *The Lion King* tonight," Bridgette reminded him. "I don't think we have time."

"But I've seen *The Lion King*, and I've never ridden in one of those. *Please?*"

They stepped out of the way of the people walking by, and she knelt beside him. "Honey, we're going to see a play, with real people, and—"

"But I see real people every day," Louie insisted. "Please, please, *please*?"

Bodhi touched Bridgette's shoulder, and she stood to talk to him. He whispered in her ear, "Would you mind if we gave him the option to make this decision?"

She looked down at Louie, who was practically salivating over the horse-drawn carriage. "Are you sure you don't mind? I can pay you back for the tickets."

"I'll take you up on that, but I don't accept cash. Think you can come up with another way to make it up to me?"

She blushed a red streak as he knelt beside Louie.

"Louie," he said in his most serious tone. "This is a big decision, and I want you to think hard about what I say, okay?"

Louie nodded vehemently, his little brows pulled together. He was so cute Bodhi wanted to smile, but he needed Louie to understand the seriousness of his decision.

"If you choose the carriage ride instead of going to see the play, you can't change your mind later. The same way baseball players have to run around all three bases to get to home plate, the driver of the carriage has to stay on track the whole way. He can't change directions and take us to the play. Do you understand what that means?"

Louie nibbled on his lower lip, nodding.

"This is your decision, little dude. Take a moment to think about which one you'd rather do, ride the carriage or see the play."

Louie looked up at Bridgette. "Mom, do you want to see the play more than ride the carriage?"

Bodhi melted a little at Louie's love for her.

She crouched beside Bodhi, giving Louie her full attention. "I want to do whatever will make you happiest, honey."

Louie seemed to think about that as he turned to Bodhi again. "Can you watch *The Lion King* movie with me and Mommy when we go back home to our real house?"

Bodhi considered himself a strong man, but that little boy was his kryptonite. He prayed he wouldn't be called in before he had a chance to fulfill his promise. "Yes. I'd love to."

A short while later, after giving their tickets to *The Lion King* to a young family, they climbed into a carriage, with Louie safely seated between Bridgette and Bodhi. Bodhi stretched his arm across the back of the seat and rested his hand on Bridgette's shoulder. She was wearing a blousy black tank top. Her skin was warm and familiar. His whole body seemed to shed tension at *finally* having the connection he'd craved all day. Their eyes met, and the fire he'd come to expect ignited between them, but that was nothing compared to the bigger emotions winding around them like a tether, binding the three of them in this moment of time. He should be worried about the powerful emotions, but after a lifetime of locking his emotions away, he wanted to soak in every second he could.

Louie marveled at all the sights during their forty-five-minute carriage ride through Central Park. And he wasn't shy about telling the driver that Sugar Lake was much prettier than the lake they rode past. He went on to tell the patient man about all the ways Sweetwater was better than New York City, and Bodhi wasn't sure he disagreed. After their ride, they stopped for cotton candy, and since Louie was yawning every few minutes, Bodhi suggested they take a cab home.

"I don't want to take a cab. I like walking," Louie said.

Bodhi stifled a chuckle at Louie's change of heart about cabs.

"It's a long walk, sweetie," Bridgette warned him.

"Several long blocks."

"I'm a big boy," Louie insisted. "I can walk long blocks."

"I like your determination." Bodhi touched Bridgette's lower back. "What do you think? Are you up for the walk?"

"Absolutely."

Louie held both of their hands and chatted about the carriage ride for the first two blocks. His chattiness slowed by the third block, as did their pace. When Louie's hand went nearly limp in Bodhi's, he stooped beside him. Louie's eyelids were heavy, and his lips were stained pink from the cotton candy, as were his shirt and hands.

"Hey, little dude," Bodhi said. "I know you can walk the rest of the way, but I'm a little cold. Would you mind if I carried you to keep myself warm?"

"Okay, but I *can* walk," Louie said with another big yawn.

Bodhi lifted him, and he snuggled in against his chest. Within minutes, his body was heavy with the weight of sleep. Bodhi had been wrong the other night when he told Bridgette that watching out for Dahlia was the same as watching out for Louie.

Nothing compared to *this*.

CHAPTER FIFTEEN

THEY WALKED THE rest of the way home with Louie sleeping soundly on Bodhi's chest and Bridgette snuggled against his side.

Dahlia was so excited to see them, Bodhi had to take her right outside so she didn't wake Louie. Bridgette changed Louie into his pajamas and tucked him into bed. He was so worn out, he remained asleep. She tucked Jeter in beside him and sat on the edge of the bed, admiring her sweet boy. He loved Bodhi the same way he loved Aurelia and their other close friends. She saw it in the way he looked at him and how he'd reached for Bodhi's leg and not hers in the elevator. She had ached a little at that, in a good way. She wanted his world to be full of love, and thinking of Bodhi and Louie's relationship in the same way she thought of Louie and her other friends helped her to put things into perspective. She heard the front door open and the heavy cadence of Bodhi's footsteps coming down the hall.

Her body prickled with anticipation.

Dahlia trotted into the room beside Bodhi. "Hi, beautiful," he whispered, and pointed to Louie, a question in his eyes.

"He's out cold."

He touched his lips to Louie's forehead. "Night, little man."

The look in his eyes was so serene, she knew Louie had affected him just as deeply as he'd affected her boy. They headed for the door, and

Bodhi patted his thigh for Dahlia to follow him out. The pup whimpered and rested her chin on the bed.

"I think your boy has won over my dog. Do you mind if she stays with him while we hang out?"

"Hang out?" Bridgette wrapped her arms around him and whispered, "Or *make* out?"

His gaze darted to Louie.

Oh, how she loved that, but she'd been patient all day, keeping the heat between them under wraps when she'd wanted to kiss and touch him every minute. *Now it's Mommy's turn.*

"He's out like a light," she assured him.

"Lie down," he whispered to Dahlia.

In one leap, Dahlia was on the bed, lying next to Louie. Bodhi took a step toward her, and Bridgette dragged him out of the room.

"Let her be," she whispered. "She's *your* dog, Bodhi. Do you expect her to be any less protective than you are? Louie will probably sleep better with her beside him anyway."

In the hallway, he trapped her between the wall and his body. His eyes glowed with a savage inner fire as he brushed his lips over hers, and her whole body thrummed with anticipation.

"Think he'll sleep soundly enough for me to do dirty things to his mommy?"

He lowered his mouth to her neck, and the first touch of his tongue earned a needy moan. She clamped her mouth shut as his hands moved down her hips, and he clutched her ass, holding her tight against his hard length.

"Feel what you do to me, baby." His breath sailed over her skin like summer heat.

"Take me to your bedroom and I'll show you how much *more* I want to do to you," she promised.

He took her hands, walking backward down the hall and raking his eyes hungrily over her, lingering on her mouth so long she salivated. His gaze slid lower, making every inch of her tingle and ache. She reached for him, and he drew her against him. Closing the door behind them, he wasted no time staking claim to her mouth. His tongue moved forcefully over hers, devouring her with such mastery, her ability to think ebbed. All their pent-up desires came rushing out as their clothes flew through the air, and they tumbled to the bed naked. They crawled under the covers in case Louie woke up, and Bridgette playfully pushed him onto his back. His eyes blazed into her as she straddled his thighs and slithered down his body, kissing his chest. He groaned and arched as she grazed her teeth over one nipple.

"You drive me crazy, baby."

"Mm. That's the plan."

He leaned up and captured her mouth, and then his hand was between her legs, dipping inside her, teasing and taunting, turning her into a wet, writhing bundle of need. He lifted her by the hips, and she guided his eager length to her center, sighing at the intense pleasure as she took in every blessed inch of him. He sealed his hot mouth over her breast, and she arched forward, clinging to him as he pumped his hips to a rhythm that took her right up to the brink of madness—and held her there. She squeezed her inner muscles, earning an utterly male and hot-as-hell groan. His hands were everywhere at once, groping her breasts, teasing her clit, touching her ass. Her body was on fire with the overwhelming sensations. In one dominant move, he shifted her onto her back and drove into her. She cried out in ecstasy, and he silenced her with his talented mouth. His hips thrust faster, deeper, until every ounce of her trembled. Just when she thought she'd burst, he angled his hips, and the next thrust sent her spiraling into oblivion. He swallowed her sounds, masterfully drawing out her orgasm, until her name tore from his lungs and he surrendered to his own release.

The kiss went from fierce to tender, and his hips pulsed slower, doling out one scintillating sensation after another, both of their bodies quaking in the aftermath of their passion. When he drew back and gazed into her eyes, there was no hiding from the truth. It wouldn't matter what words were said or how many miles apart they would eventually be. She knew what love looked like.

Bodhi lay next to Bridgette long after they made love, knowing he'd never be able to sleep in his bed again without seeing her there in his arms. Was the universe cruel, or beautiful? He thought of the day they'd met in the bakery, and how many times they'd run into each other before finally coming together. He thought about the night he'd heard her talking through the walkie-talkie. She was like a beautiful gift. The person he wanted and the person he needed. He ran his hand over her hip, reveling in the feel of her and earning a sweet, sleepy smile. A gift he could borrow but not keep. Did the cruelty of that outweigh the beauty?

He touched his lips to hers, pushing that worry away, and she snuggled closer. "Bridgette," he whispered. "*My* sweet, beautiful Bridgette."

"Can I ask you something personal?" she asked.

"Anything."

"How did you lose your father?"

For a beat his body went rigid at the unexpected question. "He was killed in the war."

She lifted her face from his chest with empathy in her eyes, softening the shock. "Is that why you went into the military? You mentioned having a degree in horticulture, and it's not exactly a natural progression, from flowers and plants to wars and guns."

"I would have gone into the military right after high school, but my mother insisted I get a degree." He and his mother had rarely argued, but as a teenager he was full of piss and vinegar, and they'd argued for weeks over applying to colleges. She'd won, of course, because there was nothing he wouldn't do for her. Thinking of how many times his mother had asked him to step away from rescue missions, he corrected his thought. *Almost nothing.*

"You enrolled after graduation?"

"Enlisted." He kissed her softly. "Yes, the day after my graduation ceremony. I spent several years in the Special Forces, and at the end of my second tour, I was recruited out by Darkbird, the company I work for now. They offered me a chance to do what I wanted to do and have a life outside the military, which I was more than ready for. Although some things remain the same. The missions are classified, which means I can't talk about where I'm going or have any outside communication while I'm gone."

"Was your father in the Special Forces, too? Did he do rescues like you?"

Bodhi felt his barriers clicking into place, and he held her a little tighter, hoping to keep them at bay.

"My father was on a special combat team. They got ambushed, and he was taken prisoner." A knot formed in his chest, but he forced himself to continue. "A rescue team went in, but the mission was compromised, and they were too late. They retrieved his body, and the bodies of two of the other guys."

"So much about you makes sense now." Pain rose in her eyes. "I'm sorry."

She pressed her cheek to his chest and embraced him. It was exactly what he needed, because he wasn't sure he could force many more words out.

When the knot in his chest unraveled, he tipped her chin up and kissed her again.

"People die in wars every day, and one day I might be one of them. That's why this has to be short-lived. I have mandatory training a week from Sunday, and I could be called in for an assignment any day between now and then. Prisoners aren't taken on schedules, and we don't just rescue prisoners. We rescue troops who are stuck with no way out, and missions aren't always successful. We've lost men, Bridge. Good, strong, smart men. A lot of them. I've seen families torn apart after they lose their brothers, sons, husbands, wives, mothers, and fathers. I heard my mother crying herself to sleep too many times, and saw her growing sad when my father's name was mentioned by friends. I'll never put you or Louie in that position."

"I know this isn't the same, but you have Dahlia, and you love her. You're her *person*. She looks at you like Louie looks at me. Aren't you worried about leaving her behind?"

"Sure, I worry about her, and my mother and Shira. But my mother watches Dahlia when I go away, and if something happens to me, my mother will take her. She'll need Dahlia as much as I've needed her, and I feel good knowing they'll have each other."

She was breathing harder, and his inclination was to soothe her with a kiss, but they needed to have this conversation, if for no other reason than to remind himself why he couldn't allow his emotions to get the better of him.

"How long are you usually away?" she asked just above a whisper.

"It depends. Several days to several weeks. What do you *really* want to know, Bridgette? What don't you understand, or what's bothering you, beyond the obvious?"

"I guess I'm curious about why you have a hard-and-fast rule about relationships. I understand and appreciate the line we've drawn, because I've lost someone I loved, and I don't want to go through that again." She pulled back, putting just a few inches of space between them, but when she lifted her chin, steeling herself for God only knew what, it felt like miles. "But I'm sure there are other women who would give anything to love you and be loved by you for whatever time they could get. Love can be the most wonderful, uplifting, life-affirming experience, and it makes me sad to think that you're against *ever* allowing yourself to go there."

Aren't I already there? hung on the tip of his tongue, but that confession had to remain locked away.

"Bridgette," he said gently, trying to quell the anger and hurt pummeling him from the inside out. "You just made love with me, and now you're selling me on falling in love with someone else? Am I missing something? Do you need an out from this?"

Her shoulders slumped, and sadness rose in her eyes, her strong facade crumbling right before his eyes. He took her in his arms, wishing things were different, that death wasn't knocking on his door with every mission.

"Is that what you really want, Bridge? Do you want me to fall in love with some other woman?"

She shook her head. "No."

"Is this too hard on you? Knowing I'll leave soon?"

"No," she whispered. "It's what we need to do. For Louie."

He knew better. It was what they needed to do for her, too, and if he were honest with himself, for *him*, as well. It was going to be hard enough leaving them, but leaving and knowing they were waiting on his return? That would distract him from doing what he needed to do for the people awaiting rescue, and that wasn't a risk any of them could afford. He bit back the despair and forced himself to do the right thing.

"That's why we have to appreciate what we have right now." He lowered his lips to hers, trying to escape the sinking feeling in the pit of his stomach. She wrapped her fingers around his arms and rolled onto her back, bringing him down over her. A stab of guilt lay buried deep inside his chest as he tipped her chin up and kissed her.

"I never should have kissed you that very first time," he whispered. "I knew it would never be enough."

"Then make it enough. Make love to me again and again until the very feel of each other is imprinted in our bodies."

"My beautiful girl . . ." There was no masking the love in his heart, or the regret in his voice.

As their bodies came together with the heat and passion of a couple on the brink of an unwanted separation, Bodhi was no longer filling moments of physical desire. He was filling his soul with her, allowing his anguish over leaving to fall away, until there was nothing but Bridgette.

CHAPTER SIXTEEN

FOR ALL THE calm Bridgette had felt in the days leading up to meeting Bodhi's mother, when Sunday arrived, she was a nervous wreck. She took her shower while Louie slept, and after she dressed, she found Louie helping Bodhi cook waffles. She stood outside the kitchen watching her little man standing on a chair, pouring batter onto the waffle iron with her big man's help. Bodhi kept one hand protectively around Louie's waist and spoke in a low, patient voice.

"That's it. Perfect." Bodhi took the measuring cup Louie was using to pour the batter from him and set it on the counter. "Now we close the lid and let it cook."

"Sometimes my mom burns my waffles."

Great. At five he was already throwing her under the bus.

"I burn them sometimes, too," Bodhi said.

Thank you for having my back.

"My grandma never burns them."

"Grandmas are pretty special. They know how to do everything," Bodhi said.

"Did your grandma teach you to make waffles?" Louie rested his head on Bodhi's shoulder.

Bridgette took out her phone and snapped a few pictures. She typed a quick text to Willow. *Ovary overload. When can you babysit?*

"No, little dude. My father did, when I was a year or two older than you." He opened the waffle maker, and steam rose into the air.

"Whoa! That's cool. Did your dad show you that, too?"

"Sure did." Bodhi grabbed a fork and used it to take the waffle out and put it on a plate. They set to work pouring more batter. "We used to have a cabin in the woods, and we'd get up before my mother and make waffles just like these."

Bridgette's phone was still on silent, and it lit up with Willow's text. She opened and read it quickly. *OMG! Cute! Wednesday night, and Zane can stay with Louie until Mom picks him up Thursday morning. Okay?*

"With chocolate chips?" Louie asked as Bodhi closed the lid on the waffle iron.

"With chocolate chips. Know what else we did? We slept in hammocks tied between two trees."

"I want to do that!" Louie exclaimed.

"Maybe one day you'll get a chance to."

Bodhi's noncommittal answer stung, even though she knew it was for the best. She'd decided last night after their talk that she wasn't going to get caught up in what they wouldn't have. She was bound and determined to enjoy whatever time she and Bodhi had left.

She replied to Willow as an idea formed in her mind. *Perfect. Thank you! Do you have Logan Wild's number?* Logan was a friend of their family, and he owned a cabin in the Silver Mountains, close to Sweetwater. A few text messages later, her plans for her Wednesday-night date with Bodhi were set in motion.

They ate breakfast on the balcony, and while Louie brushed his teeth, she and Bodhi enjoyed a handful of stolen kisses.

They packed up their belongings and loaded them in Bodhi's car so they wouldn't have to do it after the game, and then they took a long walk with Dahlia. Bridgette took several more pictures, and Bodhi asked a woman walking by to take a picture of the three of them. She was glad they'd have these mementos. After dropping off Dahlia at

Bodhi's, they took a cab to pick up his mother, and Bridgette's jitters returned. Standing outside his mother's door, Bridgette imagined all sorts of things going wrong. What if Louie misbehaved or had a melt-down? What if Bodhi's mother was abrupt, or they didn't get along? What if she saw Bridgette as an impediment? A distraction to her supremely focused son?

She put a hand on Louie's shoulder, reminding herself that Alisha Booker was a florist *and* a mother. If nothing else, they could connect on those levels and make it through the afternoon. As the door opened, Bodhi's hand found the small of Bridgette's back, as if he knew she needed that hidden comfort.

"Well, hello there, my new friends." Alisha Booker greeted them with a warm and welcoming smile, wearing a pair of jeans and a Yankees T-shirt, which instantly put Bridgette at ease. She was tall and thin, with kind hazel eyes that moved from Bridgette to Bodhi, and finally, to Louie. Her whole body seemed to sigh with pleasure at the sight of him.

Bridgette followed her gaze, surprised to see Bodhi's hand on Louie's other shoulder.

"Hi," Louie said. "Are you Bodhi's mom?"

Alisha bent at the waist. Her thick salt-and-pepper hair tumbled over her shoulders like a mane. "I am Bodhi's mother. My name is Alisha, and you must be Bodhi's friend Louie. I can see you're a fellow Yankees fan." She pulled her hand out from behind her back and slid a Yankees baseball cap on her head, instantly winning over both Louie and Bridgette.

Louie grinned and touched his own ball cap.

"Hi, Mom." Bodhi's hand pressed more firmly on Bridgette's back. "This . . . is Bridgette Dalton."

The way he paused, like he was giving a special person a proper introduction, made Bridgette's pulse quicken.

"It's lovely to meet you, Bridgette. Bodhi tells me we're going to be neighbors."

A twinge of sadness washed through her at the reminder that Bodhi wouldn't always be living right next door. Couldn't she escape reality for just a little while longer? "Yes. I think you'll really like Sweetwater."

"If I like it half as much as Bodhi does, I'll consider myself lucky. From what he tells me, you and I have quite a lot in common. I can't wait to get to know you better." She grabbed her purse from a hook by the door. "Shall we go?"

"Guess what, Alisha?" Louie didn't wait for her to guess. "A horse drove us through a park last night, and today we rode in a cab and Bodhi let me pay the man."

Alisha glanced at Bodhi with the motherly look of wonder Bridgette had seen in her own mother's eyes when she'd received the flowers from Bodhi.

"Did you know that when Bodhi was your age," Alisha said in a hushed tone, "he was afraid to pay the cabdriver? He thought if he put his hand through the window he'd never get it back."

"Bodhi's not afraid anymore. He paid the man yesterday," Louie said as they stepped into the elevator. He blinked up at Bodhi with a look so serious Bridgette wished she could whip out her phone and take a picture. "I have your back, Bodhi."

Oh, gosh. Friends, friends, friends.

Bodhi ruffled his hair. "Thanks, little dude."

And so began their incredible afternoon.

They had seats by the dugout, and Louie was beyond excited to see the players up close. He ate a hot dog and ice cream and cheered right along with the rest of the crowd. Bridgette was waiting for him to get whiny and tired, but he hadn't complained once, and they were already in the last inning. Louie stood by the railing with Bodhi as Bodhi pointed out each of the players.

"It must have been a difficult decision to sell your flower shop," Bridgette said to Alisha.

"It was, but I'm looking forward to slowing down and pursuing some of my other passions," Alisha explained.

"Like . . . ?"

"I'm not sure," she said casually, watching Bodhi and Louie. "But life is too short not to try to figure it out while I still can."

"Well, if you get bored, you're always welcome to help out in my shop. I'm having a heck of a time finding someone to hire." She brushed her hair away from her face, thinking of the last few résumés she'd negated. "Small towns are great, but I know too much about most of the people who live there. It's hard to hire someone who you know drinks too much on the weekends, or has questionable friends."

"That's because the flower shop is your baby. Like Louie. You'd never let just anyone watch him."

"You're right about that. My mother takes care of him while I'm at work, but it would be nice to find someone trustworthy so I could get home a little earlier. But you must know all about that, having raised Bodhi by yourself." She looked over as Bodhi lifted Louie to his shoulders. They seemed so natural together, it was easy to let her mind wander to a future they could never have.

"Yes, I remember the days of Bodhi doing homework in the back of the store while I worked late. But he didn't turn out so bad, did he?"

"He's wonderful, and he's so good with Louie. I can't believe he hasn't spent his whole life around children."

Alisha's expression turned serious. "He spends a fair amount of time around children with Hearts for Heroes."

"Oh?" Bridgette realized Bodhi had never elaborated on the charity, and she'd been so caught up in stealing time with him, she'd forgotten to ask.

"They help grieving military families who have lost family members. Each chapter holds quarterly get-togethers, and if Bodhi's in town, he tries to attend. He's known some of the kids for several years." Her eyes warmed, and she glanced at Bodhi. "He's helped a lot of people move on after losing their loved ones."

Bridgette's eyes were drawn to Bodhi as he lowered Louie down from his shoulders. She was sure Louie would drive him crazy. *Up and down, up and down.* Louie put both hands on the railing, riveted to the game. Bodhi stood behind him, one hand on either side of Louie's. A human shield over her little boy.

"He didn't tell you about that, did he?" Alisha asked, pulling Bridgette from her thoughts. "It doesn't surprise me. He's lived up to his name, hasn't he?"

"What does *Bodhi* mean?"

"*Bodhi* is the understanding one possesses of the true meanings of things, and the literal meaning is 'awakening.' When Bodhi's father and I chose his name, it was with the hope that he would be good and kind, and not wrapped up in hate, greed, or his own ego." She paused, smiling as if she were remembering the moment she'd chosen the name.

"You couldn't have found a more perfect name."

"Yes. I'm not so sure that's always a blessing." Alisha blinked several times. "Anyway, I'm not surprised he didn't tell you more about his work with Hearts for Heroes."

"We don't spend that much time talking." *Oh God. That sounds bad.* "I mean, when we're together, Louie is usually around, and when he's not, we—"

Alisha touched her arm, laughing softly. "Honey, I wasn't born yesterday. As a mother, you know you can't pull the wool over a mother's eyes. All it took was one look to know what Bodhi felt for you and Louie."

"It's not like that," she began, but there was no avoiding the obvious. She met his mother's gaze, and the truth came easier than she'd expected. "What I mean is, I know how dangerous Bodhi's job is. He's been honest with me about not wanting to get too involved, and frankly, Louie and I already lost Louie's father. I'm not sure we could handle loving and losing another man."

"Oh, sweetheart. I didn't know about Louie's father. I'm sorry."

"Thank you. Louie was only a baby when it happened. He doesn't remember him." Bridgette looked down at her hands, afraid her eyes would give her lie away. "I think for all of our sakes, it's better if we enjoy our time together and then go our separate ways."

"I won't pretend to know what's best for either of you," Alisha said. "But I'm not so sure *the way* you lose someone you love makes the pain of losing them any easier or more difficult. It's the emptiness they leave behind that hurts so badly, regardless of whether they deliberately walked away or were taken from us. But the heart is a wonderful, strong organ. It has the ability to heal and grow and love more than one person. The trickier part is finding someone who makes your heart *want* to love again. Someone who fills all those empty places and then some."

Alisha was so down-to-earth, Bridgette could see herself pouring her deepest emotions out to her, and she struggled to keep the rest of her thoughts about Bodhi to herself. She redirected the conversation.

"You never fell in love again after losing your husband?" Bridgette asked.

She shook her head. "But who knows. Maybe I'll find that in Sweetwater, too."

"Mom!" Louie hollered.

Bridgette looked over just in time to catch Bodhi taking a picture of Louie with his arm around Derek Jeter's neck.

"Oh my goodness!" She pulled out her phone and took pictures of Derek signing Louie's baseball cap.

"Didn't Bodhi tell you he'd called in a favor with the team manager and arranged for Derek to be here to meet Louie, even though he is retired?" Alisha asked.

"No." *Holy cow.* That was a heck of a favor!

"Babe!" Bodhi waved her over.

Alisha reached for her phone. "Go! I'll take the picture."

"But *you're* the Yankees fan," she said to Alisha as Bodhi tugged her over to the railing. Holding Louie in one arm beside Derek, he wrapped his other around Bridgette and said, "Smile, babe. This is a once-in-a-lifetime opportunity."

Louie was too sidetracked chatting with Derek to notice the endearment, but she wasn't. Nor was she too sidetracked to realize the coincidence. Bodhi was a once-in-a-lifetime opportunity, too.

Bodhi didn't believe in magic, but there was definitely something bewitching about making a little boy's dreams come true. And, he had to admit, there were also some secret powers at work when it came to Bridgette and his mother. They had talked and laughed and gotten into serious discussions during the whole baseball game. By the time they'd dropped Alisha off at her condo, the two were practically in tears over saying goodbye. That had done something funky to Bodhi's emotions, which was as unexpected as the warm and soft feeling inside him as he carried Louie up to his bed in Bridgette's house and tucked him in later that night. Louie had rehashed their weekend for most of the ride back to Sweetwater, and he'd begged to wear his signed baseball cap to bed. He'd fallen asleep only after Bridgette had agreed, about forty minutes outside town. Now he looked cute as hell lying with the covers pulled up to his chin, a small smile on his sleeping face as he snuggled Jeter.

"You made his year, Bodhi," Bridgette whispered as she wrapped her arm around his waist and rested her head on his chest. "Today's a day he'll never forget."

"I have a feeling I won't, either."

As Bridgette led him toward her bedroom, everything felt different. Things were changing so fast, like he'd been racing up and down a highway his whole life, never stopping anywhere long enough to put down roots. He'd always believed roots could be ripped out, stolen by the wind, shredded into dust. Bridgette made him question that belief. Her world had been uprooted at such a tumultuous, vulnerable time, with a tiny baby to care for, after her married life had just started, and she'd found a way not only to survive, but to thrive.

How much heartache could one person survive?

He didn't want to know the answer. As Bridgette closed the bedroom door and he took her in his arms, those thoughts fell away, and he filled his mind with his beautiful *here* and *now*.

With *Bridgette*.

CHAPTER SEVENTEEN

MONDAY EVENING BODHI and Bridgette sat in her car in front of his house making out like horny teenagers. Willow and Zane had invited them to an impromptu dinner at their house, and Roxie and Dan were bringing Louie with them. Bridgette had stopped by after work to pick up Bodhi, and he'd been devouring her ever since. He took the kiss deeper, and she reached across the seat and palmed his cock.

They'd been insatiable since their trip, and he didn't want to stop, but . . . "We're never getting out of this driveway if you do that."

She yanked the button open and pushed her hands into his briefs. "Mm-hm."

"Baby." He groaned and shifted in the seat to give her more room. "You're not going to believe this, but I've never made out in a car like this."

Her eyes flamed. "How can I stop now, knowing that?"

She lowered her mouth over the head of his cock and used her tongue to drive him out of his mind.

"Holy shit, Bridgette."

He reclined the seat, and she made a sound that vibrated through him as she stroked and licked and used her hand to intensify his pleasure.

"That's so good, baby."

She quickened her pace, then slowed to an excruciatingly erotic rhythm of dragging her tongue along his shaft, followed by a tight stroke of her hand, and finally, taking him to the back of her throat. He slid a hand beneath her shirt, and caressed along her spine. *Needing* to touch more of her, he pushed his other hand down the back of her skirt, thanking the powers above for whatever forgiving material it was made from. He moved aside her lace panties and dipped into her slick heat, earning a lustful moan as she rocked forward and back, fucking his fingers as she loved him with her mouth. He felt her thighs flex around his hand, and she sank down on his fingers, moaning through her climax while continuing her exquisite torment and shattering his control.

"Bridge—" His hips shot off the seat, and his climax crashed over him.

His body quaked and pulsed, and she stayed with him until he sank back against the seat, sated and spent. She climbed over to his side of the car, curled into his arms like she was ready to settle in for the night, and sighed. He closed his eyes, soaking in every minute they had together.

An hour later, after washing up—and getting Bridgette a clean pair of panties that Bodhi couldn't wait to take off her—they were seated at Willow and Zane's dining room table having dinner with her family. Ben and Piper had made a few joking comments about Bridgette and Bodhi showing up late, and Louie explained, in his adorably believable way, that they were probably late because they had to take Dahlia for a walk. He then went on to explain that Bodhi had to pick up the dog's poop with a plastic bag. The boy knew how to break the ice.

Bodhi glanced at Louie, who was wearing the hat Derek Jeter had signed and sitting between his grandparents, across the table from him and Bridgette, totally focused on eating while the adults all talked at once. What was it like to grow up surrounded by all this playful banter and love? He realized how smart Bridgette had been to move back home when she'd lost her husband. Everything she and Louie needed to heal was right there in that room. A twinge of guilt prickled his nerves, because he knew that soon she'd need them again, and that was all on him.

"We should send Piper to Bodhi's house to check out the quality of his work," Ben teased, elbowing Bodhi and snapping him back to the moment.

"No, we should not." Bridgette squeezed Bodhi's hand under the table.

"What's the matter?" Piper smirked, setting her eyes on Bodhi. "Afraid he won't pass muster?"

"You're welcome to come check out my work anytime," Bodhi offered.

"But not right before we leave in the mornings, because he's at our house borrowing sugar," Louie said without looking up from his dinner.

Bridgette choked on her drink, laughing and coughing, her cheeks flushed. Bodhi patted Bridgette's back and felt a grin tugging at his lips as seven sets of amused eyes turned in their direction.

He cleared his throat and schooled his expression. "Louie's right. I can't find sugar as sweet as Bridgette's at any store."

Louie looked up from his meal. "I bet Willow's sugar is sweet, because she makes the yummiest doughnuts!"

Everyone laughed, sparking conversations spoken in code about baked items, creamy fillings, and desserts eaten before dinner. Bodhi had lived with military guys for long stretches of time, and they had *nothing* on the Dalton family.

"You boys can thank my Roxie for our girls' sweetness," Dan said, eyeing Zane and Bodhi. "She's got the sweetest sugar of all, and they are her daughters."

Bodhi's mother had a good sense of humor, and there hadn't been many dull moments when he was growing up, but being around this much inherent love and laughter was a whole different world. Dan leaned over and kissed Roxie, tweaking an old sadness Bodhi hadn't thought of for a while. Was his mother lonely? He'd never thought *he* was lonely. Not even all the times when Shira had asked about it over the years. But spending time with Bridgette and Louie had taught him what it felt like *not* to be lonely. He took comfort in knowing that Bridgette and Louie would have enough family to ensure they wouldn't be lonely after he left. After this week, he and his mother would have even more in common. Would their support for each other be enough to fill the emptiness Bridgette and Louie would leave behind?

The playful banter and laughter continued through dinner. When Zane and Willow got up to clear the table, Bodhi and the others rose to help.

"Can I go watch a movie?" Louie asked.

Bodhi's instinct was to follow Bridgette and Louie into the living room, but he held back, helping to clear the table instead.

Roxie sidled up to him, looking pretty in another artsy top and a pair of wide-legged pants. The spark of mischief in her eyes reminded him of Bridgette. "I see you've been using the lotion I gave you."

He glanced at the plates covering his hands. "I have, but . . . ?"

She patted her heart and said, "It's on your sleeve, honey." She walked away humming a happy little tune.

Talia was right behind her. "You let her give you lotion?"

He set the plates beside the sink. "What am I missing?"

Zane laughed. "Apparently nothing, if you're using Roxie's lotions *and* showing up late for dinner."

Bodhi felt a hand settle on his shoulder—*Dan*. Respect straightened his spine.

"Son," Dan said, "what you're missing is that my wife has the power to charm love out of anyone, like a flute to a cobra."

Bodhi froze. Was he that transparent? He'd thought he'd been keeping his emotions in check around others, even if not in his own mind.

"Oh yeah. My Roxie knows her stuff." Dan walked away.

Ben elbowed him. "Dude, get that look off your face before the girls start planning your wedding."

"Ben," Zane said sternly. "Man, you know he's leaving at the end of the week. Don't make him feel worse for it."

"I have to admit, Bridgette has never seemed happier." Ben patted Bodhi on the back. "But when you leave . . ."

Tell me something I don't know.

"I hear we're babysitting your dog Wednesday night." Zane turned off the water and dried his hands.

"Dahlia?" This, he did not know.

Zane and Ben exchanged an oh-shit glance and converged on him in a huddle that rivaled one preceding a final play in football.

"I fucked up," Zane whispered.

"As per usual," Ben teased.

Zane glared at him. "Seriously, Bodhi. I thought you knew. You can't tell Bridgette I told you about your date."

"Jesus!" Ben chastised in a harsh whisper. "Dude?"

Zane cringed. "Shit. Well, I already blew it. Here's the deal." He glanced over his shoulder at the others talking in the dining room and spoke fast. "Willow and I are babysitting Louie and your dog Wednesday night so you and Bridge can have a night alone. I'm keeping Louie until Roxie picks him up in the morning, so you have more time together."

Holy shit. Bridgette had planned all of this? A night alone? And she'd even taken care of Dahlia? He glanced around Ben at his beautiful girlfriend, who never failed to surprise him.

"If you tell Bridgette we told you," Zane warned, "we'll have to kill you."

"Dead," Ben said.

"Body disposed of," Zane said.

"Like you never existed," Ben confirmed.

Bodhi chuckled. "You can try."

Zane and Ben glowered.

"I'm kidding," Bodhi assured them. "I've got it. Christ, you do stick together, don't you?"

They rose to their full heights and bumped fists, then they turned their fists toward Bodhi. Surprised, Bodhi bumped each of them.

"About time we had another guy around," Ben said.

"No kidding." Zane put an arm around each of them and headed for the others. "I love the girls, but it's like estrogen overload in here."

Bridgette came into view, standing in the living room with a hand on Louie's shoulder and talking with Talia and Willow. If this was estrogen overload, he'd happily drown in it.

Bodhi wrapped his arms around Bridgette from behind and rested his chin on her shoulder. "How many times did you sneak out of this bedroom?"

She placed her arms over his, laughing softly. She was giving him a tour of Willow and Zane's house, her childhood home. He father had dubbed the house the Grand Lady because it sat high on a hill, as if it stood sentinel over the rest of the homes on the street. "You don't really want to know."

He turned her in his arms, his eyes fierce, his jaw tense, but she knew him well enough by now to *feel* the difference between real and feigned tension. This was neither. It was *jealousy*, and she was loving that particular emotion more than she probably should. It reminded her of their first night together when he'd thought Ben was her husband.

"Maybe a better question would be, what did I do when I snuck out." She pushed up on her toes and kissed him. "It wasn't what you think."

His eyes narrowed, and she whispered, "I never had sex until I went away to college. I've only been with four men. Two before Jerry, and you."

He touched his forehead to hers. "It wouldn't have mattered, except that you just saved me from having to kill some poor bastard around here." His lips curved up in a sexy smile. "What did you do when you snuck out?"

"Went to the creek and partied with my friends. Danced to loud music, drank beer they'd stolen from their parents, and dreamed about growing up and getting out of this tiny town."

"Really? You didn't love living here?"

"I did love it, but I wanted so much more." She drew in a deep breath and took his hand, leading him to the window. "I used to look out this window and dream of big cities and all-night parties. I wanted more fun, freedom, and . . . I don't know. I wanted *more* in general, I guess. When I went to college, it was like uncorking a shaken bottle. All fun, all the time."

He touched his lips to hers. "How did you pass your classes?"

She held up her hand, indicating *barely* with the space between her finger and thumb. "I only completed a year and a few weeks before I met Jerry."

"Ah, the ultimate freedom." He held her tighter. "I'm glad you had that. I wish I had known you back then."

"You wouldn't have liked me. I was too wild for you."

"You have no idea what I was like in high school."

"*Please.* You were big and broody, like you are now. Only I bet you studied hard and you were the head of the football team, telling everyone what to do. I never liked those types of boys. I wanted long-haired bad boys."

His lips curved up. "I was as bad as they came."

"Uh-huh," she teased, unable to picture him doing *anything* wrong. "Bad boys don't work in their mother's flower shop."

"Wanna bet?" He rolled his shoulders back and puffed out his chest. "I was well behaved, and I did my schoolwork, but I was a cocky asshole for a while, just the type of guy you would have liked. I didn't ask girls to go out with me. I'd point to them and say, 'Friday night,' and they'd practically fall to their knees."

Her jaw dropped open. "Seriously? You're bossy, but I can't even imagine you treating girls that way."

"Yeah, well . . ." He tugged her against him. "I've got to say something to save face."

"You were a mama's boy!"

He tackled her on the bed, tickling her ribs, and she squealed.

"I was a badass!"

"Big, bad Bodhi," she said between laughs. "The mama's boy!"

He smothered her face in kisses, and she couldn't stop laughing. Suddenly Louie raced into the room and dove onto the bed, tickling her, too, and Bodhi was tickling Louie, and they were all laughing hysterically. Bodhi trapped them both beneath him, his arms around them, and collapsed on top of them in a fit of hysterics.

"God, I love you two—" bubbled out with his laughter.

Bridgette bit her lower lip, eyes wide.

A gasp drew her attention to the doorway, where Willow stood with her hand over her mouth, barely covering her smile. Behind her, Zane and the others each wore the same shocked, and happy, expression.

Don't overthink. Don't overthink. Friends love each other.

Louie wrapped his arms around Bodhi's neck, smiling so hard it had to hurt his little cheeks. "We love you, too, Bodhi!"

She met Bodhi's gaze. Her son's arms were wrapped tightly around his neck as he rose to his feet. His smile turned to something she couldn't quite read. Regret? Begging for forgiveness? Anger? If it was the latter, she knew it would only be aimed at himself, and that made her ache inside.

Bodhi didn't miss a beat. He tickled Louie's belly, earning another innocent giggle and reminding Bridgette not to make too much out of things in front of him, because Louie was just that—*innocent*. To him, the word *love* held a meaning very different from what it meant to her and Bodhi.

It was the man holding him, and the way he was looking at *her*, that had her stomach tied in knots.

"High five, little dude." Bodhi held a hand up, forcing a smile that didn't come anywhere near reaching his eyes.

Louie slapped his hand.

Bodhi turned a genuine smile on her family, who were watching the three of them like they were on the big screen. "I guess the cat's out of the bag. I totally dig *all* my new friends."

Bodhi, *the rescuer*, had just saved her heart by protecting her son's.

Bodhi, *the man*, however, wasn't fooling anyone else.

Least of all her.

CHAPTER EIGHTEEN

BODHI HAD STEPPED on a land mine, and he was terrified of making a move. He hadn't meant for his feelings to tumble out, but for the briefest of seconds he'd forgotten who he was and what was at stake. Bridgette looked like she was going to fall apart any second, and he needed to get to her without making things worse.

"Who wants dessert?" Roxie burst into the room, reaching for Louie, and saving Bodhi's ass.

"Me!" Louie cheered, and happily climbed out of Bodhi's grip and into hers.

"Good idea," Willow said, her eyes darting between Bodhi and Bridgette. "We'll—"

Ben pushed to the front of the group and herded them toward the stairs. "Downstairs, everyone. The ticklefest is over." He glanced over his shoulder and gave Bodhi a look that told him he had his back.

When they were safely out of earshot, Bodhi quietly closed the door and went to Bridgette as she sat down on the edge of the bed. He stood before her and took her hands in his, telling himself it would be easier for her if he covered up his feelings. He met her gaze, and the hope and fear in her eyes brought him to his knees before her. He gazed up at her, love seeping out of his pores. His gut clenched with the realization that he was an asshole after all, because he wanted her to love him back, even if only for their last few days together.

"I never meant to fall in love with you," he admitted, and her eyes went damp. "I thought I could do this, but you and Louie . . ." Overwhelmed by his emotions, he paused to try to regain control and cradled her face in his hands. He was probably holding her too hard, but he was afraid to let her go—and afraid not to. Tears streamed down her cheeks, slipping over his fingers. "I fell, Bridge. I fell so hard I feel like I'm breaking apart. I love you and Louie, and I know I shouldn't, and it's unfair, but—"

She crushed her mouth to his, silencing his confession. Her salty tears slipped between their lips as they tried to hide from reality.

"Don't say it," she said into the kiss.

"Bridgette." He sank back on his heels, lifting her onto his lap as they kissed. "You're mine, and I'm yours. Right now we have this."

She cried harder, all the while kissing and touching him all over as he was touching her, like they were each making sure the other was real.

"I never meant to hurt you." His devastation came out loud and clear, and he hated himself for putting them in this position.

"I know." She drew back, a shaky smile appearing and disappearing in quick succession. "I fell, too, Bodhi, and I know it's not fair to Louie."

The pain inside him erupted, piercing him with the force of a hundred wild beasts trying to claw their way out.

"Maybe we can make it work," she said through her tears. "I can handle being apart a few weeks at a time."

"Baby." His throat thickened to the point of every breath causing pain, but he loved her too much to gloss over this subject. He held her face again, gentler this time, brushing his thumb over her lower lip, then pressed a soft kiss to it. "I know you can handle a few weeks, but can you handle not knowing if I'll live or die every time I go to work?"

She swallowed hard.

"Can you handle when they show up at your door and tell you the man you love is never coming back? Can you imagine telling Louie I'm gone?"

She turned away. He guided her trembling chin back toward him, and she closed her eyes.

He kissed her wet cheeks. "Please look at me, Bridge."

Her eyes opened, and he nearly drowned in the despair in them.

"The ball is in *your* court," he said as firmly as he could. "Do you honestly want to go through that . . . *again*?"

"It might not happen," she said angrily.

A memory he'd buried long ago raced through his mind. It was the last time his father had been home on leave. *Dad, you'll come back, right?* His father had looked him in the eyes and said, *I sure hope so.* Hope wasn't good enough for Bridgette and Louie. He couldn't do that to her.

"You're right," he relented, then forced himself to man up and take the hit. "But if it does? Baby, we went into this relationship with our eyes open, remember? Can you look me in the eyes and tell me you want this? That you're willing to risk the devastation of losing me? Maybe not in a month, or a week, but every single time I go to work, it's a risk. Are you willing to put Louie through that?"

Her chin fell to her chest, fresh tears sliding down her cheeks, and she shook her head. "I can't do that to Louie," she said so quietly he almost missed it. She fisted her hands in his shirt and met his gaze. "But I want more time with you."

"I know. I do, too. But I have to report for a week of training Sunday night."

"I know." She sat up a little straighter, killing him with her strength. "We promised each other every night until you left. Willow and Zane said they'd babysit Wednesday, and I asked them to take Dahlia, too. I planned a special night. And the Peach Festival is Saturday. Can we just have that? Can you stay until Saturday evening?"

"My sweet, beautiful Bridgette. Every day I stay will make it that much harder when I leave. Are you sure that's what you want?"

Her eyes brightened and she nodded vehemently, her hair tumbling around her face. "I want whatever I can get. A day, a week, an *hour*."

His gut told him to say no, to make it easier on her, but as it had been doing all evening, when he opened his mouth, the truth poured out. "Then I'm going to love you every second we have left, so you never regret it."

He wrapped her in his arms, trying to escape the torment between them, and for the first time in his life, he questioned his career choice.

CHAPTER NINETEEN

AFTER FIELDING HER family's overprotective phone calls for two days, Bridgette was thrilled to get away with Bodhi Wednesday night. She loved her family and appreciated their concerns, but she wanted to enjoy these last few days with Bodhi without thinking about how much it would hurt when he left Saturday evening. They knew the reason for her situation. Bodhi had taken the time to talk with each of them Monday night. Bridgette had been floored to find out that while she was on the couch with Louie, Bodhi had told them about the dangers that came with his job and about losing his father.

Later that night, after Louie was asleep in his bed, and after they'd made love, they'd stayed up for hours talking. She'd wondered if he'd ever considered doing something else with his life, though she hadn't voiced the question. He'd told her about the friends he'd lost and the families they'd left behind. He'd gone on to tell her about the men and women he'd rescued, and she'd heard in his voice the fulfillment it gave him, answering her silent question.

Every time a mission is successful, I know my father didn't die in vain. His death made me strive to be the best at what I do. And because of that, someone else gets to live. She held on to that statement like a lifeline when her decision about sticking to their plans of *here* and *now* felt like she was swallowing glass. Her family understood, but they worried she might regret that decision later.

Bridgette couldn't worry about regret. She had a little boy's feelings to protect. The second Bodhi had asked if she could handle being notified of his death, and having to explain that to Louie, her choice had become clear.

Now, as they drove up the narrow mountain roads, she decided not to think about his leaving.

"Slow down." She pointed to the fork in the road up ahead. "Turn right there." She was glad they'd taken his truck so she could snuggle against him as they drove to Logan's cabin. The sun hung just above the horizon, slicing through the umbrella of trees in fits and spurts and spreading a romantic hue over their evening.

"This would be much easier if you'd just tell me where we're going." Bodhi squeezed her shoulder.

"But it wouldn't be nearly as much fun." She'd wanted to surprise him with the overnight trip to Logan's cabin. All she'd told him was to dress for the outdoors and pack a bag. She glanced at the walkie-talkie hooked to the waist of his jeans, and she wondered if it would work this far away. Louie hadn't needed to call him to say good night recently, as Bodhi was at their house nightly, playing games, tossing a ball in the backyard with Louie, or watching movies, as he'd promised.

"You sure you're okay with being away for the night?" he asked.

"I'm more than okay, and Louie's in good hands. Zane's like a big kid. He'll keep Louie up too late, feed him too much sugar, and let Dahlia sleep on the bed. Louie might never want to come home." She saw the driveway up ahead and said, "Take the next right, but take it slowly."

"I love it when you give orders." He cocked a sexy grin and pulled her closer.

He stopped the truck in front of the iron gates that led to Logan's driveway and set a narrow-eyed stare on Bridgette. "Where *exactly* are we going?"

She pressed a button on the key fob, and the gates opened. "You'll see. My friend Logan Wild's place." She motioned with her hands for him to continue driving.

"Why does he have iron gates, Bridge?" he asked as the gates closed behind them.

"He's a PI and ex–Navy SEAL. He has this thing about safety. Remind you of someone?" she teased. "He owns two hundred acres and has all sorts of surveillance equipment set up around the property. That's how he found Willow skinny-dipping on his property."

Bodhi laughed. "Seriously? I bet Zane loved that."

"That was before she and Zane started going out. Besides, Logan and Willow became fast friends, and in the years since, his family has become like part of ours. Piper keeps a set of Logan's keys to the cabin, and she checks on it when he's away for long stretches of time." She didn't tell him that she'd asked Piper to come up yesterday and do a few special things for tonight.

"Surveillance? So, we need to behave while we're here?" The darkness in his eyes made her body heat up.

"Hardly. Logan promised to turn everything off except around the perimeter of the property."

"Nice." He kissed her temple as he drove up the long, forest-lined driveway and parked in front of the rustic two-bedroom cabin. His lips curved up, and he sank back in the seat as if he'd just arrived home after a long trip away. "Bridge . . . ?"

He stepped from the truck and lifted her out. Even after being carried by him too many times to count, she still got a rush of adrenaline when she was in his arms. He set her on her feet and held her hand as they walked toward the cabin. Ever watchful, he scanned the property.

He stopped midway to the porch and hauled her against him.

"What is that to our right?" he asked with a serious tone.

She laughed softly. "A hammock. I had Piper put it up for us."

He lifted her up to eye level, her feet dangling above the ground. "Someone is a very good eavesdropper."

She wrapped her legs around his waist and brushed her lips over his, the way she knew drove him mad. "I'm really good at other things, too."

"No, babe, you're incredible at everything you do. I would have been happy to stay at one of our houses. I don't care where we are. I just want time with you. But this? This is beyond what anyone has *ever* done for me."

"I wanted to give you a night you'd never forget."

"How could I ever forget a second we've spent together?" He traced her lower lip with his tongue, sending rivers of heat through her veins. "Everything about you is unforgettable."

He kissed her again, and she soaked in as many as he'd give, hoarding them for later, when she'd be forced to survive on memories of his kisses.

"Before I open that door, give me an idea of what you have planned. Otherwise I'm taking you directly into the bedroom."

"Forget my plans."

He fumbled with the keys as they devoured each other. The door flew open with the force of their bodies, and he broke the kiss long enough to push it closed. Then his mouth was on her again, kissing her fiercely as he backed her up against the wall, crushing her with his hard body.

She tugged at his shirt. "I need to feel you."

"Baby, I want to feel *all* of you." He turned with her in his arms, looking toward the kitchen and the bedroom to the left. "Bridgette," came out rough and disbelieving.

She followed his gaze to the ingredients for chocolate chip waffles sitting next to the waffle iron on the kitchen counter.

He took her in a demanding kiss and strode past the kitchen and into the bedroom. He laid her on the bed and came down over her, his gaze boring into her. "What are you doing to me?"

"Not nearly enough." She curled her hand around the back of his neck, drawing his mouth to hers.

They kissed and kissed until Bodhi's erection ached so badly behind his zipper he couldn't stand it. He pushed from the bed and wrestled with their boots, tossing them across the room. He tugged off their socks, nearly falling over as he pulled his second sock off.

Bridgette laughed, and he silenced her with a kiss, stripping away her sexy cutoffs and panties and feasting on every inch of flesh as it was revealed until she was naked and flushed, her breasts heaving with every inhalation.

He made quick work of removing his clothes, visually devouring her gorgeous body and slowing himself down at the immensity of this moment. They were completely alone. There was no sleeping child down the hall, no reason to rush beyond the desires coursing through them.

He stood at the edge of the bed, gazing at her and trying to tamp down the grenades exploding inside him at the thought of leaving her. There was no holding back the truth, even if he had to love her from afar. "You're so deep under my skin, I'll never really be without you."

She sat up and kissed his stomach. Her lips were warm and tender as she kissed around his erection. She wrapped her hand around his cock, with a wicked look in her eyes, and licked him from base to tip, causing his whole body to shudder. She did it again, and the air left his lungs with a hiss. She continued licking until his cock was slick and throbbing. When she finally took him in her mouth, it was hell trying not to rock deeper. He pushed his hands into her hair, letting her lead but holding tight as she moved in a torturous rhythm. She was exquisite, the pleasure immense, but it wasn't nearly enough.

His love for her was too consuming to watch and not touch. "I need *you*."

He lifted her into the middle of the bed and came down over her, perching on his forearms, their mouths a whisper apart. "Hi, beautiful."

"Hi." She smiled up at him.

He brushed his lips over hers. "You smell sexy enough to eat."

Her cheeks flushed, and he took her in a slow, tantalizing kiss. He cupped the back of her head, intensifying his efforts to feverish heights. He kissed her hungrily, nipping at her lips and searing a path down her chest, slowing to love all of her. Her hands moved in his hair, over his shoulders, as she arched and rose off the bed with every touch of his lips. He kissed around her belly button, slicking his tongue lower, around her damp curls, and down her inner thigh, sucking her soft skin until she bowed off the mattress.

"Bodhi, *please*. I swear you could make me come just like that."

A primal growl rose from his lungs, and he lowered his mouth to her sex. He played her body like his favorite instrument, loving and teasing, unraveling her one lick at a time. He pushed his fingers into her tight heat, stroking over the spot that made her legs flex and his name fly from her lungs. "Bodhi—"

She fisted her hands in the sheets, bucking and making those sexy sounds that drove him out of his mind. He moved over her, settling his hips between her legs. She was trembling like a live wire, her hair fanned out on the pillow, and she was looking up at him like he was her world.

He gazed into her eyes, his chest full to aching. "Baby, I will love you until I have no more breath to give."

Their mouths came together in wild kisses, and he buried himself to the hilt in one hard thrust. He pried her hands from his arms and laced them with his, holding them above her head. She bowed off the mattress, and he loved her hard and fast, then titillatingly slow, until she came undone. Her sex clenched tight and hot, and he was right there with her, so in love with everything about her, he couldn't think, could barely breathe, as pure, explosive pleasure tore through him.

They lay wrapped up in each other's arms for what felt like hours, their bodies damp from their lovemaking. Bodhi ran his fingers down Bridgette's back, bringing rise to goose bumps and causing her to snuggle closer.

"I love when you touch me." She pressed her lips to his chest.

"I could hold you like this all night and be perfectly content." He kissed her softly. "But that would hardly be fair, since we have only one night alone together and you've gone to all this trouble." He kissed her cheek and worked his way around to the nape of her neck. "I want to experience everything with you."

"Everything," she said breathily. "I like the sound of that." Her stomach growled, and her eyes bloomed wide.

He chuckled and kissed the tip of her nose. "How about we shower and then I make you some chocolate chip waffles?" He took her hand and led her into the bathroom.

He turned on the shower and kissed her while the bathroom steamed up around them.

"I can't get enough of you," he said.

Their mouths fused together as they stepped beneath the warm shower spray, their slick bodies sliding and grinding. His appetite for her was insatiable, and he was hard in seconds.

"I need you, baby." He lifted her into his arms and lowered her onto his shaft. "Christ, I could live inside you."

They made love beneath the warm shower spray, fervently taking everything the other was willing to give. Bridgette came again and again, pulling Bodhi over the edge as her third climax gripped her. He held her against the tile, resting his head on the pillow of her breasts as he caught his breath.

She smiled down at him, the water pounding against his back. "I *really* love you, Bodhi. I hope you feel it as strongly as I feel it from you."

"I do, baby."

He set her on her feet and turned so she was beneath the warm spray. He soaped up his hands, marveling at her body's reactions. Even after they'd made love twice, her body trembled beneath his touch as he moved behind her, washing her shoulders and back and working his way south. He washed between her legs, and she spread her legs wider, turning and tempting him with her sex. He couldn't resist taking another taste of her. Her back met the tile wall as she opened herself up to him again.

"Bodhi," she pleaded as he ate at her. Her hands pushed into his wet hair. "I swear I love you for more than your incredible sexual skills, but *ohmygod . . .*"

She yanked him up by the hair and crashed her mouth over his, trying to go high enough up on her toes to sink down upon him. He lifted her into his arms again, falling deeper and deeper in love as they surrendered to their passion.

CHAPTER TWENTY

BRIDGETTE LOOKED CUTE as hell sitting at the counter in one of Bodhi's T-shirts, eating chocolate chip waffles. Her hair was still damp, and she wore the sexy cutoffs she'd had on earlier. She had the hazy look of a contented lover, and he knew he'd remember that look forever.

She finished eating and pushed her plate to the side.

He leaned in for a sticky, syrupy kiss, and she laughed against his lips.

"That, Bridgette Dalton, is one of my favorite things about you."

"Sticky kisses?"

He kissed her again. "You're not afraid to laugh when we're kissing. You're not afraid to be yourself, or speak your mind, or talk about difficult subjects." *Or make hard decisions.* "Bridge, I'm blown away by what you've done tonight. This cabin, the waffles . . ." He tucked her hair behind her ear and pulled her closer. "Thank you for not being afraid to let my memories of my father into our lives."

"A very special man once told me that real love never dies. I think all love should be celebrated."

He took her left hand in his, rubbing his thumb over her fingers. "I agree. Close your eyes for me, baby."

She closed her eyes and sat up straighter. "What are you doing, Bodhi Booker?"

He took out the silver bracelet he'd had made for her and hooked it around her wrist. He ached even as he filled up with happiness, making the moment bittersweet. "Okay, open your eyes."

Her eyes searched his first, and he wondered what she could see clearest, the ache or the love. A small smile lifted her lips. Only then did she look at the bracelet. Her brows knitted at the engraving.

"It's the longitude and latitude of Sweetwater, and the date we first met at the bakery."

Tears filled her eyes. "Bodhi." She wrapped her arms around his neck. "I couldn't love anything more. It's perfect, thank you."

"I hope you don't mind, but I've got something I'd like you to give to Louie after I leave." He pulled his dog tags from his pocket and placed them in her hand.

"Bodhi . . . ?"

"It would mean a lot to me for him to have them. You can wait and give them to him when he's older. Whatever you want."

"Okay." A single tear slipped down her cheek, and he embraced her.

"Let's call Louie and say good night," he suggested. "The walkie-talkies won't work this far, and I don't want him to be bummed. Then we can go outside and take a walk or hang out in the hammock."

After they called Louie, who was having a marvelous time with Willow, Zane, and Dahlia, Bodhi carried in their bags from the truck, thinking about the call. He'd miss those few minutes of catching up each night. He wondered how his father had done it for all those years. Granted, he hadn't always been away on tour, but Bodhi remembered him being gone more than he was home.

He set the bags in the bedroom and peeked into the bathroom, where Bridgette was blow-drying her hair. Her hair was so many shades of brown and blonde, even after all this time together he couldn't come up with the right word for it. He wrapped his arms around her from behind, and she turned off the hair dryer and set it on the counter, smiling in the mirror at him. "It's chilly tonight. You'll need a sweatshirt."

"Okay."

He gathered her hair over one shoulder and kissed her neck. "I've been trying to figure out a name for the color of your hair, but nothing fits."

She turned in his arms, her cheeks pink with warmth from the hair dryer, her eyes bright with love. She wrinkled her nose and said, "Boring and confused?"

He nipped at her lower lip, and she squealed.

"Don't you call my girlfriend's hair those things." He kissed the spot he'd nipped. "Your hair is gorgeous. It's like sand from all the world's prettiest beaches blended together."

"That sounds so much better than my choices." She ran her hands over his chest, and his body heated up again. "Don't you need a sweatshirt?"

"Hardly. You keep me so turned on, I'm surprised my clothes don't burn off."

"Best answer ever. Now get out of here and wait in the living room. I have a surprise for you."

He held her tighter. "A naughty surprise?"

She laughed. "Maybe later, but for now . . ." She playfully shoved him toward the door. "Go."

She joined him in the living room a few minutes later, carrying something wrapped in a blanket, wearing *his* sweatshirt, and smiling like she had won the lottery.

"Ah, a blanket. A perfect surprise to snuggle under on the hammock."

She pulled the blanket out of his reach. "Your surprise is *in* the blanket."

"Maybe once you're under it, it will be." He held her close as they went outside. "So now you're a sweatshirt thief and an eavesdropper?"

"Do you mind?"

"Not even a little."

Moonlight dusted the area in front of the cabin, providing just enough light to find their way to the hammock strung between two tall trees. He inhaled the scents of pine trees and crisp, mountain air, bringing rise to memories from his youth.

Bridgette set the bundled blanket on the hammock. "Can we skip the walk and hang out here? I just want to be close to you, and I'm excited to give you your gift."

He lifted her onto the hammock in answer.

"Whoa!" She pressed her hands flat against the canvas as it swayed beneath her. "We need to sit up. How can we do that without flipping this thing?"

He shifted her so she was facing the side of the hammock and climbed up beside her, causing the hammock to dip. With an arm around her, he pulled her against him in the center. "Like that."

"Is there anything you can't figure out?"

"I can think of a few things." *Like how to have you and Louie* and *my career.*

Excitement rose in her eyes as she spread the blanket over their legs. "Are you ready?"

"Always." He leaned in for a kiss, and she gave him her cheek.

"No lips until you see this, because once we start kissing, we never stop. Close your eyes."

He did, and he felt her place something on his legs. "I like our endless kisses."

She pressed her lips to his, taking him by surprise, and he held her there, deepening the kiss until she pushed away.

"Wow," she said breathlessly. "Me, too. Okay, open your eyes."

He found her watching him. "Lips," he said sternly, and pulled her in for another kiss. "Thank you, babe."

"You haven't even looked at the gift yet."

"I don't need to. It's from you. I'll love whatever it is."

She sighed. "You have ruined me for all other men. You're the perfect mix of manly and romantic. It must be all those romance novels."

Man, he liked hearing that, which made him a jerk, so he said nothing.

He lowered his gaze to the gift, and lost his breath at the picture of the three of them, taken at the baseball game, set in the center of a leather photo album. Bodhi had one arm around Louie, the other around her. Louie was smiling at the camera, and Bodhi and Bridgette were gazing into each other's eyes.

He ran his fingers over the edge of the album. His throat was so thick with emotion, he didn't even try to speak.

"Your mom sent me the pictures she took at the game, and I've taken so many, I thought you'd want to have them, too. Open it up."

He opened the album and was met with a page full of red tulips, a declaration of love. His name was written above them, and below, Bridgette had signed her name.

She tipped her sweet smile up, and he kissed her. "Thank you."

He looked at pictures of the three of them, each with handwritten notes above or below. There were pictures of Bodhi looking at Louie—*I love you for never seeing Louie as an impediment*—and Bodhi and Louie walking Dahlia in the city, taken from behind, Bodhi's hand covering Louie's on the leash—*I love you for teaching Louie how to be a good, careful person*. He could still feel Louie's little hand clinging to the leash beneath his.

He tipped Bridgette's chin up and pressed his lips to hers again. He flipped the page, gazing at the picture a passerby had taken of them that same afternoon—*I love you for your laugh, and your strength, and your generosity*. He didn't know how much more he could take without breaking down. He turned the page, and got his answer with the pictures of Louie and Derek Jeter. Louie looked like he was ready to jump out of his skin—*I love you for making Louie's dreams come true.* He warmed all over at more pictures of the three of them at the game—*I love you for making these last few weeks feel like forever.* On the last page was a picture of Bridgette holding the flowers he'd sent her—*I love you for caring enough to let us go, when I know in my heart it's the last thing you want to do. I will always love you, Bridgette.*

CHAPTER TWENTY-ONE

THE NEXT MORNING Bodhi and Bridgette woke before the sun to the sounds of leaves rustling. Bridgette curled up against Bodhi as a skunk made its way across the yard. After it disappeared into the brush, Bridgette couldn't resist knocking "have sex on a hammock" off the bucket list she *didn't* have, and Bodhi was all too happy to help her out with the precarious proposition. After nearly tumbling off the hammock and ending up in hysterics—and somehow still producing two incredible orgasms—they went inside and showered.

Bridgette called Willow, who she knew would be getting ready to start baking, and checked on Louie. He was still fast asleep. After thanking Willow so many times they ended up laughing, she and Bodhi went for the walk they'd missed last night.

They sat on the rocky ridge overlooking Sweetwater and watched the sunrise. "How is it possible that we've only had a little more than two weeks together and it feels like years?"

"Time is a funny thing," Bodhi said. "You were all I thought about between the day we first met at the bakery and when I came to Sweetwater. I swear every day in between lasted fifty hours."

"Really? You thought about me? I thought I was alone in my lusting."

"The baked goods were a gift for my Realtor. After I dropped them off, I was supposed to go straight back to the city, but I took a detour. I went by the bakery, hoping you were still there, but the place was locked up and the lights were out. *That's* how much you'd affected me in those few minutes we'd connected. While I was in the city fantasizing about you"—he stole a kiss—"I tried to convince myself I'd never see you again, so it was fine to think about you all the time. And when I found out you were my neighbor, I tried like hell to keep my distance."

"Some things are just meant to be."

She cuddled against him, thinking about how lucky she was. Some people never experienced love at all, and she'd experienced it twice. She gazed out at the glassy lake anchoring the small town where she'd spent most of her life. She knew every street, practically every pothole. In the two years she'd been away, nothing had changed. It was like she'd never even left. A blip in time, during which she'd lived a lifetime, like her time with Bodhi. But somehow she knew that after Bodhi left, nothing would ever be the same again.

On the way home, Bridgette decided to take Friday off so they could spend it together.

"Are you sure you can afford to do that?" Bodhi asked.

She shrugged, knowing it would cost her, but she didn't care. She wanted as much time together as possible. "What's the benefit of owning my own shop if I can't take a day off now and then? The shop is closed Saturday for the festival, so I'm not taking any orders for the weekend."

"If you're sure, then let's make a day of it and take Louie peach picking. I make a mean peach pie."

"Of course you do," she teased. "There has to be something you don't do well."

"Let's focus on my strengths." He squeezed her thigh.

"We can donate a pie for the pie-eating contest at the festival. Louie would love that."

"Great. Sounds perfect. But if that's our plan, then I'll drive you in now and help you out in the shop so you don't fall behind."

She wanted every minute she could get with him, and gladly accepted. Since Roxie was picking up Louie from Zane's, she was in no hurry to share Bodhi. She decided to skip her usual breakfast chat with her sisters in the bakery and go into the flower shop through the back door, giving her and Bodhi a little more private time before customers began arriving. Bodhi called Zane to ask if he could pick up Dahlia in a few hours, and Zane said he could leave her all week if he wanted. Apparently they'd had a great time, too. Bodhi made plans to pick up Dahlia after he finished helping Bridgette.

"Wait a second," Bridgette said as she unlocked the back door to the flower shop. "Don't you have to finish your mom's house?"

"It's done." He followed her inside.

"But how? You're at my house until one or two o'clock every morning." She set her purse and keys beneath the counter.

A wicked grin formed on his handsome face as he pulled her closer. "Let's see. When I go home alone after making love to you, my options are climbing into an empty bed, where I'll lie wishing you were with me, or working off my frustration until I'm too tired to stay awake. Which would you pick?"

He nibbled on her neck, making her hot and bothered all over again.

"How are you not completely exhausted?" she asked, craning her neck and giving him better access to devour her. "You're at our house by seven every morning to borrow sugar."

"How can I be exhausted when I have you to look forward to?" He lifted her up on the counter and stood between her legs. "What can I do to help you out this morning, *boss*?"

"Um . . ." She hooked her finger in the collar of his shirt, tugging him forward. "You have already helped me out this morning more than once."

"I wasn't aware there was a limit, but I meant workwise. I know you're overloaded, and I want to help."

She wrapped her arms around his neck and said, "I don't know if I should be thankful or disappointed."

He lifted her into his arms. "I'll never leave you disappointed. Where's your office?" He spun around so fast she nearly flew out of his arms, both of them laughing.

"Bodhi!" She clung to him as he traipsed toward the office.

"If you think I'm going to pass up making love to you on your desk, you're out of your mind."

"Hey!" Piper yelled from the front of the store, where she stood with Willow. "Put the girl down and no one gets hurt."

"*Now* you can be disappointed," he said to Bridgette, but he didn't put her down. "Or . . . ?" he challenged Piper.

"Or . . ." Piper looked at Willow, who shrugged. "We got nothing. You can carry her all day."

Bodhi looked pleased with that response.

"You should put me down," Bridgette whispered in his ear.

"I liked Piper's response better." He reluctantly set her on her feet.

"We thought someone had broken in," Willow said. "I'm glad it was only you guys."

"Bodhi's helping me out today." It felt strangely natural and exciting to say that. "And guess what?"

"You're pregnant?" Piper said.

Willow elbowed her.

"Christ," Bodhi mumbled.

"Why do you always go for the most shocking thing you can think of?" Bridgette asked.

"That was not even close to being the most shocking thing I could think of." Piper grabbed Willow's arm. "Should we leave you alone to get back to your office romp?"

Yes. "We weren't going to have an office romp."

Bodhi leaned closer and whispered, "Fibber."

Bridgette told them she was taking Friday off, and they made plans to meet up at the festival on Saturday. After Piper and Willow left, Bridgette and Bodhi made their way to the office . . . and christened her desk.

CHAPTER TWENTY-TWO

FRIDAY MORNING WHEN they headed over to the Love Family Orchard, located at the edge of town, Bodhi worried it might already be picked clean. They were greeted by several friendly, older dogs and a crowd of people milling around an old-fashioned pole-barn-turned-fruit-stand that reminded Bodhi of the orchards he'd visited as a kid. It was busy from the minute they arrived, but with acres of fruit trees, there were plenty of peaches to go around. They'd been there for almost two hours, and had spent more time playing with the dogs than picking peaches. But they'd picked enough for at least two pies.

"Bodhi?" Louie asked as Bodhi lifted him up to pick a peach from the top of a tree.

"Yeah, buddy?" He felt Bridgette's hand on his back. They'd been sneaking touches all morning, and he almost hated to lower Louie to the ground after he picked a peach, wanting more of Bridgette. They'd gotten good at hiding their relationship, but Bodhi had caught himself reaching for Bridgette so many times, she felt like a natural extension of himself.

He lowered Louie to the ground and watched him inspect the peach. He rubbed it on his shirt, the way Bodhi had taught him, and held it up. His face and shirt were stained with sticky juice from the last two peaches he'd eaten. "Can I eat this one?"

Bodhi looked at Bridgette, wondering how many peaches one little boy could eat.

"You might get a bellyache," she said. "How about if you eat half?"

Louie nodded and handed it to Bodhi. "Can you please break this in half?"

Bodhi pulled out his pocketknife and cut the peach in half. He took out the pit, tossed it to the ground, and handed half to Louie and half to Bridgette. She held his gaze. The heat between them had changed since he'd confessed his love for her. It burned hotter and deeper, like a lifeline. She looked beyond beautiful in a light-blue tank top that made her eyes look even bluer, a pair of denim shorts, and the sexy boots she'd been wearing the first time they'd met. She hadn't taken off the bracelet he'd given her, and he was glad. He liked seeing it on her as much as he liked knowing she'd be wearing his T-shirt and sweatshirt after he was gone. She'd packed them in her bag at the cabin, and when he'd noticed, she'd shrugged in that adorable way she had and hugged them to her chest. If it were possible for a person's insides to melt, his had, right then and there.

"Thanks." Louie bit into the fruit, and juice dribbled down his chin and onto his shirt.

"Don't you want a bite?" Bridgette asked Bodhi.

He wiped the blade of his knife on his pants and put it away as he stepped closer, inhaling the scent of jasmine, and lowered his voice so Louie couldn't hear him. "I want much more than a *bite*."

She flashed her sexy smile. She had so many different smiles— sweet, sassy, mommyish, seductive, and flat-out hot as sin—and he'd memorized every one of them.

"Bodhi?" Louie squinted up from beneath his Yankees cap. "When you go home, will I be able to call you on the walkie-talkie?"

Louie had been asking a lot of questions about when Bodhi was leaving, and Bodhi was careful not to make any promises he couldn't keep. He crouched and looked Louie in the eyes. "You know what, little dude? The walkie-talkies won't work that far apart."

"Can I call you on Mommy's phone?" He chomped into the peach, like he wasn't ripping Bodhi's heart out one question at a time.

"When I leave here, I'll be going back to work. This has been a vacation for me. Like summer break from school. But I'm not allowed to bring my phone to work. So, if your mom says you can call, you can try, but I don't want you wondering why I'm not calling you back. The only reason would be that I'm not able to. Okay?"

Louie nodded, chewing the last of his peach. "What work do you do?"

"I'm like an army guy." He wiped Louie's mouth with his hand.

Louie tipped his head up toward Bridgette. "When I grow up, maybe I'll be an army guy, too."

Bodhi was as touched as he was worried. As he prepared to leave the next evening, the repercussions of his not returning had taken root. He loved what he did for a living, but now that he knew what he was missing out on, he wouldn't wish his life on Louie.

Bodhi took him by the shoulders and looked into his innocent eyes. "Listen, buddy. You focus on baseball, okay? That way one day your mom can go see you playing for the Yankees. Can you do that for me?"

Louie nodded. "Bodhi?"

"Yeah?"

"My belly hurts."

Bodhi lifted him into his arms. "How about we take our peaches home, and you can lie down for a while. When you feel better, we'll make the pies."

Louie nodded and rested his head on Bodhi's shoulder.

"Want me to hold him?" Bridgette asked as she picked up the basket of peaches.

"I'd really like to carry him, if you don't mind." He settled his hand on her lower back, wondering how a man prepared himself to leave behind everything he cared about.

Bridgette's kitchen looked like it had been through a food fight, but she couldn't have cared less. With her favorite country music playing in the background and her favorite big and little men preparing the dough for the peach pies on the counter, she wouldn't trade this mess for anything in the world.

Bodhi stood behind Louie, with his hands over Louie's on the rolling pin as they pressed the dough flat. Bodhi was not a skimper when it came to baking, any more than he was in any other part of his life. Where Bridgette would have sliced the peaches and left the skin on, Bodhi showed them his trick of putting the peaches in boiling water for sixty seconds, then immediately setting them in ice water. The skins had slipped right off.

"Look, Mom! We made the crust!" Louie grinned, a toothy bundle of pride.

She took out her phone and snapped a picture, wishing Bodhi had come with a warning sign or wearing big red flags. A man this irresistible shouldn't be allowed to roam the streets.

"How about we give Mama a chance to learn?" Bodhi suggested.

Louie scooted off the chair and pressed his flour-drenched hands on Bridgette's butt, pushing her in front of Bodhi. He picked up her phone and climbed onto the chair next to them.

"Honey, you'll get—" She swallowed her words. She didn't care if her phone got gunky and sticky. She wanted those pictures.

Bodhi hammed it up, pressing his cheek to hers, then giving her bunny ears, and making a flour handprint on her stomach. Louie giggled up a storm as he took pictures that probably cut their heads off.

Bodhi's deep laugher filled the air, and she hoped her house might soak up their love the same way her parents' home did. When Bodhi scooped Louie into his arms and tickled him silly, Bridgette thought she might liquefy.

"Okay, little dude, now I get to take a picture." He touched Louie's nose, leaving a dab of flour, and pulled Bridgette against his stomach. He took out his own phone and snapped a picture of the three of them. Louie pressed a kiss to Bodhi's cheek as he took another.

Knowing Louie would think it was a game, Bridgette touched her lips to Bodhi's cheek, and felt his entire body sigh as he took another picture.

"Can we enter a pie in the contest tomorrow?" Louie asked.

"How about if we donate one pie to the pie-eating contest instead?" Bridgette suggested. "Auntie Willow is tough competition in the baking contest."

"Yeah!" Louie wiggled free. "I'm gonna go play!"

He headed for the playroom, and Bodhi lifted him off his feet. "I think you'd better wash up first."

He tucked him under his arm like a football, earning another round of laughter from Louie, who put his arms out to his sides, his legs sticking straight out behind him. "Look, Mom! I'm flying!"

"How about you fly right up to the bathtub?"

Bodhi carried him up and left Bridgette bathing Louie while he finished making the pies. Half an hour later, while Louie played, Bridgette went to help Bodhi clean the kitchen. She found him gazing down at his phone. He shoved it in his back pocket and reached for her.

"Is the little guy all clean?" He backed her up against the counter.

"Yes. He's in the playroom."

"Perfect."

He kissed her deeply, his hands moving along her sides in a mesmerizing pattern, brushing against her breasts, then squeezing her hips. He kissed his way to her ear, slicking his tongue over the shell, and pressed his body against hers, holding her tight as he took her in another toe-curling kiss. He lifted her onto the counter, sliding her forward and kissing her so tenderly it made her ache for more.

"I'm going to miss you, baby," he said softly. "Every second of every day."

She closed her eyes against the sting of already missing him. He kissed her lids, and she felt his prickly whiskers against her cheek again.

"Was it worth letting me in?"

She nodded, unable to speak, and clung to him. He cradled her face in his hands, the lump in her throat expanding to a painful throb as she met his gaze.

"No regrets?" he asked.

She shook her head, afraid to try to speak.

"I never knew I could care about two people so much." He brushed his thumb over her lips, a smile lifting his. "Don't be sad, Bridge. Real love never dies, remember?"

Louie's fast footsteps sounded in the hall, and she pushed from the counter, working hard to contain her emotions.

"I made you a present." Louie thrust a piece of yellow construction paper toward Bodhi.

"Thanks, buddy." Bodhi knelt beside him, and Bridgette peered over his shoulder.

Louie pointed to one of the three smiling stick figures he'd drawn. It had a thick blue body, brown hair scribbled straight across the top of its head, the longest fingers of all the figures, and a big scribble of black beneath one hand. "This is you."

Bridgette moved to Bodhi's side just in time to see the love and admiration in his eyes, bringing new life to the lump in her throat.

"It looks just like me," Bodhi said.

Louie beamed with pride. He pointed to the biggest of the three figures, standing between Bodhi and a dog. The figure's head was twice as large as the others and had a full head of brown hair. He'd drawn circles for feet that were angled up, as if he were jumping spread-eagle. "This is me." He pointed to the third stick figure, with yellow-and-brown hair and long brown eyelashes. "This is Mom, and this is Dahlia." Dahlia had a huge oblong head and body, and five legs. Bridgette wondered if one was the tail.

Bodhi put an arm around him and pressed a hard kiss to his cheek. "Thanks, buddy. I'll hang this up at home."

"It's us at the park. See?" Louie pointed to the scribble of black beneath Bodhi's hand. "That's Dahlia's poop."

Bridgette covered her mouth to keep her laughter from escaping, because her little boy's and Bodhi's faces were so darn serious.

Louie raced to the back door. "Can we go outside and play?"

"Sure." She watched him run outside and returned willingly to Bodhi's arms.

"I'm framing this," he said sternly.

"As well you should."

He was still so serious she wondered what was going through his mind. "I never thought poop could stir up so much emotion."

Laughter fell from her lips before she could stop it. "Oh my gosh. I'm in love with a pooper scooper."

Bodhi grabbed her ribs and she shrieked, laughing as he chased her out the back door.

CHAPTER TWENTY-THREE

LATER THAT EVENING, Louie and Bridgette played superheroes in the backyard, donning capes and eye masks and chasing invisible villains, while Bodhi cooked hamburgers—and imagined Bridgette wearing that mask later, in the bedroom. He knew he should start putting up barriers, find that cold place he'd lived within for so long, but no part of him wanted to do that. He'd spent a lifetime being strong. Didn't everyone deserve to be weak at some point? At least for a little while?

They packed the burgers and a picnic dinner, and took Dahlia down to the lake. Large white tents were set up along the fairgrounds, and orange cones marked off the parking area, in preparation for the Peach Festival tomorrow. They set out their blanket by the water and ate dinner while Louie told them about plans he and Zane had made to build a tree fort in the backyard. Jealousy gnawed at Bodhi over another man, even an uncle, being the one to do those things with Louie. As he listened to Louie's excitement, his mind skipped forward to a dark place he hadn't allowed it to go before. After he and Bridgette ended their relationship for good, she would one day fall in love with another man. He wanted that for her. A lifetime of happiness with someone stable who would be there to watch Louie grow up and go away to college, or play baseball, or whatever it was he chose to do. He wanted her to be adored by a man who would never intentionally hurt her or put her second. In his mind, all those thoughts were real and true and born of his love for her, not clouded with jealousy. But in his *soul*, he couldn't even begin to try to picture her in another man's arms.

He wanted to be that man more than he wanted his next breath.

So much had changed since he'd come to Sweetwater, he wasn't even sure he was the same person he'd been when he'd arrived. He hadn't gone for a run in two nights. Usually that would leave him restless and edgy, but tonight all he felt was thankful that he hadn't been called in for a mission during the last couple of weeks. He looked at Bridgette, who was watching Louie with a serene expression as he chased Dahlia a few feet away. She was leaning back on her palms, her gorgeous legs crossed at the ankles in those sexy leather boots that made her look like she belonged on a ranch. He could imagine her on one, leading horses and showing Louie how to ride. He wondered if they'd ever been riding. There were so many things he'd like to know if they'd done, or seen, and even more than that, things he'd like to do with them.

Louie tumbled to the blanket giggling, breaking Bodhi's train of thought.

"Whoa." Bridgette leaned back as Dahlia leapt over her, onto the middle of the blanket, and pushed her nose under Louie's belly, causing another fit of giggles.

"Dahlia." Bodhi motioned for her to lie down, and she sank obediently to the blanket. "Good girl." He petted her and touched Bridgette's hand. "You okay? Did she scratch you?"

"I'm good. She just startled me." She glanced at his hand on hers, and when he went to move it away, she hooked her index finger over it. "This has been really fun."

Louie put his hand over theirs. "Super fun! Can we have a sleepover with Bodhi and Dahlia?"

A sly smile lifted Bridgette's lips, and he knew she was thinking the same thing he was. A sleepover sounded perfect, but he and Bridgette would do very little sleeping.

"Please?" Louie pushed to a sitting position and crawled onto Bridgette's lap, holding her face between his little hands, the way Bodhi did when he wanted her full attention. "We can make a fort in the living room and show him how we watch a movie in it. We can play games, and he can read me a bedtime story, and I promise to be good!" He was talking so fast it was hard not to chime in and beg *for* him.

Bridgette put her arms around her excited little boy and smiled. "Tonight is Bodhi's last night in town. He probably has a lot of things to do at his house to get ready to leave tomorrow evening."

Louie turned hopeful eyes to Bodhi. He crawled across the blanket and perched on his knees in front of him. "Are you too busy to spend the night with us?"

Bodhi glanced over his shoulder at Bridgette, who looked as conflicted as he was. The eager little boy asked for so little, and he *wanted* to share this special night with him. But he also wanted to make love to Bridgette one last time. To hold her in his arms and feel her love for him in every way possible.

Louie bobbed to the side, directly into his line of sight. "Bodhi? *Please* can you and Dahlia have a sleepover with us?"

The memory of his last few minutes with his father slammed into him. *Dad, you'll come back, right?* If Bodhi hadn't been so young, he would have seen what he saw now when he recalled his father's face as he'd answered, *I sure hope so.* He would have noticed the way his father's eyes had darted to his mother before landing on him. He would have understood the uncertainty in them, and maybe then he could have done something differently. Hugged him longer. Said something more meaningful than, *Okay, see ya when you get back.*

Bodhi could no sooner look Louie in the eye and deny him this than he could have left them there waiting for him. "I'm not too busy, buddy. I'd love to have a sleepover with you and your mom, and Dahlia. But we'd better make a pretty big fort."

Bridgette should have expected that Bodhi was a master fort builder. After giving Louie a shoulder ride back home from their picnic, they put Dahlia in his yard and then set to work building their fort. She and Bodhi hadn't had a second alone to talk, and even though he wasn't acting as though he was bothered by their plans, she wanted to make sure he didn't feel pushed into this sheet-fort sleepover. She was disappointed not to have the evening alone with Bodhi, as she'd been thinking about being in his arms all day. But one look at her bright-eyed little boy set those selfish thoughts aside. *At least for now.*

"The first thing we have to do is clear the area to build the fort. I need your help, little man." Bodhi showed Louie where to put his hands and stood behind him as he pushed the furniture to the perimeter of the living room.

"Come on, buddy."

He carried in the chairs from the kitchen, letting Louie hold one side. The pride in Louie's eyes was worth the time Bridgette was missing in Bodhi's arms. She helped Bodhi move the kitchen table into the living room. She was a little worried they wouldn't have enough space to sleep, but Bodhi moved from one thing to the next like he'd come up with a plan on their walk home, so she went with it.

"The thing about forts," Bodhi explained, "is that when you sleep outdoors in a real fort, you don't want to sleep on the ground if you can help it." He tied sheets together and wrapped them loosely around the width of the table, creating a giant sling underneath.

"Come here, little dude." He pushed down on the sheet hanging beneath the table. "Climb into this hammock. Let's see if you like it."

"Wow! Look, Mom. A hammock like the one in Grandma and Grandpa's yard!" He climbed into the hammock with a wide grin. In the yellow sheet he looked like a banana in an open peel. "There's even room for Jeter!"

"If you were out in the woods, you'd tie the two ends of whatever you have—a tarp or blanket—around two trees to make a hammock," he explained.

"That is pretty awesome," Bridgette said.

He cocked a brow.

She rolled her eyes. "Okay. It's *very* awesome."

He chuckled, and they spent the next hour stringing sheets, using the couch and chairs as anchors, until the entire living room was one giant fort, with Louie's hammock in the center. They covered the floor of the fort with blankets and pillows and brought Dahlia in from the yard.

"I think we've constructed the coolest sheet fort in the history of mankind. Louie"—she pointed to the ceiling—"run up and change into your pajamas and brush your teeth so we can watch the movie."

Dahlia followed him upstairs. When he was safely out of earshot, Bridgette said, "I'm sorry, Bodhi. I hope you didn't feel pushed into all of this."

He drew her against him. "I didn't, and I hope you're not too disappointed. But he hasn't asked me for anything, and I didn't want him to think I was too busy for him."

"I'm a little disappointed. Aren't you?"

"More than a little at not having another night alone with you, but I think this is good for Louie. Did I do the wrong thing by agreeing?"

"You're so careful. You never do the wrong thing."

He gave her a chaste kiss, and she slid her arm around his neck, pulling him in for another and deepening it before he could pull away.

"I can think of plenty of things I've done wrong, but leaving Louie unhappy hopefully won't be one of them. Besides, now I can wake up beside you again. That's two times more than I thought we'd ever get."

Louie and Dahlia came downstairs, and Bodhi took a step back, the longing between them as tangible as a living, breathing person.

Dahlia lay across the opening to the fort, guarding them as they played Candy Land and Uno. Bridgette and Bodhi passed furtive glances, brushing knees as they played. When Louie began a string of yawns, they put the games away, and he curled up with Jeter in the hammock to watch the movie.

Bodhi covered him with a blanket and kissed his cheek. "I'm going to say good night now in case you fall asleep during the movie. Thanks for inviting me to sleep over, little dude."

"Good night, Bodhi. I love you."

Bodhi held her son's gaze like he wanted to be sure Louie heard him, and said, "I love you, too, Louie."

He put a hand on Bridgette's back as they switched places, and she realized how much they were asking of each other with their *here* and *now* relationship. It was clearly as difficult for him to stay on the right side of the lines they'd drawn as it was for her. She wondered what it would be like to have a relationship where Louie was aware of their feelings and could trust and count on them. She knew that could never be with Bodhi, and she pushed the thought away as quickly as it had come.

"Good night, honey. I love you." She leaned in to kiss Louie, and he threw his arms around her neck, kissing her hard.

"I love you, too. Thanks for letting us have a sleepover. Bodhi, my mom's kisses are magic. They keep bad dreams away." Louie yawned. "Mommy you should give Bodhi a good night kiss."

"Yeah, Mommy. I want one of those magical kisses." Bodhi pulled her down and kissed her just as hard as Louie had, making a dramatic *mwah* noise and earning a sleepy laugh from Louie.

"If you get uncomfortable up there," he said to Louie, "you just climb out and sleep right here." He patted the space between him and Bridgette.

Bridgette turned on *Finding Dory* and returned to her spot, an appropriate distance away from Bodhi, wondering how a handful of inches could feel like the enemy.

When he was sure Louie was asleep, Bodhi moved closer to Bridgette. They lay facing each other, her knee tucked between his thighs, kissing and whispering.

"When Louie's grown up and madly in love," he said, "you need to tell him what you sacrificed for him tonight."

"He's not going to ever grow up. He's staying five forever. It's easier that way."

"You're going to have a hard time when he starts getting into trouble, kissing girls under the bleachers, and sneaking out."

She scowled. "Who are you kidding? I'm going to have trouble when he starts kindergarten next month. Besides, he's never going to sneak out, because I'm going to buy one of those house-arrest cuffs and put it on him."

"Says the rebel who snuck out all the time." He kissed her softly. "Do you remember your first kiss?"

"Yes. It was a total disappointment. I had gone to a party in ninth grade with this boy, T. C. Calloway. I waited all night for that kiss, and when he walked me to the door, he kissed me on the lips. It was the wettest, most Dorito-smelling kiss I've ever had. To this day, I can't eat Doritos. Do you remember yours?"

"I do, and it was the best kiss of my life." He watched disappointment rise in her eyes. "She had the sweetest mouth, the most luscious lips, and when I held her, she made these sounds that drove me out of my mind."

"I don't really need to hear all the details," she said, pulling away.

He held her tighter. "I remember not wanting the kiss to end. She kissed me softly, but her body—*Jesus, her body*—was glued to mine. To this day, I've never met anyone sexier. Anyway, she pressed against me so hard, I couldn't help but take the kiss deeper—"

"Bodhi!" She tried to push out of his hands.

He tipped her chin up, smiling because he knew how pleased she'd be when she heard his next words. "We were so into each other, she stumbled, and her back hit a brick building."

She stilled, a smile curving her lips. Then she pushed at his chest again and whispered, "That was cruel! I thought you were being a jerk, telling me about some other girl."

He pressed his lips to hers and felt her smile.

"Do you *really* remember your very first kiss?" she asked.

"Your kisses have erased my memory of anyone else."

"Now that's the best answer you could give." She snuggled closer, and they lay in silence for a long while.

"Bodhi?"

"Hm?"

"Thanks for giving Louie tonight."

"I should be thanking you two."

He wanted to give Louie years of tonights. There was a world of want inside him, and he was trying his hardest to shove it all behind a door and bolt it closed with a heavy chain. But every thought brought another. *Louie should have siblings, like you do. Surround him with enough love that he'll never be alone.* He wanted to make it so she never had to work late and could be home when Louie was sick. He wanted to ask about her hopes and dreams and fulfill every one of them. His wants filled the room inside him, pushing against the door and rattling the chain.

Her uneasy expression told him her mind was circling tomorrow, just as his was. He covered her mouth with his, reveling in her touch, her taste, her *heart*. Before he knew it, they were greedily groping each other all over. He forced himself to break the kiss before he took things too far.

"Baby," he whispered, and kissed her forehead, tucking her against him to try to regain control. "Louie can't wake up and find us like this, but I want to hold you a little while longer."

"What if I say I want to wait for you?" she asked breathlessly. "What if I tell you I can't say goodbye tomorrow?"

He glanced at Louie, his entire being heavy with regret. He didn't respond, because he knew he didn't have to. He held Bridgette as they drifted off to sleep.

Bodhi awoke before dawn to the feel of Louie climbing between them. Bodhi wrapped them both in the safety of his arms and closed his eyes, wishing here and now could last forever.

CHAPTER TWENTY-FOUR

THE PEACH FESTIVAL was one of many community celebrations in Sweetwater, and every year Bridgette tried to remember why those celebrations had felt too *small town* for her when she was younger. She hadn't missed the festivals until she'd returned home and attended them with baby Louie in her arms and realized how wonderful their close-knit community actually was. All the local businesses shut down for the event, and practically the whole town showed up, which had given her a renewed sense of safety and comfort that she'd never thought she needed. Now, as they gathered along Main Street, climbing into flatbed trailers full of hay for the annual Peach Parade, she knew she'd rely on this community again after Bodhi left later that afternoon.

The trailers had been decorated by local middle- and high-school kids, painted with pictures of peaches and orchards, with orange and red streamers hanging beneath signs on the sides that read, SWEETWATER PEACH FESTIVAL, HAVING A PEACHY TIME, and boasted the names of local businesses sponsoring the event. The winner of the Peach Queen Beauty Pageant rode in the first trailer, wearing a short pink dress and a silver crown, waving to the crowd as they led the procession around the block. Bodhi sat beside Bridgette atop a hay bale, one arm around her—*I need to make sure Mommy doesn't fall off*—and one around Louie, who was happily perched on his lap and waving to the crowd. Her family always rode together for the parade, and today was no different. Her parents sat on the far end, her father's arm around Roxie, and beside them, Willow and Zane snuggled together. Piper, Talia, and of course, Aurelia, who was like family, were laughing. Ben sat on Bodhi's other side, chatting with him. It was easy to imagine a life with Bodhi, and today she allowed herself to do just that. *Every love deserves to be celebrated.*

She played with images of attending future festivals and Winter Wonderlands. She saw nights with cookouts, a bedroom with both of their belongings, and Louie jumping in between them on the mattress in the mornings. She imagined working at the shop alongside Bodhi, their newborn baby in her arms.

But if anyone knew the truth, it was her. Wishes didn't bring futures.

After the parade, Bodhi helped her down from the trailer, his black T-shirt straining over his biceps and chest as he lowered her to the ground, and whispered, "Hi, beautiful. Want to hide out behind the haystacks with me?"

Yes, please.

"Why don't Grandpa and I take Louie to get his face painted?" Roxie suggested. "That'll give you kids some time to do adult things."

"Yeah!" Louie hollered.

"Okay." Bridgette kissed the top of his head. "But you have to listen to Grandma and Grandpa."

"He always does," Roxie said as she took Louie's hand. "Come on, sugar pop. Let's see if we can convince Grandpa to get his face painted, too."

Ben nudged Bodhi and Zane. "Fifty bucks says I can kick your asses in the pie-eating contest."

Bodhi's chest expanded, exchanging a challenging look with Zane.

"Cockfight," Piper said over Bridgette's shoulder.

"My man will win," Bridgette replied.

"Hardly," Willow said.

"I've got this, Wills." Zane winked.

Aurelia pointed to the guys. "It's like the Hulk, Brad Pitt, and . . . Lord, I've got no idea what to call Ben. Good Time Dalton?"

Every love deserves to be celebrated.

"This ought to be fun." Talia looped her arm through Bridgette's.

Bridgette couldn't take her eyes off Bodhi. But it wasn't just because of his broad back scaling down in a perfect V to his dark jeans, which hugged his powerful legs and ass deliciously, although that was an impeccable sight. Seeing him with Ben and Zane added images to her *future* wishing bank.

Talia leaned closer, her hair tumbling over her shoulders. "How are you holding up?"

"Surprisingly well." It wasn't an outright lie. As long as she didn't dwell on the fact that they had merely a few hours left together, she was okay.

"Denial," Talia said flatly.

"Let's call it postponing reality."

Bodhi glanced over his shoulder and blew her a kiss.

"My goodness, Bridge," Talia said in a hushed, serious tone. "He's so into you. How can he *leave* you guys?"

"He's not leaving us," she said more easily than she expected. "He's actually protecting us from the worst-case scenario."

"But what if the worst case never happens?" Talia asked. "You're okay with giving him up?"

A pang of sadness cut through her. "I have to be, because if we stayed together and the worst case happened, I'd never survive it."

Bodhi kept his eyes on Bridgette as he settled into his seat, looking giant between Ben and Zane. He had a few inches on them, but it was the breadth of his shoulders, the size of his bulbous muscles, and his granitelike features that made him look like he could take anyone on. Bridgette felt like she was playing a game of Which One of These Things Is Not Like the Others. Bodhi *looked* like he belonged on a battlefield even as they draped an apron over him and he put his hands behind his back, preparing to attack the pie with the same determination as he did everything else.

"You're the strongest of all of us," Talia said. "Everyone thinks it's Piper, but I know better."

As they cheered for their men, Bridgette remembered something her mother had told her after she'd moved back home with Louie. *You don't know what strength is until you've put aside your greatest desires for the good of your child.*

Bridgette ran her fingers absently over the bracelet Bodhi had given her, watching her man gobble down pie and dreaming about all the sweet, peachy kisses she'd get afterward. Bodhi's hands shot up in the air, declaring victory before anyone else had even finished half their pie. She wondered if there was a saying about the strength of men. Not that it mattered. She knew she was looking at the strongest man of all.

And she secretly wished they were both a little weaker.

The afternoon passed too quickly, with potato-sack races and tasting everything from peach tea to peach barbecue sauce. Bodhi should be sick of peaches, but he wasn't, because this day would forever be remembered as one of his best. He knew even the word *peach* would remind him of sneaking behind haystacks to kiss Bridgette, and racing with Louie through the obstacle course. He glanced across the picnic table where they were eating dinner with the rest of Bridgette's family and friends. Louie's face was painted with the Yankees logo on one side and a peach on the other. His clothes and hair were filthy from rolling in the grass and hay and eating sticky peaches, and the glimmer of happiness in his eyes made it all worthwhile. Bodhi wanted to be there tonight when he conked out, too exhausted to move. He wanted to fall into bed with Bridgette and reminisce about all the adorable things Louie had done before taking her in his arms and making up for the lovemaking they'd missed last night. But he had to leave if he was going to have time to drop off Dahlia at his mother's and get everything else done before reporting to training the next evening. He'd already packed up his belongings. All he had to do was say goodbye, pick up Dahlia, and get on the road.

It was the saying goodbye part that had him tied in knots.

Bodhi squeezed Bridgette's hand beneath the table, wanting desperately to pull her against him. Her hair was tousled, her skin was bronzed from a busy day in the sun, and when he leaned closer, more than a hint of sadness shone in her eyes.

Bridgette whispered something to Roxie that Bodhi couldn't hear. Then a forced smile formed on her face, and she said, "Louie, honey? Bodhi has to go back to the city. Are you ready to say goodbye?"

Everyone pushed to their feet as Louie ran around the table and jumped into Bodhi's arms.

"'Bye, Bodhi. I love you," Louie said.

Bodhi closed his eyes against unexpected tears, hugging him tight. "I love you, too, buddy. You be good for your mom, okay? Remember, you're the man of the house. That means you always do the right thing."

Louie nodded vehemently.

Bodhi reached into his pocket and pulled out the blue ribbon he'd won in the pie-eating contest. "Think you can hang on to this?"

"Yes." Louie handed it to Bridgette. "Mom, don't lose this."

Everyone laughed.

"Okay, buddy. I need to get on the road." He kissed his cheek one last time and set him down.

"It's been a real pleasure," Bridgette's father said, embracing Bodhi. "You be safe, you hear?"

"That's the plan."

"Okay, Grandpa," Roxie said. "Take Louie over to the petting zoo. I'll be right there."

"Yay!" Louie took his grandfather's hand, and off they went.

Bridgette seemed to relax a little after Louie left. Bodhi wanted to take her in his arms, but Roxie embraced him before he had a chance.

"If only goodbyes were as easy for adults as they are for children." Roxie drew back and smiled up at him. "You're a special man, Bodhi Booker. We'll be waiting for you to come back."

A ripple of sadness wove its way from Bodhi to Bridgette. "I don't know if or when I'll be back, Roxie. How about you take care of Bridgette and Louie for me?"

"I can do that." Roxie took his hand in hers, holding it for a long moment, and her smile faded. She drew him into her arms again and whispered, "Please be careful."

"I know we're not supposed to refer to the future," Ben said as he pulled Bodhi into a manly embrace. "But we're holding your spot, man. Three dudes, whenever you're around."

"Thanks, Ben." Bodhi had military buddies he'd known for years, and somehow, in less than a month he'd become just as close to Bridgette's family and friends.

Zane hugged him hard. "What he said, man."

"Thanks. Good luck with your screenplay."

Talia cried as she embraced him, tearing at his heartstrings a little more. "I'm so happy you had this time with Bridgette and Louie. Love is good, no matter how long it lasts. Be safe, Bodhi. You'll be in our thoughts."

"Thank you." He was going to lose it if they kept this up. Piper embraced him, and he expected her to give him hell, but all she said was, "Don't die, you big bastard."

"You guys act like you'll never see him again," Aurelia said. "I'll see you in the city, but give me a hug anyway, Hulkster."

"Until you move here and partner with Willow," Ben said, yanking Aurelia's shirt so she stumbled back beside him.

Bodhi reached for Bridgette's hand. "Ready, beautiful?"

"No," she said solemnly, then forced a smile and said, "Yes."

Talia touched Bridgette's arm as they walked by and mouthed, *Love you*.

That show of support made leaving Bridgette easier *and* more heart-rending. While Bodhi was glad her family would be there for her, he hated knowing she'd need them.

CHAPTER TWENTY-FIVE

"I'D RATHER GIVE birth again than say goodbye to you," Bridgette said as they stood in his living room waiting for Dahlia to come in from the backyard. The house felt hollow without Bodhi's tools and Dahlia's dog bed. "And believe me, it's painful pushing a little human out of your body."

He tugged her against him, hating himself more with every passing second. And the worst part about it was that even the thought of her having babies made him want them to be his. *Man up. Face this head-on and get the hell out of here.* The hard-ass in him was no match for his heart. He held her tighter.

"Bodhi?" she said shakily. "Is this really it?"

He put enough space between them to see her face. *Christ, that was a mistake.* Tears spilled from her eyes, slicing him right down the center of his chest. "I'm sorry, baby. I feel like I'm staring down the barrel of a gun. If we stick to our *here* and *now* plan, the gun goes off when I drive away. Once and done. And if we don't, it'll be pointed at you and Louie every time I get called in for an assignment, over and over again."

He wiped her tears, and she shook her head.

"Once and done," she said. "I don't want to know if you get called away. I can't lose you that way. This is better."

His mouth descended upon hers to silence their reality and allow them to live within the confines of each other's arms for their last few moments. She returned his efforts eagerly, her greedy hands traveling all over his body, igniting his every sense. Her kisses were sweet and hot, and her body conformed to his with practiced perfection, making him out of his mind with longing and desire. He wanted to stay right there, holding her, and let tomorrow pass them by. He lifted her into his arms, and her legs circled his waist. Her fingers moved along his neck, and he moaned with the familiar and scintillating sensation, wanting so much more than he could take.

He slowed their kisses, intending to break the connection and do the right thing, but he couldn't tear himself away. Overwhelmed with emotion, and with nowhere else to go, he sank down to his knees, holding her as they kissed. He threaded his hands into her hair, gazing into the eyes of the woman who had trusted him with her son, and her heart. He wanted to say so many things—*I will always love you. I wish things were different. I don't want to leave. Find your happily ever after. I want that for you and Louie*—but he couldn't form a single one.

She buried her face in his neck, both of them rocking in anguish as she whispered, "I know," to his silent confession. He knew she did.

Dahlia bounded into the house far too soon. The air between them was so thick with sadness, it was like walking through quicksand as they made their way to the truck. He put Dahlia in the passenger seat, his belongings piled in boxes on the floor, behind the seat, and in the bed of the truck.

He held Bridgette's beautiful face in his hands one last time. "You turned my world upside down and made me feel things I never thought I would. You are my here and now, baby, but I will *always* love you."

"I love you, too." She clung to him, trembling, rivers of tears wetting her cheeks.

They held each other for so long, he wasn't sure he could pull away, and then his strong girl did it for them. She touched his face, a genuine smile lifting her lips despite her tears.

"Get out of here. Geez, Bodhi. You suck at saying goodbye."

Laughing and fighting tears of his own, he pressed his lips to hers one last time and climbed into the truck, feeling like he was leaving his whole world behind. Bridgette stood on the grass crying, her arms wrapped around her middle, watching him drive away.

He never knew a heart could actually hurt. Falling back into the armor he'd once worn without thought didn't come easily as he made his way toward the highway. Dahlia whimpered and nudged him with her nose. He petted her, spotting the photo album Bridgette had given him in a box on the passenger-side floor as he reached over. A stab of longing took up residence in his chest.

"Bodhi?" Static crackled in the air. "Are you there?"

He thought he'd imagined Bridgette's voice, but her broken voice came through again. "Bodhi?"

He shoved his hand beneath Dahlia in search of the walkie-talkie he'd meant to return. "Bridgette?"

"I will always love you."

Tears welled in his eyes. "I will always love you, too, beautiful. I meant to give you this back."

"I'm glad you"—static broke through the transmission—". . . talk to you until I can't."

"I miss you so much already, Bridge." He released the button, and static filled the line as he drove out of Sweetwater. "Bridgette?" he said urgently, the pit of his stomach sinking like lead as he tried one last time. "Bridgette?" But the line was dead.

Bridgette had promised herself she wouldn't fall apart when Bodhi left, and she felt like she'd held herself together pretty darn well despite her tears. At least she hadn't stolen his truck keys and locked him in her bedroom, as she'd contemplated in their last moments together. She lay on her couch, swiping at her eyes, and gulping for air as another round of sobs racked her. Her phone vibrated, and she bolted upright, hoping it was Bodhi. Talia's name flashed on the screen, and her hope fell away. She read the message. *Are you okay?*

Was she kidding? She texted back. *No.*

She was glad she'd asked her mother to keep Louie for a few hours. He didn't need to see her like this. She lay back down on the couch and closed her eyes, but the tears kept spilling out.

A few minutes later, her front door opened and her sisters walked in. The knot in her chest loosened a little. She sat up and wiped her tears. "You didn't have to come over."

Willow plunked two bottles of wine on the coffee table. "Of course we did," she said as she went into the kitchen.

Talia sat beside Bridgette and reached for her hand. "What can we do to help?"

"Want me to go after him and drag his ass back here?" Piper asked.

"Yes, please." Bridgette managed a smile.

Willow returned with four wineglasses and set them on the coffee table.

Bridgette watched Willow pour the wine, glad her sisters had come to her rescue. Bodhi was wrong. She did need rescuing, because she was drowning in sorrow. "I knew this was coming. It shouldn't hurt this bad."

"Why not?" Piper asked. "Just because you knew doesn't make it better."

"But it should." Bridgette sobbed. "There should be a switch inside us that we can flick when we know we're going to get hurt. We did the right thing. Didn't we?"

Her sisters exchanged a troubled look that made her feel worse.

"You think we should have stayed together?"

"That's a hard one, Bridge." Willow sat down beside her. "We've never seen you so happy. It's hard not to want that for you, no matter what the cost."

"But there's a *huge* cost, Willow." Bridgette guzzled her wine. She set her empty glass down and refilled it.

"Maybe," Talia said gently.

Bridgette slumped back against the couch. "Yes, *maybe*. I was hoping you guys would just agree and tell me we did the right thing. But I forget, you have no idea what it's like to lose the person you love. Imagine it, Willow. Zane's not away on location, or gone for a few weeks, but bury-him-in-the-ground *dead*." Sobs bubbled out again, and she futilely pressed her lips together in an effort to stop them, but the idea of Bodhi getting killed made her cry harder. "I'm sorry. That was a horrible thing to make you imagine. But I can't go through that again, and Louie definitely doesn't need to get attached and then lose Bodhi like that."

"Okay. I'm sorry," Willow said. "You did the right thing. I don't know what we were thinking."

Piper refilled Bridgette's glass and sat on the coffee table in front of her. "Admittedly, I know nothing about love—"

"Or dating," Talia added.

Piper scowled. "That's by choice. Anyway, back to my point. I don't think you two are done. I just don't. What kind of guy talks to your whole family about how much he loves you and Louie and then disappears?"

Bridgette sighed heavily. "The kind that loves us enough to save us from more pain later." She wiped her tears and forced the confession she didn't want to make. "This wasn't a one-sided decision, even though I'm bawling like *he* left *me*. I mean, maybe at first, but at Willow and Zane's house he gave me the choice of waiting. And he asked again before he left. I made this decision, too. But that doesn't mean it doesn't hurt." *Or that I don't regret it.*

"Then there's only one thing we can do." Piper picked up her glass and held it up in a toast. "Bash or laugh?"

Bridgette felt a flicker of lightness inside her at the reference to the game they'd started when they were kids. Whenever one of them would have a bad experience, they would either bash everything about it until they were no longer angry or upset, or they'd make so many jokes they laughed until they cried.

"Fine," Bridgette said. "But if even one of you tries to bash Bodhi, I'll go all crazy, psycho girlfriend on your ass."

"Laugh it is," Piper said. "Remember the night I told you not to wear mom panties?"

Tears flooded Bridgette's eyes anew.

"Red alert!" Willow yelled.

"I got it!" Talia yelled. "Remember when he blurted out he loved you in front of everyone?"

Bridgette buried her face in her hands. "Remember when I said I could do friends with benefits?" She looked up with teary eyes, knowing there was no quick fix for this broken heart.

The room went silent.

"If that wasn't the biggest sack of shit I've ever heard, I don't know what is," Piper said, and finally, Bridgette smiled.

It was a start.

The start of a very long road she didn't want to walk alone.

CHAPTER TWENTY-SIX

BODHI DROVE WITH the music blaring and the window down, anxious for any distraction from the ache eating away at him. But there was no escape from thoughts of Bridgette. She'd already become as vital as the air he breathed. Too edgy to be trapped in the truck, he pulled off at the next exit and found a grassy area to walk Dahlia. He paced the lawn, wondering why he was putting them both through this. He should get his ass back in the car, drive back to Sweetwater, and tell her he was wrong, that he didn't want to let their love go.

"Come on, Dahlia." She jumped into the truck.

Bodhi glanced at the photo album and knew he couldn't drive away. What if it was months before he was called in for a mission? He wanted whatever time he could get with Bridgette and Louie.

Feeling like he'd pushed a five-hundred-pound gorilla off his back, he climbed into the truck and pulled out his phone to call Bridgette. He petted Dahlia again and drew in a deep breath. Maybe they'd get lucky and have several months together before he was called away. Yes, it would be harder to leave months from now, but at least they'd have more time.

As he scrolled to his contacts, his phone rang. Darkbird's number flashed on the screen, setting that fucking gorilla back in the middle of his chest as he answered the phone.

"Booker." He closed his eyes as he listened to his orders to report for duty immediately. He half listened, debating calling Bridgette, but every scenario led to the same outcome. The outcome he'd worked so hard to avoid—Bridgette and Louie waiting for him to come home.

An hour later, feeling like he'd swallowed a bucket of nails, Bodhi dropped off Dahlia with his mother. He gave her the keys to her house in Sweetwater and caught her up on the completed work. Anything to avoid the obvious. He crouched beside Dahlia, saying goodbye for what could be the last time. It had never been easy, but now, as he gazed into his dog's eyes, Bridgette's voice whispered through his mind, making it a hundred times harder. *You're her person. She looks at you like Louie looks at me.*

"You be a good girl." He kissed her on the center of her snout, hugged her one last time, and rose to say goodbye to his mother.

Worry lines mapped Alisha's forehead. She was wringing her hands, the way she always did when he got called in, but it felt different. This time he didn't see a proud mother who knew he was doing the right thing. Instead, he saw a mother who had lost her husband and knew she might also lose her son.

"Thanks for taking Dahlia," he managed. He embraced her, remembering all the times she'd asked him to change careers—and all the times he'd told her he'd do this until the day he died. He hoped to hell this wasn't that time.

Her body was heavy with sadness. "I hoped that bringing Bridgette and Louie here meant something."

"It did. It meant *everything*. But it's over now, and I've got to go." He grabbed the bag he'd brought up with him and withdrew the photo album.

His mother's hand covered her heart. "Oh, honey."

He nodded curtly, needing his armor more than ever as her eyes misted over and she tugged him into another embrace. "You can't save everyone, honey. At some point you need to accept that. No matter how many people you save, you'll never bring your father back."

"I'm not trying to bring him back. I'm just trying to make sure no one else gets left behind. Mom, I've really got to leave. I haven't been home yet, and I need to report for duty."

She released him, her eyes more troubled than before. "Does Bridgette know you got called in? Or does she think you're going to be training?"

"Training. It's better anyway." He bent to love Dahlia up one more time, then nodded toward the photo album. "Keep it safe. I love you."

"Bodhi," she said just above a whisper, tears welling in her eyes. "I'll keep it safe, but you come back to me. You hear? You've already made your father proud. You don't need to keep—"

He cut her off with a quick hug and reached for the door, unable to listen to one more plea. "I love you."

When he arrived at his condo, memories of Bridgette and Louie slammed into him. He stalked down the hall with his eyes trained on the floor to keep from glancing into the guest room and remembering Louie tucked in beside Dahlia. In his bedroom he focused on packing, and not on the memories of making love to Bridgette that pummeled him every time he caught sight of the bed. He hated fending the images off when he wanted to revel in them. But now was the time for focus and determination toward his mission. He couldn't afford to be sidetracked.

After packing, he sat down at the kitchen table and wrote a letter to his mother, and one to Shira, as he'd done before every assignment. He wished he'd received something from his father, in his father's voice, that he could have turned to in those early days after losing him. But while Bodhi had always been more comfortable with letters than talking about his emotions, his father was the opposite. As warm as his father had been, he was not the type to pour his emotions out in something as tangible as a letter. *Funny*, Bodhi thought. *Until Bridgette, I'd never been the type to verbalize my feelings.*

He set aside the letters and pulled another piece of paper from the stack, staring at it for a long while before finally putting into words all the things he'd wanted to say to Bridgette and couldn't. He sealed it up tight, set the letters in the cabinet above the refrigerator, with the others from missions gone by, and hoped he'd live long enough to write more. Then he called Shira.

"You're back from your love nest?" she teased.

His gut knotted up. "I was called in."

"Goddamn," she said in an angry whisper. "Bodhi, what about blondie and her son?"

"Bridgette and Louie. It's over." Momentarily hurt into silence, he sank down to the chair, hands fisted. "We knew we had to end it."

She was silent for a long moment.

"Shira . . ." He drew in a deep breath. "I'm already fucking torn up. Don't make me feel worse."

"I'm sorry. It's not that. I just . . . I thought she might change your mind. She met your mother, Bodhi. No woman has ever met your mother."

He ground his teeth together. If he hadn't gotten the call to report to duty, Bridgette would be in his arms right now, even if only for another few hours, days, weeks. Whatever it was, he'd wanted it. "You know the deal—"

"I know. I get it. And you probably did the right thing, but it sucks. She must be devastated."

"Yeah. It seems to be going around. I've got to go, but please tell me you'll get the letters."

"I'll get the letters. But you better fucking come back."

"That's the plan."

CHAPTER TWENTY-SEVEN

"HANG ON," BRIDGETTE said to Talia, who was on speakerphone. She made a U-turn and came to a fast stop on the side of the road in front of Chopstix. Her laptop and purse flew off the passenger seat. "Darn it. One sec." She put the car in park and leaned over to pick up her things. The bracelet Bodhi had given her slid down her wrist, and a pang of longing shot through her. She hadn't heard from him since he'd left almost two weeks ago. Not that she'd expected to, but she'd thought his training was only for a week, and she'd hoped he might be as lonely for her as she was for him. When she'd bought Louie his new backpack for kindergarten, he kept talking about how he couldn't wait to show it to Bodhi, piling more longing onto the already mountainous ache. Every night when she put Louie to bed and tucked him in with Jeter, his Yankees hat hanging on the bedpost, she had to stifle her heartache. She'd cried herself to sleep more nights than not, but she considered getting up, showering, and working all day a major success. Dinners, however, were another story.

"What are you doing?" Talia asked. "It sounds like you're all worked up."

"I'm late picking up Louie, and I almost forgot to get dinner. I stopped too fast and all my crap fell off the seat." She set her things on the seat, feeling rattled. "Okay, I'm back. Remember when you mentioned advertising outside of Sweetwater? Can you help me figure out where to advertise? I thought things at the shop would slow down, but it's been really busy."

"Of course. I'll do some research tonight and let you know what I come up with."

She breathed a sigh of relief. "Thank you."

"How are things? Any word from Bodhi?"

Bridgette grabbed her purse and got out of the car. "No, but I didn't expect to hear from him. I just hoped."

"I know. Maybe his training ran longer than expected."

"Or maybe he's better at sticking to plans than I am." She leaned against the car, knowing she should be rushing into the restaurant, but she needed a moment to tamp down the burning in her chest.

She'd needed lots of moments lately. She didn't want to admit to Talia that she'd been using the jasmine massage oil her mother made on a nightly basis, hoping her love potion might work its magic. Or that she'd broken down and sent him a text last week, saying she thought they'd made a mistake and she wanted to talk. The fact that he hadn't responded should have made it easier for her to move on, but she'd come up with a hundred excuses in her mind about why he hadn't, and that ridiculous tactic had given her hope.

"I'm sorry, Bridge. Want me to come by tonight and hang out?" Talia asked.

"No. It's okay." Her sisters had come over every night for the first week to try to cheer her up. Sometimes it worked, until they left and she was alone in her bed, staring at Bodhi's romance novel she'd never read and the walkie-talkie that couldn't reach him. And her phone. Her stupid phone. She'd looked at their pictures too many times to count.

"You sure?"

"Yeah. I don't want you messing up my nightly routine of being strong for Louie and then falling apart like a loser."

"Oh, Bridgette. You're not a loser. You're sad, and you have every right to be."

Tears threatened. *My cue to get moving.* "Thanks for helping me with the ads. I have to run or Mom will give Louie ice cream and cookies for dinner."

She raced through picking up dinner and Louie, and as she drove up the hill toward her house, she held her breath at the sight of Bodhi's truck pulling out of his mother's driveway. She sped up, hoping to catch him. The truck slowed as it passed, and she stopped her car, hope swelling inside her. The driver, an older man with gray hair, stopped beside her car, and her whole body slumped.

"Everything okay?" he asked.

No. I'm stopped in the middle of the road with my heart in my throat, and you're not Bodhi! "Yes," she said meekly. It was then she noticed a sign on the side of the truck for a roofing company.

She rolled up her window and parked in her driveway, on the verge of tears again. She hadn't even given Louie the dog tags from Bodhi. It made the end of their relationship feel *too* real.

Louie unhooked his seat belt and thrust a picture over the seat. "See what I drew with Grandma?"

She took it, trying not to let him see her sadness. "Great, honey."

"Aren't you going to look at it?"

As she lowered her gaze, he said, "That's me and you and Bodhi and Dahlia. See what I'm holding, Mom? What do you think it is?"

Emotions clogged her throat, and she tried to swallow past them. Louie had been fine with his *friend* Bodhi leaving. He didn't need to see her lose it.

"It's Jeter! I miss Bodhi and Dahlia, don't you?"

A tear slipped down her cheek, and she turned away. "Uh-huh."

"Why are you crying, Mommy? Because you miss them, too?"

She shook her head. "No. I just had a hard day."

He climbed over the seat and wrapped his arms around her neck, making her cry harder. *I suck so bad.* She held her breath, trying to stop crying so she wouldn't upset Louie.

"I'm sorry you had a hard day, Mommy."

He was so sweet. He didn't need to see this. Wasn't this what she and Bodhi were trying to keep from happening? Wasn't this the exact reason they'd made their here-and-now plan? She wiped her eyes and straightened her spine, forcing herself to pull her shit together for her son's sake.

"We can make a fort and eat dinner in it," Louie suggested. "Or make green slime. Or we could play superhero. Want to play superhero?"

Life was so easy in his eyes. Friends came and went. The road to happiness was paved with slime and forts and pretending to be someone else. She brushed his hair from in front of his eyes and kissed his cheek.

"You can be Spider-Man, and I'll be Batman," Louie suggested.

Spider-Man sounded a lot better than Sad Mom.

"Yes. I would love to play superhero. I want to be the best superhero there is." *The kind who never cries in front of her son.*

The smell of sulfur permeated the cold night air. Rapid gunfire and heavy artillery blasts sounded like deadly fireworks, competing with the sound of blood rushing through Bodhi's ears. His team had successfully completed their first mission and were redirected to help a task force of Special Forces soldiers and Marines who had captured two suspected insurgent leaders. They were ambushed, and trapped in the kill zone. The enemy pummeled them from three sides with machine-gun fire. Bodhi shouted commands into the encrypted satellite radio as he ran out from the cover of his truck, armed with seventy-plus pounds of equipment, to rescue a fallen soldier. He hoisted the man over his shoulder, returning gunfire as he carried him to safety inside the truck. An explosion rang out, sending Bodhi into the air and blowing him back with magnum force. He slammed into the earth, and his head snapped back. Bodhi cried out in agony as he tried to open his eyes, pain searing through his limbs and chest. One eye refused to open; the other was blinded by sand. He tried to sit up—his mind racing to the soldier in the truck. He listened for other members of his team, but the gunfire and chaos were too immense. Bridgette's voice sailed through the darkness—*I will always love you*—just as another explosion rang out, and the world faded to black.

CHAPTER TWENTY-EIGHT

"WHAT'S UP, STINKY butt?" Louie said when they walked in through the back door of Willow's bakery Wednesday morning.

"Louie Dalton, you apologize to your aunt right this second." Bridgette shook her head, sharing a silent laugh with Willow.

"I'm sorry," Louie said despondently.

"Isn't kindergarten wonderful?" Bridgette bent at the waist, hugging Louie around his shoulders from behind. "In the span of three days he's learned all sorts of new phrases."

"Wait until middle school." Willow motioned with her finger for Louie to come closer.

He walked over with a serious, worried expression. "I'm sorry, Auntie Willow. I won't call you stinky butt anymore."

Willow pointed to her cheek. "Put a little sugar on it." He kissed her cheek, and she said, "What does Mom say Mr. Smarty Pants can have this morning?"

"I had French toast." Louie grabbed his stomach. "I'm too full to eat."

Willow's eyes widened. "French toast?"

"Uh-huh, and we have show-and-tell today." Louie rummaged through his backpack.

"Does that mean you got some sleep last night?" Willow asked Bridgette.

"No. It means I'm trying to put things into perspective."

Louie held up his walkie-talkie. "Look what I'm bringing in to show my class!"

Roxie walked in the back door, and Louie raced over to her.

"Grandma Roxie, can we go to school early? I have show-and-tell today, and I don't want to be late. I'm bringing my walkie-talkie."

"I can see that." Roxie ran an assessing eye over Bridgette. "Give me one minute and then we'll take off." She sidled up to Bridgette and lowered her voice. "The boy wants to go to school early? Whose child is he?"

"Talia's," Bridgette and Willow said in unison.

"You got that right," Roxie said. "Honey, I was in the grocery store last night, and two people asked if you were okay. Apparently your shop is full of *blue* roses?"

Bridgette shrugged, but there was no denying she'd been channeling her sadness into her business. Blue roses signified the *impossible* or the *unattainable*. "I think they're pretty."

Roxie arched a brow.

"Fine," she relented, and lowered her voice. "What's wrong with them? They *are* pretty. I'm trying to move on, but it has to come out somewhere."

Roxie hugged her. "I'm not asking you to move on." She gazed into her daughter's eyes and smiled. "I'm merely telling you what your customers think. I, on the other hand, would just like you to eat some doughnuts so you don't wither away. Gardening is healthy, honey, but don't count that man out just yet. He wore his heart on his sleeve." She glanced at Louie, busy playing with his walkie-talkie. "I don't think he's done with either of you."

"He's not coming back, Mom. It would be easier for me if you'd accept it, too."

"What do you mean, 'too'?" Roxie patted Bridgette's cheek. "A mother always knows." She planted a kiss on Willow's cheek. "Wedding plans, sweet pea. We need to start making them."

"I know. Soon, I promise," Willow said.

"Come on, Louie." Roxie waved him over to the door. "Let's go freak everyone out. It's been *years* since a Dalton was early for school."

As soon as she was out the door, Willow grabbed Bridgette's hand. "What did you mean you're putting everything into perspective?"

She lifted one shoulder. "I've been texting Bodhi, and he hasn't responded *once*. I told him I made a mistake and that I want to get together and talk and see if we can figure out how to make things work. But he's gone into radio silence. I even caved and let Louie leave him a good night message the other night."

"How did Louie handle it when he didn't call him back?"

"The boy puts me to shame." She grabbed a doughnut from the tray, but she had no appetite and set it beside her on the counter. "He said Bodhi would call him back when he could."

"That's good, Bridge. You don't want him to be sad."

"I know. It's wonderful how resilient kids are. Every night he snuggles in with the stuffed dog Bodhi gave him and whispers good night to Bodhi and Dahlia. But he never gets sad." She ran her finger over her bracelet. "I envy him, Willow. I don't want to be sad, either."

Blinking against damp eyes, she said, "I'm trying. I'm really trying to move on, but I see him everywhere. I *feel* him with me. It's like he's right there, but he's invisible, and I know that's crazy and unhealthy. I made my choice, but I regret it. I regret it so badly I can barely breathe sometimes. Every morning I expect to hear him knock on the door to borrow sugar. I actually *hope* for it. And every morning I get this huge letdown, even though I *know* it's ridiculous. Stupid, I know."

"That's not stupid, Bridge. You miss him."

Tears slid down Bridgette's cheeks, and she swiped angrily at them. "The other night I heard a dog bark and I bolted out the front door, thinking it might be him and Dahlia."

Willow embraced her. "I'm sorry."

"What am I going to do? I feel like I did when I lost Jerry, only this time I have no idea if he's alive or . . ." She pushed back and wiped her eyes. "I'm doing exactly what I said I would *not* do. I can't cry over him every day. It's been almost four weeks. That's enough. *Please* tell me that's enough."

"I can't do that. Only you can know when it's enough."

Bridgette groaned. "I hate you a little right now. I need tough love. I need someone to slap me across the face and tell me to grow up. I'm going to figure this out. I swear I will." She inhaled deeply and blew it out fast. "And until then, I'm going to make as many blue flower arrangements as I damn well please."

Bridgette locked up the flower shop half an hour early and leaned against the glass doors thinking about Louie. He'd started kindergarten without a hitch. No crying about being away from Bridgette or his grandmother, no exhaustion from the full day of school. Nothing but excitement. Tonight she would pick him up on time and make him a real dinner. Maybe even lasagna. Memories of the night Bodhi had made him lasagna came crashing in, bringing waves of sadness. Okay, so she wasn't ready to go that far yet. *Spaghetti.* Louie loved spaghetti. She was determined to take control of her emotions, and that started with baby steps. Dinner felt more like a giant leap, but she could handle it. It felt good to have a plan, no matter how small that plan was.

She strolled around the shop, trying to see it through the eyes of customers. There definitely were a ridiculous number of arrangements with blue roses. But they helped her get the pain out in a way other flowers couldn't, or at least, *hadn't*. This was just another reason she needed to hire someone as soon as possible. Then she could deal with her sorrow in private. She was surprised by the number of applications she'd gotten from the ads Talia had helped her place in the city and surrounding areas. As she walked through the shop, another plan developed. After Louie went to sleep, she would review the applications, and even if she wasn't completely sold, she was hiring someone by next week. Period.

She went into the office, remembering when Bodhi had helped her in the shop. He'd fit in seamlessly, making arrangements and handling orders like a professional florist, and best of all, he'd dragged her into the office when there were no customers for some secret kisses and sexy time. She sank down in her chair, memories appearing in her mind one after another. Their first dance, first kiss, first *everything*.

Our last kiss.

She could still feel Bodhi's arms around her, his mouth on hers, could still feel the moment the sadness had become too much and he'd sunk down to his knees. A burning ache started in her chest, spreading like wildfire and bringing an onslaught of tears.

How could they end something they'd just started?

He hadn't returned her texts.

It was really *over*.

With shaky hands, she fumbled through unhooking the bracelet. She had never taken it off, and it felt like she was tearing off a layer of skin. Her fingers curled around it, and she pressed her fists to her forehead, tears puddling on her desk like memories refusing to be forgotten.

It hurt too much. She couldn't do this. Her fingers unfurled, and she looked at the silver bracelet, seeing the inscription on the inside for the first time. You are my forever. BB

She heard a tortured wail and realized it was coming from her. Fumbling with the bracelet, she desperately tried to hook the clasp, as if it were a salve to an open wound. It *clunked* to the desk, and she tried again. But it was no use; she was shaking too badly. She needed Willow's help. She stormed out of her office, smacked into a rock-hard chest—and screamed.

Bodhi dropped his crutch and wrapped his arms around Bridgette as she struggled and punched, trying to wrench free. With a bandage over one eye where he'd taken shrapnel and his left arm and leg casted, he wasn't exactly a sight for sore eyes. And that was just the damage she could see. He held her too tight, but he didn't care. He was never letting her go again.

"Bridgette. It's me, beautiful."

"What happened?" Willow's voice preceded her as she flew into the shop, stopping short at the sight of them. "Holy shit."

Bridgette looked up at Bodhi with a bewildered expression. Her mouth opened, but no words came. She started pummeling his chest again. "I . . . I've been texting you."

He grabbed her hands, tears welling in his eyes. "I got called in to a mission the day I left," he said quickly. "I was going to come back, but then the call came and I couldn't do that to you. But I couldn't leave for good, Bridgette. When I landed in the States, I came directly here. The back door was open. I didn't mean to frighten you."

Her eyes moved over his face, as if she was seeing it clearly for the first time. "You're hurt. Your eye. Oh my God. You're really *here.*"

"I'm here, and I'm not going back to rescuing."

She reached for his face with both hands and went up on her toes. He lifted her into his arms, and her legs wound around his waist. For the first time in weeks, he felt whole again. He didn't care that he could barely breathe from his healing broken ribs, or that balancing was a problem. Bridgette was finally in his arms again.

"I thought it was over," she said between sobs and kisses.

"Real love never dies, baby. How could it be over? You're my here and now, and I'm standing right *here*, right *now*. I left you and Louie behind once, and I'll never do it again. If you let me, I'll spend the rest of my life making it up to you both."

He gazed into her eyes, seeing the woman whose voice brought him home. "I want to build the tree fort for Louie and be there for his first kiss and when he sneaks out and drives you crazy. I want to see your belly round with our babies and teach our children the secret language of flowers before they need it and sleep in sheet forts watching silly movies."

Holding tight to Bridgette, he tried to sink down to one knee. Willow rushed over and helped him maneuver his cast and find his balance. Her face wet with tears, she stepped away, Bridgette's silent supporter.

Bridgette gulped for air, her body trembling, still wrapped up tight around him. "I love you, Bodhi."

"I love you, baby, and I should probably wait for Louie and talk to him about this or something, but I can't wait."

She laughed while she cried.

"I don't want to miss another day with you, baby. I want to be the man you and Louie can count on, right beside you for the rest of our lives. My sweet, beautiful Bridgette, will you marry me?"

Sobbing, she nodded and wrapped her arms around his neck. "Yes! Yes, I'll marry you!"

He brushed his lips over hers. "I don't have a ring yet—"

"I hear you, and you'll need to fix that," she said with a laugh. "But right now shut up and kiss me."

EPILOGUE

BRIDGETTE SLITHERED INTO her dress and gathered her hair over one shoulder. "Bodhi, can you please zip me up?" It was Thanksgiving, and they were late for dinner at her parents' house, where Louie had spent the afternoon helping his grandparents prepare for their first holiday in their new home. Bodhi's mother had moved in next door, and she, too, was at Bridgette's parents' house helping them prepare.

Bodhi slid his hands inside her dress and groped her breasts, feeling her up from behind.

"Hey, Handsy Jack. You just *had* me." She turned her face, and he captured her mouth in a sweet, loving kiss.

"Your point?" He brushed his thumbs over her nipples, reigniting the inferno he'd just finished smoldering. His hips pressed against her ass.

"My point"—*Lord, that feels good*—"is that we're already late. And your mother and Shira are both waiting for you to arrive." She'd met Shira shortly after Bodhi had returned, when she'd come to spend the weekend, and they'd hit it off like sisters.

"For us to arrive," he corrected her.

It had been more than nine weeks since Bodhi had returned, and six weeks since he'd officially accepted his new position strategizing and training rescuers one week per month, with no chance of being sent away. He wasn't starting that position until after the new year.

Only for You

Apparently Darkbird paid incredible amounts of money for former Marines and Special Forces soldiers to risk their lives and rescue others. Bodhi had been channeling much of his income into his charity and still had enough saved that he didn't need to work full-time. But Bridgette knew that Bodhi had never been motivated by the money. He worked for the things he believed in, and now he would be helping in a different way.

Dahlia lifted her head from her dog bed beneath the windows.

"Relax, Dahl," Bridgette said. "We don't have time to mattress hop right now. You can go back to sleep." They'd been so loud earlier when they were making love—enjoying the freedom of a child-free house—that Dahlia had bolted from the room.

Bodhi reluctantly zipped her dress, kissing her neck until she was panting again. Her phone rang, and she snagged it from the dresser. *Mom* flashed on the screen. She wiggled out of his hands and answered the phone as she pushed her feet into her heels.

"Hi, Mom. We're on our way."

Bodhi went for her neck again, and she closed her eyes.

"Honey, are you okay? You sound out of breath."

"What?" She pushed from his arms, and his eyes darkened. He hauled her against him, kissing her neck again and making her laugh. "Yes, Mom. I'm fine."

She ran her hand over his handsome face with its new battle scars. He'd undergone surgery on his eye before coming home, and another since. His vision had returned, and his other injuries had healed, though his scars were a daily reminder of how close she'd come to losing him. Not a day went by that she didn't thank the powers that be for bringing him back to her and Louie.

"Bridgette?" her mother said, jolting her back to their conversation.

"We're on our way, Mom. Sorry we're late." She took Bodhi's hand and dragged him toward the stairs. Dahlia trotted after them. "We got a little hung up."

She promised they'd be there in a few minutes and ended the call as they descended the stairs. They stopped to love up Dahlia for a few seconds before hurrying out the door. "Bodhi, you can't kiss me like that when I'm talking to her. It's like announcing to my mother that we're late because we were fooling around."

He grabbed her in the middle of the driveway and brushed his lips over hers. Even after all this time, it still caused a shiver of heat to tickle down her spine.

"Like she doesn't know?" he said, and kissed her again.

He helped her into the car and leaned in for another kiss, taking her hand in his. He lifted it to his lips and pressed a kiss to her fingers. The stunning ruby-and-diamond engagement ring he'd had made for her sparkled between them. The band was engraved with roses and bellflowers, signifying eternal and unchanging love.

"Are you sure we need to go have turkey?" Bodhi asked with the wolfish grin she loved. "I'm hungry for something much sweeter."

"Oh, shoot! I forgot the pie."

Bodhi ran inside and grabbed the pie, and they hurried over to her parents' house. Her father was carrying the platter of turkey to the table when they arrived.

"There's my girl and future son-in-law." He set down the platter and hugged her. "You look beautiful."

"Thanks, Dad. I'm sorry we're late." Bridgette caught a smirk from Piper.

"Finally," Louie exclaimed as he climbed into his chair. "I'm starving, and Grandma said we had to wait. What took you so long?"

Bodhi ruffled Louie's hair. "We forgot the pie and had to go back for it."

Louie went into a long explanation about how they'd made the pie together as everyone came into the dining room.

"You have hand marks on your butt," Willow whispered to Bridgette.

Bridgette turned to check out her ass, and Willow laughed.

"Really?" Willow whispered. "You did it in the kitchen?"

"No," Bridgette snapped. "Yes. At first. *Shh.*" They'd christened the kitchen table and worked their way upstairs. Christening the stairs along the way, and the bed, the shower . . .

"Funny, Bodhi never used to be late for anything," Shira said with a conspiratorial glimmer in her eyes. "You are the absolute best thing that has ever happened to him. Thank you for getting my bestie to stop risking his life."

Bridgette glanced at Bodhi, who was talking with Zane, and a rush of heat flowed through her. "Thank you for not sleeping with him," she teased.

"That's an easy 'you're welcome.' No offense, but *ew*. He's like my brother." Shira laughed. Bridgette had told her how she'd thought they'd slept together when Shira had visited, and—after she laughed hysterically—Shira had assured her that sleeping with Bodhi had never been on her to-do list.

"Your brother, however . . ." Shira eyed Ben, who was talking with Aurelia. "What's his deal? Are he and Aurelia a couple?"

Bridgette caught Ben stealing a glance at Bodhi's tall, blonde, and beyond gorgeous friend. "Your guess is as good as mine."

Roxie and Alisha were discussing Roxie's new fragrances. They had gotten along fabulously from the moment they'd met. Roxie had been showing Alisha around town, and in the process, Alisha had begun helping Roxie with her business, and getting close to Louie in the afternoons when they babysat. They both looked at Bridgette, and she had a feeling they were talking about her and Bodhi. Their warm smiles told her more than words ever could. She and Louie were truly blessed to have Bodhi and his mother in their lives.

They took their seats. Shira and Alisha sat across the table from Bodhi and Bridgette.

Talia sat beside Bridgette. "You look really happy, Bridge."

"I am." Bridgette took in her sister's perfectly done makeup and thick, shiny hair hanging loose over her shoulders. "And you look gorgeous. Do you have a date later?"

Talia smiled, but she shook her head and shifted her eyes away, making Bridgette curious about her plans for the evening.

"I want to sit with Uncle Benny," Louie announced, and climbed onto a seat beside Ben, who was sitting next to Aurelia.

"Benny?" Ben said.

"That's what your girlfriend calls you," Louie said, looking at Aurelia, who looked as shocked as the rest of them.

Aurelia had been joining them for holiday dinners since her grandfather had suffered a stroke and moved into a rehab facility on Long Island. Willow and Zane were also seated across from Bridgette and Bodhi, and as Bodhi leaned in for a kiss, she remembered how hard it had been to hold back her affections the first time Bodhi had joined her family for dinner.

"Buddy, Aurelia's not my girlfriend," Ben said. "We're just friends."

"But she's a girl, and she's your friend. My teacher said you can have girlfriends or boyfriends," Louie explained.

"He's got us all figured out." Aurelia tapped Ben's chest and winked at Louie. "You call him Benny all you want, buddy." Her hand flattened on Ben's chest, and Bridgette glanced at Piper and Willow, who were exchanging curious looks.

"Oh yeah," Piper said under her breath. "That boy has got a nose for hookups, all right."

"Piper." Roxie glared at her with the don't-tease-your-sibling look she'd honed when they were growing up. She sat at one end of the table and reached for Talia's and Louie's hands. "Our first Thanksgiving in our new home. This feel *so good*, and we have a lot to be thankful for. Two new almost sons-in-law, everyone's healthy and happy, and Aurelia's moving back to Sweetwater in a few weeks."

"Speaking of," Piper said, "we need to schedule a time to discuss the renovations so I can get started."

"How about after I get settled in?" Aurelia asked. "I still have some financial things to work out."

Ben's brows knitted. "You do? I didn't know that."

"What are you? Her keeper?" Piper teased. "Let's do our thankful rounds so we can eat. I'm starved. Talia, why don't you start and we'll go around the table."

"Okay." Talia looked around the table, her eyes settling on Willow and Zane, and then on Bridgette and Bodhi. "I'm thankful that two of my sisters have found such wonderful men, and I'm hoping one of them has a friend they might wrangle into coming to Sweetwater."

Soft laughter filled the dining room.

"Can I go next?" Louie asked.

Bridgette opened her mouth to say he should wait, but then she realized that some things—like gratitude and *I love yous*—shouldn't ever have to wait.

Bodhi leaned closer to Bridgette and kissed her cheek, whispering, "That's your boy."

Bridgette smiled and said, "That's *our* boy."

Would he ever get used to how that made him feel? He looked across the table at the little boy who stole his heart more times each day than he could count, and he knew he never would. Alisha smiled at him with the grateful look she'd had in her eyes ever since he'd decided to step down from handling covert missions. He'd thought he'd miss it. But everything he needed to be happy was right here in this room—almost. Dahlia was at home waiting for them.

"I'm thankful for Bodhi," Louie practically shouted. "Because now I'm going to be a big brother."

There was a collective gasp, and all eyes turned to Bodhi and Bridgette. Excitement rose in Bodhi, surprising him. They hadn't talked about having children, and he knew she was on the pill, but there was that one percent . . .

He turned to his beautiful fiancée with an arched brow.

Bridgette looked like she'd swallowed a frog. "What? No!" She shot a look at Louie. "Louie, Mommy is *not* having a baby."

"Yes, you are," he insisted. "Molly Graynor's mommy is getting married, and she told Molly that's what you do when you're going to have a baby."

"Molly Graynor's mommy has had three babies out of wedlock," Piper said. "I don't think you should take advice on the birds and the bees from her."

"What's wedlock?" Louie asked.

Bodhi couldn't help but chuckle.

"Piper." Bridgette sighed and nibbled nervously on her lower lip. "Louie, babies aren't born because men and women get married."

"Then how *are* they made?" he asked.

Oh shit.

"Oh my," Roxie said with a laugh. "He's definitely your child after all, Bridgette."

Bodhi knew nothing about how to handle this, but Bridgette was turning white, and he couldn't let her flounder.

"I've got this," Bodhi said. "Louie, when two people love each other very much, they make babies out of their love."

"Really?" Louie pointed at Willow. "Then Auntie Willow and Uncle Zane will have babies, and Uncle Benny and Aurelia. And maybe even Uncle Benny and Shira, because he keeps looking at her the way Bodhi looks at Mommy *all* the time. And Grandma and Grandpa will have babies. I'm going to be a big brother lots of times!"

Aurelia glared at Ben, Shira blushed, and there was collective laughter and a round of comments about making babies.

Bridgette excused herself to go to the bathroom, and the pit of Bodhi's stomach told him something was up. He hoped he hadn't totally screwed up his answer and went after her.

He caught up to her by the bathroom and drew her close. "Hey, beautiful. Are you okay?"

"Yeah." She smiled, and as always, it cut straight to his heart. Then she trapped her lower lip between her teeth and touched his chest. "Louie just freaked me out for a minute. We haven't really talked about having kids."

"I just assumed you'd want more. Do you not?"

She ran her finger along the stretch of tanned skin between his open collar. "With you?"

He scowled. "No, with some other neighbor-turned-fiancé."

"Let me think about my other neighbors." She tapped her chin.

He grabbed her ribs and stifled her shriek with a passionate kiss.

She dragged him into the bathroom and locked the door behind them. He swept his arm around her again and said, "Babies?"

The idea of having babies with Bridgette made him near giddy.

"Babies mean stinky diapers and sleepless nights."

"I'll change them." He nibbled on her neck.

She scrunched her nose and looked up at the ceiling, feigning deep concentration. "They get up a *lot* at night."

He pressed his lips to hers and felt her smile. "I'll get up with them. I'm a great night owl."

"Gee, I don't know," she teased, and put her arms around his neck. "Maybe you should try harder to convince me."

He lifted her into his arms, and her pretty dress gathered around the tops of her thighs. "Baby, I plan on doing just that."

"It's going to take a *lot* of convincing."

He gazed into her beautiful green eyes, and as he lowered his lips to hers, he said, "Then it's a good thing we have forever."

A NOTE FROM MELISSA

I have been excited to write Bridgette's story since I first met her in Logan Wild's book, *Wild Boys After Dark: Logan*. I knew she needed a very strong, independent man, someone who had the ability to love her son, Louie, with his whole heart and bring out the side of herself that she'd ignored for so long. Bodhi Booker surpassed my greatest hopes, and I hope you loved reading their love story as much as I enjoyed writing it.

Each of Bridgette's siblings will be featured in their own books. Sign up for my newsletter to keep up to date with new Sugar Lake releases and to receive an exclusive short story (www.MelissaFoster.com/News).

If this is your first Melissa Foster book, you might enjoy my big-family romance collection, Love in Bloom. Characters from each series make appearances in future books, so you never miss an engagement, wedding, or birth. A complete list of all series titles is included at the start of this book.

Happy reading!

Melissa Foster

ACKNOWLEDGMENTS

Writing Bodhi and Bridgette's story was very difficult for me, as I don't usually write about couples who agree to break up. My heart ached for them, and I'd like to thank Lisa Bardonski and Lisa Filipe for giving me tough love during the writing process and convincing me to stick to my guns. I needed it. A special thank-you to fan Sas Mitchell, for help with research on flowers and their meanings.

I chat with fans often in my fan club, and they inspire me on a daily basis. If you haven't joined yet, please do. You never know when you'll end up in one of my books, as several members of my fan club have already discovered (www.Facebook.com/groups/MelissaFosterFans).

If this is your first Melissa Foster book, you have many wickedly sexy and fiercely loyal heroes and sassy, empowered heroines to catch up on in my Love in Bloom big-family romance collection. You can find a full list of my books on my website (www.MelissaFoster.com/Melissas-Books).

If you don't yet follow me on Facebook, please do! We have such fun chatting about our lovable heroes and sassy heroines, and I always try to keep fans abreast of what's going on in our fictional boyfriends' worlds (www.Facebook.com/MelissaFosterAuthor).

Remember to sign up for my newsletter to keep up to date with new releases and special promotions and events and to receive an exclusive short story (www.MelissaFoster.com/Newsletter).

For publication schedules, series checklists, and more, please visit the special reader goodies page that I've set up for you at www. MelissaFoster.com/Reader-Goodies.

A special thank-you to editor Maria Gomez and the incredible Montlake team for bringing another Sugar Lake story to life. As always, heaps of gratitude to my editorial team and, of course, to my own hunky hero, Les.

ABOUT THE AUTHOR

Photo © 2013 Melanie Anderson

Melissa Foster is a *New York Times* and *USA Today* bestselling and award-winning author of more than sixty-five books, including *The Real Thing* in the Sugar Lake series. Her novels have been recommended by *USA Today*'s book blog, *Hagerstown* magazine, the *Patriot*, and more. She has also painted and donated several murals to the Hospital for Sick Children in Washington, DC.

She enjoys discussing her books with book clubs and reader groups, and she welcomes an invitation to your event. Visit Melissa on her website, www.MelissaFoster.com, or chat with her on Twitter @melissa_foster and on Facebook at www.facebook.com/MelissaFosterAuthor.